Zhang Dynasty:

# SEDUCTION OF THE PHOENIX

## Michelle M. Pillow

**Futuristic Romance**

New Concepts

Georgia

Be sure to check out our website for the very best in fiction at fantastic prices!

When you visit our webpage, you can:
* Read excerpts of currently available books
* View cover art of upcoming books and current releases
* Find out more about the talented artists who capture the magic of the writer's imagination on the covers
* Order books from our backlist
* Find out the latest NCP and author news--including any upcoming book signings by your favorite NCP author
* Read author bios and reviews of our books
* Get NCP submission guidelines
* And so much more!

We offer a 20% discount on all new Trade Paperback releases ordered from our website!

Be sure to visit our webpage to find the best deals in e-books and paperbacks! To find out about our new releases as soon as they are available, please be sure to sign up for our newsletter (http://www.newconceptspublishing.com/newsletter.htm) or join our reader group (http://groups.yahoo.com/group/new_concepts_pub/join)!

The newsletter is available by double opt in only and our customer information is *never* shared!

Visit our webpage at:
www.newconceptspublishing.com

Seduction of the Phoenix is an original publication of NCP. This work has never before appeared in book form. This work is a novel. Any similarity to actual persons or events is purely coincidental.

New Concepts Publishing, Inc.
5202 Humphreys Rd.
Lake Park, GA 31636

ISBN 1-58608-777-0
March 2006 © Michelle M. Pillow
Cover art (c) copyright 2006 Eliza Black

NCP books are available at special quantity discounts for bulk purchases for sales promotions, premiums, fund raising, or educational use. For details, write, email, or phone New Concepts Publishing, Inc., 5202 Humphreys Rd., Lake Park, GA 31636; Ph. 229-257-0367, Fax 229-219-1097; orders@newconceptspublishing.com.

First NCP Trade Paperback Printing: March 2006

OTHER TRADE PAPERBACKS FROM NEW
CONCEPTS PUBLISHING BY MICHELLE M.
PILLOW:

CAUGHT

GHOST CATS

REDEEMER OF SHADOWS

THE JADED HUNTER

ULTIMATE WARRIORS

THE BARBARIAN PRINCE

THE PERFECT PRINCE

THE DARK PRINCE

Dedication:

To Brent, because we survived childhood with only a few scars, because I now can defend myself with a stick, because I'm *cough* sorry for the whole 'baby, baby, nice, nice' thing when we were infants, but mostly because I'm kissing up for when you are rich and I need a loan.

## Chapter One

*Imperial Palace of the Zhang Dynasty, Honorable City,
Muntong Territory, Planet of Líntiān*

Prince Zhang Jin watched the women bowing before him,
one right after another. Their long sleeves trailed over their
hands, falling gracefully to the floor. The delicate silk of
their traditional gowns only complemented their beauty.
White powder hid their complexions, accenting their red
painted lips. They were all lovely, each sent from the far
reaches of his home planet of Líntiān to present themselves
in the Hall of Infinite Wisdom located at his home in the
Imperial Palace.

"Yang Ping," the herald announced as another woman
stepped forward.

Jin kept his eyes forward as Yang Ping bowed before him.
The yellow silk surrounding her added a pleasing light to her
face, as the orange glow of the palace torches reflected
lightly off her. The torchlight was only to add ambiance to
the ceremony and wouldn't truly be needed until nightfall.
Above, the outside sun was reflected in through small holes
in the ceiling. They were so tiny and inlaid into the intricate
design that it was impossible to see them.

The herald spoke again, but Jin didn't catch the woman's
name. He bowed as was expected, bored to the point that his
mind had gone numb. Absently, he traced the gold statue of
a warrior god standing by the entranceway and imagined the
life-size bust to be on the verge of attacking the hall. Jin
wasn't one for violence, but the prospect was more
entertaining than bowing and smiling.

This was the *Qi-zi* ceremony and he was to have his pick of
the women for his bride--if he so chose. What none of the
elders seemed to realize was that he did not wish to be
married. Still, he and his brothers were eligible, each year
they'd send women for his inspection and each year he'd
send them away as unworthy. He'd done it so many times

that he was beginning to recognize some of the women from years before, though they wore different makeup and clothing.

At least he wasn't forced to endure the tradition alone. His brothers stood next to him, each feeling much the same way he did. They did not wish for brides either. Why marry when they could spend their days at leisure in the arms of a concubine? However, according to their father, when the time to take a bride presented itself, they'd be guided by their ancestors and would have an uncontrollable compulsion to claim her at any cost.

"Yu Xiang," the herald announced the next eligible lady. A woman covered in a long blue gown shuffled forward and bowed respectfully. The four princes nodded their heads in return. She was pretty, but her virtue was indeed in question. Some experience wasn't necessarily a bad thing in a bride, but the princes knew well Xiang had enough experience to rival that of all the princes combined--a very great feat. Though, looking at her now, she appeared as unsullied as a virgin. That was another thing he didn't like about the ceremony. How did you really know anything about a woman by watching her bow? Just a look was supposed to capture his interest and make him want to know more? How could that be possible after so many women came before him? Their faces would blur into one and he wouldn't remember a Shu Fang from Ting.

Xiang batted her eyelashes at them while pursing her lips. Hearing a noise, Jin looked out of the corner of his eye. His oldest brother, Zhang Haun, winked in his direction. Jin tried not to return the insolent look with one of his own, knowing his father, the Emperor of the Muntong Empire, was watching them carefully. Next to Haun stood the youngest prince, Shen, and then their brother Lian. They also had two sisters, Mei and Fen. Mei was off in space with her husband, a foreign prince, but even if she had been home she wouldn't have been present. The Zhang princesses weren't forced to endure these ceremonies.

"Jia Wan," the herald said and Jin tried not to yawn.

Traditional music, passed down for many generations, played over the quiet hall. The sound of the flute mingled with that of the harp. It was beautiful and archaic. It was tradition. Jin knew that without tradition the people would lose all connection to the past. It was important for them as a royal family to rule in accordance with ideals and to honor the old customs. That is why they never protested coming to stand for hours to watch women parade before them. As much as he loathed it, he out of all his siblings was blessed with a powerful understanding and respect for the past.

The Zhang palace was hidden behind great walls in what was known as Honorable City. Aside from when duty demanded it, Jin never left the city. Why would he want to? The city was a fortress. He was comfortable in his home, surrounded by his family and his scrolls. His needs were tended to and every whim fulfilled. On the outside, the palace walls were protected by a thick moat and there were only two known entrances inside--one in front and one in back of the large rectangular complex.

The Hall of Infinite Wisdom was only one building within the palace walls, located in the center. It was the largest structure, set high upon stone to tower over the surrounding courtyard and gardens. Also within the compound were practice halls where the royal family and imperial guards could exercise. There was a hall where they paid homage to their ancestors, a library, archery range, the Exalted Hall used for weddings and special private ceremonies. Barracks for the guards were near the weapons chambers, which were located close to the royal chambers where the Zhang family lived.

"Dong Xia He," the herald said, as a woman clad in red shuffled forward. Jin took a deep breath, eyeing the long line waiting behind her.

Emperor Zhang and Jin's mother, the empress, sat in high thrones above the hall. Carved golden dragons coiled around the royal couple. His father had a long mustache that hung down the front of his tunic. They wore matching yellow embroidered silk decorated with Imperial red dragons and ancient symbols. Just like when their people had lived on Earth long ago, red and gold were the colors of royalty, representing fortune and wealth. The emperor's clothing matched the buildings, all of which had yellow tiled roofs and dark red walls.

"Let go of me, you son of a Lophibian whore!"

Jin perked up at the very feminine cry. The language wasn't that of Líntiān but he understood it well enough. It was a star language, from a culture that long ago shared the planet Earth with his people. When they were growing up, the emperor had demanded that all his children upload language files into their brains. They'd been on a very strict educational schedule for most of their childhood--but that had been decades ago.

"I'll kick your ass, you tyrannical brute!"

Jin narrowed his eyes, concentrating on what the woman screamed. The translations shouldn't have been difficult to do, though it had been a long time since he had used them. Was she really screaming insults or were the translations harder than he thought?

"Zhang Jin," said an authoritative, old voice. The words were soft, carried as if on a gentle breeze.

Jin turned, seeing the transparent figure of his dead grandfather, Zhang Manchu, standing beside him. Instantly, he placed fist to palm and bowed in respect for his ancestor. "Grandfather."

Tension curled in his gut. What was his grandfather doing here? Now? At this ceremony? Did the bearer of the female voice bring danger with her? He knew he'd much prefer facing a life and death battle than finding a bride.

"Jin?" Haun asked. His brother's eyes glanced to Jin's side. Jin knew his brother couldn't see the spirit. The ancestors only showed themselves to those they wished to guide.

"Grandfather Manchu," Jin answered. Haun frowned, but nodded once in complete understanding. The commotion grew louder and the sound of a struggle ensued, distracting Jin from his grandfather's spirit.

"Takes five of you brutes and a blow dart to subdue a little girl like me? Your parents must be so proud! Is this all you got? Huh? Huh! "

The line of awaiting women parted in a flurry of blue, green and yellow embroidered silk. Their bodies created a pathway to the large gold doors leading from the hall. Five Imperial guards dragged a woman by each of her limbs, the fifth holding her masked head to keep it from thrashing about. Even clad from head to toe in black, it was easy to see by her curves that it was a female--that and the sound of her ungodly curses as she fought their hold.

"Let go of me you, Kaokin scum." The woman freed an arm and tried to punch the guard holding her head. The man jerked to the side, wrenching her into a strange angle. She didn't scream at the painful twist of her body as Jin expected she might, but only got madder. "You'll pay for that."

Feeling a hand on his shoulder, Jin looked once more at his grandfather. The dead man appeared apologetic, but didn't take his eyes off the female. Jin turned back to the show.

"What's the matter? Can't understand me? Well see if you can't understand this!" The woman kicked violently, jerking the guards back and forth with her weight. "*Cào nǐ zǔxiān shí bâ dai!*"

Everyone in the hall gasped. Jin couldn't believe the audacity of the woman. To insult a person's ancestors, let alone eighteen generations of them, was a striking offense indeed. Either she was very brave or very foolish.

With great effort the guards thrust the woman down before the emperor, shoving her to her hands and knees while forcing her head to bow low in submission. A gold feather dart stuck out from her side. Jin knew the men had tried to subdue her with the tranquilizer dart, just acquired less than a decade ago for use in palace security. From the looks of it the dart wasn't having much of an effect.

The prisoner squirmed, fighting to get free. The guards twisted her arms back, pulling until she cried out in pain. Jin didn't move, though he stared with interest. His grandfather's hand tightened on his shoulder until it felt as if his ghostly fingers were dipping beneath his skin, burning into his flesh. He tried to lower his shoulder to stop the feeling, but his grandfather held tight.

"What is the meaning of this?" the emperor asked calmly, eyeing the prisoner. No one made a move to help her and she did not look around as if she wanted to be helped. Jin suppressed a smile. This one was stubborn, maybe foolishly so. He wished he could see her face. He'd like to look at the woman behind the mask.

"It is time, Jin," his grandfather said.

"Time?" Jin asked confused, prying his eyes from the woman to study the departed man once more.

Everything moved as if in a blur. His grandfather's fingers dug deeper, holding him in place, even as his fingers slid over Jin's heart to his throat. Jin froze, unable to move or speak. He opened his mouth to protest but all that came out was a long hiss of air. A chill worked over his entire body, growing like a frost over his throat and shoulder, down his lungs and into his hips and legs. Gasping for breath, he was helpless as his grandfather's spirit entered into his eyes, crowding his soul as the ancestor took residence inside him. Before he knew what was happening, his body was taken over, jerkily moving with a will outside its own.

"Cease!" His voice commanded harshly, but the words did not come from him. His body moved forward on the platform, out of his control. He tried to pull back to his spot by his brothers, desperately wanting to reach to them, but he no longer had power over his body.

*Grandfather!* he thought. *Tiānna! What are you doing?*

*I told you, Jin. It is time,* his grandfather's voice answered in his head. The man sounded sad, if not a little apologetic.

*No,* Jin began to protest, but his brother's harsh voice interrupted the thought.

"Jin?" Haun said quietly from between his teeth. "What are you doing? Come back here!"

Jin desperately wanted to obey. He'd never felt so helpless in his life. Every part of him tried to resist the possession, but his grandfather's spirit was too powerful for him to resist. The will inside him was strong, but his grandfather's hold over him was stronger.

A murmur of sound flowed over the hall, rising and falling like a crescendo of music. His body was forced down from the platform and he was moved before his parents. Jin was only a mere mortal and did not possess the knowledge of the spiritual plane. There was no way to fight off the attack, no way to tell the others what was happening to him. The emperor and empress watched him approach, their expressions blank.

*Grandfather! Cease at once! I order you!*

The faint sound of laughter in his grandfather's voice was the only answer he received.

"I have chosen," Jin announced out loud, bowing respectfully to his parents. He looked down at the woman completely covered in black, as his hand lifted to motion to her. Despite his best effort to keep his mouth pressed tightly shut, his lips moved, forming words that filled him with dread and anger. "I have found my bride."

His parents didn't move. The hall was still at the declaration. Out of all the children, he was the first to declare marriage. Princess Mei was married, but she'd defied tradition when she took the foreign prince as her husband. They had been joined in space, away from Líntiān in some foreign Var ceremony of joining.

Jin struggled to regain control, but it was no use. It was too late. To take it back now would be to dishonor himself and his family. He looked down at the woman, unable to see her face. It was hard to tell anything beyond the fact that she'd been arrested and had what appeared to be a tight little body beneath the black clothing she wore. Jin felt his body stir with passion. The mocking sound of his grandfather's laughter filled his head once more. Jin wondered if the desire was his own, or that of his possessor. Even as he wondered, he knew. He desired the woman before him. Her mere presence rocked the foundation of his safe, protected world. The danger in her excited him.

The prisoner's eyes darted up to stare at him. It was possible the declaration had just saved her from death, and she didn't look at all grateful for the gesture. Her gaze pierced inside him, jolting him with the anger that her eyes held. They were the color of jade, the precious green jade their ancestors had brought with them from Earth. The only pieces that survived were in the Sacred Chamber, protected by Zhang An, his long dead great-grandmother. To even look upon it was an honor.

*Is this a sign?* Jin asked his grandfather. *What does this mean? Her eyes, they....*

*It is done,* his grandfather's voice interrupted, reminding Jin that he stood in the middle of the palace hall. Jin held tense, ready to reclaim his body. To his annoyance, his grandfather didn't act like he had any intention of getting out right away.

*This goes too far, láotou. Make yourself known to my family and take it back. I will not be married to this woman. She is unworthy of my family. She is a thief!*

*It is too late, my grandson. What had to be done is now done.*

Jin wanted to scream, but couldn't, as the old man held him in silence.

\* \* \* \*

*I have found my bride.*

The words echoed through Francesca La Rosa's head over

and over. She was sure that's what the prince had said, but her Líntiānese was faulty due to an imperfect upload and she couldn't be positive. At least, she really didn't want to be positive.

*I have found my bride.*

Couldn't the man just fight her instead? Or shoot her with some more of those fun darts?

Francesca glanced at her side. The thing was as sharp and annoying as a giant thorn, but she didn't give them the pleasure of watching her remove it. Let them think it didn't bother her. By sheer mental will alone did she keep from passing out as the drugs flowed through her body.

If the rumors of the royal family held true, he would be a skilled warrior proficient in many martial arts. Francesca glanced up to the prince. She knew what he was. It was clear with just one look. He was handsome, like his brothers, dressed in the royal color of red. The dragon tunic looked to be made of silk brocade. It was absolutely gorgeous with perfect details. Golden flames were embroidered around the oriental dragons. The long tunic fell to mid thigh, the material so light it caressed his muscled chest and trim waist perfectly.

She tried to tell herself she was unaffected by his physical form, but even so, she looked him over from head to toe. His silk pants were red, trimmed in gold. They were loose, as was the style of the Muntong court, and he wore black ground shoes.

Francesca stared at his hips in disbelief. His weight shifted slightly. Was he aroused? Is that what this was about? He wanted to sleep with her? The prince was handsome and strong, she'd give him that much, and he appeared just arrogant enough to be fun between the sheets. No untried virgin, she could see the merit in his plan, but this dramatic display was hardly warranted.

Though, now wasn't the time for such thoughts. Her life hung in the balance and she needed to stay focused if she were to escape. Francesca had no doubt she would succeed in getting away. She always did.

Slowly, she drew her gaze back up to meet his. His eyes were dark, piercing, almost burning with an inner fire as he stared at her through the strands of his chin length hair. A strange look passed over his face, but he did not turn away.

That's when she noticed the hall had gone deadly still.

"So shall it be," the emperor announced, breaking the silence.

Francesca gasped, knowing her mask hid her expression as her eyes turned upward to the throne. Someone roughly pushed her head back down. She gritted her teeth. If she got a hold of those ponytailed guards, she would pull their hair out one by one. Staring at the emperor was considered an offense. However, since she'd just gotten caught not only stealing the royal jewels, but using an outlawed form of Wushu to do it, impoliteness was the least of her worries.

*Besides, they can do nothing worse than what has already been done to me.*

"My son, Zhang Jin, has chosen a bride," the emperor continued in Líntiānese. "Hang the banner of good fortune at the palace gate, so that all may know of our happy day. Inform the matchmaker and summon the astrologers to the palace at once. Guards, take her to my son's chambers."

"Father," one of the princes asserted from the platform. Francesca gritted her teeth as the egotistical prince motioned toward her. The emperor shook his head once. The gesture was all that was needed to silence the man. With fist to palm, the prince bowed, saying no more.

"There will be time for you to offer your blessings after the astrologers read their futures, Prince Haun," the emperor said to the man who had spoken. It didn't take a genius to know that was not what prince Haun had tried to do. He'd been protesting his brother's actions.

*Ah, come on, Emperor. Let the man speak.* Francesca gave a short laugh. *I for one happen to agree with him.*

The hands on her body loosened and Francesca wiggled free. She'd fight every man in the hall if she had to. "I--"

The words never left her as fingers clamped down on the back of her neck. Shivering, she looked up to find that Prince Jin touched her. His lips pressed into a harsh line, but other than that his face was expressionless. Very sternly, he said in her language, "It is done, do you understand? Cause no more trouble."

*Who in the hell does this fuck-nut think he is talking to?*

Francesca opened her mouth to retort. Jin let go of her, only to grab the front of her neck. He pushed at the soft spot in her throat and she instantly felt lightheaded. Her vision blurred. Speech became impossible. Though she still saw colors and heard voices, she was too numbed to move. The prince jerked the dart from her side, holding it up so she could see him pass it to a guard.

"Take her," Prince Jin ordered. Her body was lifted up and she felt herself being carried from the silent hall. Hands pressed into her, digging into her flesh, and she couldn't even find the will to scream at them, let alone fight.

* * * *

Jin turned to the emperor. When his grandfather moved his hand to touch the woman, he'd sent a shock of energy over her, making her helpless and compliant. However, it also left his grandfather's spirit weakened and Jin was able to cast the man out. The departure left him feeling dizzy.

He opened his mouth as he gasped for breath, but it was too late to stop what had been done. His father had acknowledged his supposed choice in bride. The astrologers were called, the banner hung to show that one of the princes had chosen a new princess. News would spread over the countryside. To take it back now wasn't an option.

Glancing around the hall, Jin saw that Manchu's spirit had gone completely. He took a deep breath. How dare his grandfather possess his mortal coil, declare a bride for him and then leave without so much as an explanation as to why he chose *this* particular woman? The hall was filled with eligible Líntiānese bachelorettes, so why pick a stranger? Why a foul-mouthed, disrespectful foreigner?

"Leave me with my family," the emperor ordered the quiet hall. The women were the first to go. Some looked upset by the interruption in the ceremonies. He knew that they would pout that he'd chosen, after all these years, a woman not like them. Most likely, they would consider it an insult that a criminal would be his bride over the richest, most well-bred women in the land. Jin hated to admit it, but *he* found it to be a bit of an insult. He again glanced around for his grandfather. The man was gone.

*See if I ever leave you offerings again, old man.*

When the royal family was alone, the emperor relaxed. Stepping down from his throne, he went to his son. Jin's brothers followed suit, joining them on the hall floor. The empress stayed on her seat, not moving as she looked at her boys.

"Jin, are you crazy? She's a criminal. We don't even know what she was arrested for," Haun said. "How could you pick her?"

"Her crime has to be serious, if the guards dare to interrupt the ceremony for it," added Shen. He was the most contemplative of the brothers and often spoke with a sound mind.

"Jin--" Haun demanded.

"Stop," the empress broke in, standing. She slowly made her way down from the raised platform from her throne. Their mother was regal and beautiful--a true ruler. Gracefully, she touched Jin's cheek, running her finger lightly over his jaw. "He could not help himself, could you my son? You saw her and just had to have her."

"Grandf--" Jin began. His mother slid her hand over his mouth, leaving her palm pressed against his cheek as her thumb moved to still his lips. She shook her head, her serious eyes telling him to be quiet.

"Lian," the emperor ordered. "Go retrieve the guards. We must find out what Jin's bride is charged with. And see if they know who she is. If they don't know, you have my permission to access the intergalactic database to find out."

Lian obeyed. Jin knew his father was worried about the family honor. The emperor would not want the scandal of his son marrying a criminal. If her deeds weren't that bad, she could be pardoned in light of the situation.

"There is still time," Haun said. "The astrologers' readings.... Madame Eng could announce the obvious imprudence of the match. Undoubtedly the stars will not agree with such a joining. She isn't like us."

"Let us meet the young woman first, my sons," the empress said, still studying Jin, "before we are to judge her. There is a reason Jin was compelled by her. Perhaps this is fate."

Haun nodded once, but he wasn't happy. Jin was surprised to hear his mother talk favorably about fate. He knew her to still be bitter about Mei's departure. It was a fact she blamed on her own grandmother, Zhang An, who guarded the Sacred Chamber and often divined the family's futures. An's prediction with Mei hadn't been completely forthcoming as she manipulated the situation. If the empress had her say, Mei would have been married to a Líntiānese prince, Song

Lok, whose family lived across the Satlyun River, ruling the only other dynasty on the planet.

"Shen, go tell your sister Fen of this news and send a communication to Mei," the empress said. "We must appear pleased in this, otherwise there will be suspicion of our family. Haun, I beseech you, go welcome the woman to our palace and make sure her every comfort is met."

To any other, it would seem odd sending Haun to greet an arrested woman, but Jin knew his mother sent the oldest prince to ascertain the security risk she posed. Haun was an honorable man and the greatest of warriors. He might be a harsh judge, but he would be fair. And, should the woman continue to prove volatile, he would be able to easily subdue her.

"She is not to be allowed to roam free, not until we know more," the emperor said. "Jin, it will be your responsibility to see to her."

Jin would've smiled if he wasn't so irritated. When he was alone with his parents, he said, "Grandfather Manchu came to me, or more to the point, took over me. I had no will to stop this."

"We warned you about the compelling force of the ancestors when a match was to be made," the emperor said. His lips curled slightly, as if he was suppressing a laugh at the thought.

"Compelling is one thing, but possession?" Jin shook his head. "Certainly if we announce what happened, the people will understand. I can't be expected to marry a … a criminal."

"No, my son, the people will not understand. They will believe it an even stronger sign that you are meant to be together. One does not dispute the ancestors in such things," his father said.

"All ancestors were once human and not all humans act with logic," Jin mumbled.

"Very true," the empress agreed.

"Maybe your grandfather knew you needed a push." His father smiled, giving a small laugh. He didn't even try to hide his amusement. "How many years now have you been avoiding even considering finding a bride? You and your brothers walk in here, eyes bored as you look through each and every woman presented. You have never considered the possibility. Perhaps your grandfather knew that."

"He should have told us beforehand," the empress said, "before meddling."

"And perhaps it was just time," the emperor stated. "The one meant for you presented herself. What else could be done?"

"He's an old fool, that's what he is!" All eyes turned to the keeper of the secret chamber, Jin's great-grandmother, Zhang An. The three living royals bowed to the woman in respect, though the empress' movements were stiff. Empress Zhang was not talking to her dead grandmother whom she blamed for leading her daughter Mei away.

The spirit was dressed in the old style. Her long sleeves swept over the floor as she drifted to them. The delicate silk gown was made even more so by the fact that it traveled on air. Every movement was silent, like the breeze. Her wrinkled, pale face was transparent, shading with each subtle movement until it appeared smooth as a young girl's. She shifted over them, as if threatening to blow away completely. Long, dark hair streaked with white flowed around her shoulders. Tradition from her time of life would have had her put it up, but An was proud of her locks and, being dead, didn't have to listen to tradition.

"She's a thief of the worst kind," An accused. "She is not fit to be part of this family."

"What do you mean, thief?" The emperor stepped closer to her, studying the old woman carefully.

"Exactly that," An returned in irritation. Out of all his ancestors, they saw Zhang An the most. Since her death, she had been residing in the sacred room hidden within the walls of the Hall of Infinite Wisdom behind the thrones. However, lately she'd been of sour temperament--ever since Empress Zhang refused to leave her offerings of wine. "She tried to steal the phoenix. If not for my guarding it, she would've succeeded in taking one of the last pieces of precious jade! And you know what that will do to this family's reign. Emperor Song wouldn't hesitate to claim what is ours if he feels we are no longer capable of ruling. Within a generation our time would be over."

The comment left them speechless. The phoenix was a symbol of not only their royal power, but also a receptacle to that power. It fed them, guided them. Jin closed his eyes.

What cruel game was this the spirits played? Were they so bored as to guide him to a woman who wished to take all his family had? What had she to gain by taking such an important artifact? There were other things in the palace that were easier to get to for a thief and would provide just as much profit. Why the Jade Phoenix?

Then an idea struck him. An mentioned Emperor Song. He was the only man who had anything to gain by his family's fall.

Emperor Song was ruler of the only other dynasty on Líntiān. It was located across the Satlyun River, which flowed through the exact center of their planet, separating the territories of Muntong in the east and Singhai in the west. The river circled from north to south. It was a marvel of nature, so wide it was impossible to swim across. It was one of the reasons that the two empires did not fight. Though they didn't agree on much, peace was something the Líntiānese cherished. Or so the Zhang family had thought.

Was Emperor Song tired of peace? Did he yearn to rule all of Líntiān? Jin had never met the Emperor of Singhai, but Haun had. His older brother didn't seem too impressed with the man. He said he was a snob. Or was Emperor Song still angry that Haun had discovered the drug, chandoo, was being produced in his Lin Yao Mines? The Zhang family fought hard to protect the masses from the drug. It lured you in, made you feel alive, but eventually would rot your brain and wear you down into a worthless mass of nothingness. Emperor Song denied knowledge of the intergalactic drug traders, but the Zhang family was unconvinced.

Was this just a plot to dethrone the Zhang family?

Slowly, Jin noticed all eyes were on him. He shook his head. This day was supposed to be a day like any other. But now, he was engaged to a woman he knew nothing about, to a woman whose face he'd not even seen. The memory of her eyes pierced him. Jade, just like what she tried to steal from them.

"By my will or not," Jin said, taking a deep breath as he tried to figure out his path. "By my will or not, the words left my lips. Everyone heard them. I will honor my decree and take the woman as my bride."

"You cannot!" An shook, her transparent figure rippling. "To do so will grant her immunity from this. This is not the path. It can't be! I would have seen it. For once she is your bride she won't be put on trial for taking what becomes hers as well as yours. Our possessions will become hers and hers ours. Not that she could possibly have anything we want. Think about what you are doing!"

"I must, Grandmother." Jin turned to his parents, knowing full and well he was changing his tune from a few minutes before. "To back out of my word now would be to dishonor the Zhang name. The declaration was public and witnessed by many. How would it look if the first of your children to declare marriage backed out later like he was indecisive? The people will be angered."

"You are wise, my son," the emperor said, nodding.

"What? No!" Zhang An screeched. "What if she steals the jade and leaves you? You don't know these outsiders. They are not like us, Jin. They are deceitful, liars--"

"Odd, Grandmother. When you sent Mei to marry an outsider, you didn't seem to mind them. What is it? They're fine, so long as you choose them?" the empress demanded.

"I did not choose for Mei. The fates chose. I only told her of her destiny," An said, lifting her chin. "Do not be angry with me, child, for divining the future. You are lucky I tell you anything at all." The spirit's face became tight as she mumbled, "Ungrateful woman, refusing to give me my offerings."

Jin hid his smile. Zhang An liked her 'offerings'. Wine in particular.

"Perhaps Father spoke for the fates as--" the empress began. Jin sighed, his grandfather hadn't said anything about fate.

"Zhang Manchu is my son," An interrupted, her image fluttering. "I think I know what--"

"Please," Jin tried to insert into the argument. He wasn't in the mood to listen to them fight about Mei's marriage. Prince Jarek was a good man, the empress knew that, but he'd taken Mei with him into space. His sister was happy and in love with a child on the way. To Jin, there wasn't really anything else to discuss about the matter. Mei had chosen her fate, accepted it with open arms. Jin wished he could do the same. But his situation was different.

"What if she was tried for her crimes before you married?" Zhang An glided forward, her words merely a whisper on the breeze that came with her. Her milky eyes stared into him, eerily searching his depths. Jin had to look away before the woman saw too many of his thoughts. Her voice low, An continued, "If she were to receive death--"

"Death?" Jin repeated, frowning. He recalled his new bride's eyes. They haunted him with their anger. A pain unfurled in his gut and he couldn't bare the thought of killing her. It was strange that he'd feel such, but there it was. "Isn't that a little severe?"

*I just want to discover her purpose. My defense of her has nothing to do with the fact that her body sets mine on fire.*

"Such a harsh punishment when she didn't even succeed in her crime?" the empress asked.

"I told you not to defend your father's actions to me," An told the empress. "He was my son and even I don't understand why he would betray us in such a way."

*Grandfather betrayed them by making him choose a bride? That makes no sense. If An said the man was bored and meddled, he'd understand that. But betrayal? What exactly was going on? What was this all about? And what were the ancestors not telling them?*

It wasn't odd for the spirits to disagree, especially if they'd disagreed in life, but Jin didn't like the almost desperate look on his great-grandmother's face.

"Enough!" Emperor Zhang demanded. Both women jumped.

"But death, Grandmother?" Jin repeated, not wanting his elders to fight. "Do you really think that--?"

"She was caught in the act," An argued. A slow smile spread over her features. "The crime of attempted theft may not be enough for such a sentence, but the fact that she used the ancient form of Wushu when doing it would be. Long ago, it was declared illegal. For the safety of the people, those who practice must be put to death. We cannot risk its teachings being passed on. Read the scrolls, they will tell you. Law is the law."

"And I am emperor, not you," his father answered.

An's lips pressed tightly together. Jin took a deep breath. He didn't know much about the Wushu Uprisings, except what he had read about in the ancient scrolls and he didn't remember the death law An spoke of.

"There are many things for us to consider," his father said

at last. The emperor ran his fingers over his mustache, looping a long piece over his forefinger. He pulled his hand down, stroking the long whiskers before patting them against his chest. "If she is gifted in Wushu as you say, we must find out how she learned. If her master taught one person, he could've taught more." Turning to his son, he continued, "I leave it to you to discover what we must from your bride. For now you must be attentive to her. Show the people that you were serious in your word. And, if the courts deem her guilty and she is put to death, you will go into mourning for her. I am sorry, my son, but there was a reason you were guided to do as you did. It might not be for marriage, but to watch her and discover her secrets. If she was hired to take the jade, we must know by whom. And if she truly practices Wushu, we need to know who trained her."

"This is ridiculous," An protested. "We should be rid of her at once. If my son wouldn't have interfered, she would be tried and hung for her crimes."

"No offense, Grandmother, but the world belongs to the living." The empress studied the woman with a calm expression. "Your duty is to guide, not to dictate."

An's already translucent features paled and dimmed. A sensation of anger washed over Jin. His great-grandmother was upset by his mother's harsh words. If he didn't know better, he would have said her eyes teared. "Very well, my child. See how well you fare without my guidance in this."

With a strong gust of wind, the woman dissipated into thin air, leaving them alone. Jin wasn't worried. The spirit might be angry now, but she would come back. She always did.

"You should not have said that to her," Emperor Zhang said to his wife. "I know you are upset with her, but she is still our elder and we must respect the dead."

"And why shouldn't I remind her of her place? The woman is dead and yet she intrudes in our lives like she is still ruler of this house. Her guidance is welcome, but I will not be dictated to. The sooner she learns that, the sooner this will be a peaceful household. She had her time of rule, this is ours." The empress turned to her son. "Jin, this argument is not for your ears. You are a good man, my son. You are wise and we trust you to do what you must. Right now your duty is to introduce yourself to your bride."

Placing fist to palm, Jin bowed. His mother was right and he would do what he must. As he walked from the hall, he glanced around for his grandfather's spirit. The old man was nowhere to be found.

## Chapter Two

Francesca was livid. Whatever Prince Jin had done to her with his hand had left her body weak and a little achy. Once the lightheadedness had passed, she was able to concentrate, but her limbs didn't move. It was all she could do to rock her head back and forth on the mattress.

Glaring at the ceiling of the lavish room, she cursed herself for getting caught. Everything had gone so smoothly. Francesca had slipped into the Sacred Hall undetected as the Líntiānese royalty had their little 'show off the new concubine'--or whatever it was--ceremony. No one had seen her, she was positive of that. Then how in the world did they know she was there? Motion detectors? Cameras? She closed her eyes, running through every little detail. She would have seen a camera and surely she would've known if she tripped an alarm.

If this was prison, it was the nicest one she'd ever been in. The walls were lined with silk and gauze. In truth, it looked more like a brothel than a penitentiary. There were a couple thin sliding doors, but they were pulled closed and she couldn't see into the other rooms. However, the main door was different than the others in that it was dark and thick with gold inlay. This section of the palace was obviously the prince's personal living quarters. Which meant all the other royal children would sleep in this building as well. The emperor and empress would have their own building nearby.

*If that man thinks I'm going to screw him just to get out of a hanging, he's seriously mistaken!*

Because of her lethargic state, the guards had carried her effortlessly out of the Hall of Infinite Wisdom, following the walking paths that led from the large center building, through the beautiful gardens, to the sleeping chambers of the royal family. Looking past the guards, she'd seen the strange flowers lining the paths. All of them were delicate, fragrant blossoms--some as pink as a maiden's blush and others shaped like an eight-point, dark blue star with a golden center. Tiny winged creatures fluttered over the petals. Their bodies were so small compared to their large black wings. The shape of the number '7' formed when their wings bent forward in flight.

Each building had a name, but she couldn't remember what this one was called. When she'd memorized the palace map, she never thought she'd see this area. In fact, she didn't think she'd come face to face with the royal family.

*That will teach me to be unprepared.*

Unprepared was a little harsh. She'd studied the layout endlessly, not just memorizing the forty plus names of the buildings inside Honorable City. She had visualized her escape, had planned each aspect perfectly. What in all the galactic refuse heaps had happened? Did one of those spoiled brat princes really declare that she was to be his wife? What was that all about? It had to be a joke. Her Líntiānese wasn't that great. She did get the upload of it from the black market on Torgan but it had been an incomplete copy. Maybe she'd mistaken his words.

*I have found my bride.*

No, she was pretty sure that was what the man had said.

*I have found my bride.*

*Bride?*

*Bride?!*

"Bride?" Francesca swore, trying to force her weak body into sitting up. All that lifted was her neck. She dropped her head back down in frustration. Nothing made sense. Why would a prince choose to marry a stranger? A thief?

Her?

*Couldn't he have just said sex slave? I think I'd prefer that. At least I could respect it. What kind of prince threw his future away on a girl like her? What kind of man gave his word so flippantly?*

The guards hadn't touched her beyond carrying her to the room and tossing her on the bed. She still wore her mask and her dark clothing. Francesca closed her eyes and took several deep breaths, willing herself to move with her mind. If she concentrated hard enough, perhaps her mind would take over her body. Most injuries were mental anyway. It was part of the fight-through-the-pain mentality she'd been trained with. The feeling in her neck was slowly beginning to work its way down her shoulders. It felt like prickling needles along her shoulder blades. Hopefully, it wouldn't be long before she could move.

Hearing a noise, she turned to look at that door as it slid open. It was one of the princes, but not the crazy one who made her his bride. No, it was the other one, the sane one who had wanted to protest the marriage--Prince Haun. He too wore red and gold, only there weren't any dragons in the patterned design. Even if she hadn't seen him in the hall, it was clear by the superior look on his face that he was royalty. Only a man with power could look that arrogant and sure of himself. Francesca knew how to read people. In her line of work, she had to.

*I knew I shouldn't have come yet. I needed more time to prepare. If I were ready, I'd be gone by now with the Jade Phoenix. I should have waited.*

Who was she kidding? She was addicted to the adrenaline rush stealing gave her and she was as ready as she'd ever be to steal the Zhang artifact. Being 'on the job' was the only thing in the world that could make her feel alive. Odd that to feel alive she had to be in the clutches of death. Irony was nothing new to her. Neither was facing death. Life was a game and she did love to play.

She closed her eyes briefly. Perhaps *love* was too strong of a word. Compelled by a will outside of herself was more like it.

"Your name," the prince stated, speaking her language. His tone was husky and thick with his Líntiānese accent.

Francesca snorted and looked at the ceiling. Forcing complete disinterest into her tone, she said, "You first."

"I am Prince Zhang Haun, future Emperor of the Muntong Empire," he said. "You will answer my questions."

Francesca smirked. Did he honestly think his title would intimidate her? There was nothing he could do to her that was worse than what had already been done. Titles meant nothing to her, nor did the people who bore them--using status as a means of power over those who were weaker.

"Your name," he insisted, standing rigid by the door.

"Princess Zhang Mei," Francesca said, mocking his accent as she stared once more at the ceiling. There was something inside her, daring her on. It was the same thing that made her such a great thief. So what if she was reckless with her life? It was her life--such as it was. "Do you not recognize me, dear brother?"

"You dare to impersonate my sister?" the prince demanded. "You are not her. I spoke to her this morning."

"Your brother dares to claim me for a bride?" She mimicked his hard tone.

"What is your name, thief?"

"Princess Song Jia." Francesca could feel his frustration radiating over her. She tried to lift her hand. It was still plastered to the bed. Half expecting the prince to slap her for her obstinacy, she peeked at him from under her lowered lashes. His face was red and his fists were clenched at his sides. Oh yeah. He was livid.

"Fine. Do not answer. But you should think about your position here. Thieves are not welcome, even if my brother did claim you for his bride. Until the marriage is final, you can still be executed for your crimes. I suggest, for your sake, you tell him more than you are telling me." Prince Haun turned and left her alone.

Francesca rolled her eyes. Loudly, so the prince could hear her, she said, "Well, as long as I can't go anywhere, I might as well take a nap. Do you think you could have one of those nursemaid guards bring me an extra pillow?"

\* \* \* \*

Jin met his brother's eyes as they passed in the hall. Haun's lips were tight and he shook his head in obvious exasperation. His brother didn't have to say a word. Jin knew he was angry. Since Haun didn't get upset easily, he could only guess that the woman had really gotten to him. He wondered what she had done.

Sighing, he stopped by the door to his chamber, pressing his forehead against the cool gold inlaid entryway. From the corner of his eye, he watched Haun leave the royal chambers through the front entrance.

The guards had brought the woman to his room, as ordered. Jin wasn't sure he wanted her in his bed. Sure, she had beautiful eyes, but he had yet to see her face. And, even if she was the most engaging creature in the galaxies, it didn't mean he wanted to be married to her. He didn't want to marry any woman. Not yet.

"Why, Grandfather?" Jin whispered, staring at the door. "Why me? Why her? Why this?"

He waited for an answer that didn't come, but wasn't surprised. The ancestor was avoiding him.

"Fine, old spirit, play your game, but know that one day I too will be in the afterlife and then you won't be able to escape me."

Placing his hand on the door, he slid the barrier easily to the side. His eyes instantly went to the bed. Spread out on the silks was the woman. The stark black of her tight outfit was a startling contrast to the bright blue and gold silks of his bed. He searched the mask for her gorgeous eyes, but they were closed.

Jin waited, hands hanging by his sides as he stood in the doorway. He didn't expect her to be sleeping. She was a thief caught with her hand around the jade and she ... *slept?* It didn't make sense. He'd dealt with his fair share of criminals over the years and this was not how they acted.

He took a deep breath, shutting the door behind him. His family was depending on him and he wasn't sure where to start. What did he say to her? Sorry, I didn't mean it. I was possessed. Care to tell me who hired you?

Slowly, his eyes drifted down to her chest. It rose and fell evenly. He watched, counting to see if she faked rest. When it became apparent that she didn't, his examination went from investigative to curious. Jin found himself eyeing the gentle slope of her breast more than her breathing. The soft curves molded into a flat stomach and rounded hip. She was not shaped like the typical females of his planet. Her body was made up of lush curves, and yet was tight with muscles that he longed to explore for himself.

Jin glanced down her legs and back up to her hips. He was fascinated by the shape of them. Taking a step closer to the bed, he didn't think as he reached out to touch her. She didn't move. Lightly, he let the tips of his fingers glide over her hip. The woman's body was warm, causing his hand to tingle as the nerves came alive. A trail of desire worked its way over him, shooting up his fingers and stirring his loins. Without exploring further, he pulled back. She was still sleeping.

Jin knelt on the bed, his knee close to her unmoving arm as he stared at the mask that hid her face from view. Curious, he drew the backs of his fingers over her covered cheek. The mask was warm, caressing every subtle curve. He could see her tanned skin through the eye slits, or at least the part that wasn't covered by dark shadow. Her eyes were rounder, larger than his people's. Tracing his finger over the impression of her lips, he drew along to the other side. The mask didn't appear to have a seam to pull it free and expose her features.

"Please tell me you're above raping an unconscious woman."

Jin stiffened. It took him a second to translate the words as he fought down his desire for her. The woman hadn't moved and her eyes were still closed. However, he felt her cheek shift when she talked.

"Otherwise," her low voice continued, dripping with sarcasm, "I might regret your beautifully dictated proposal. It's not every day a woman is ordered to marry a tyrant. I have to say, I was very touched by the whole affair."

"You know who I am." Jin pulled back, moving to stand beside the bed. The woman chuckled and her lids opened. Her jade eyes stared directly at him, devoid of fear. In that moment he knew. She hadn't been sleeping. She'd been waiting. "How? You didn't look at me."

"I smelled you," she chuckled, "and by the sound of your walk."

"Impossible. You do not know me well enough for such things." Jin hid his surprise the best he could, but had a feeling she would sense it anyway. There was an eeriness to the way she looked at him, so lacking in emotion.

"In the hall. You touched me. I smelled you then and I smell you now. Not bad, I might add," she said, her tone low. She took a deep breath, making a show of sniffing him. "You exercised this morning. Not hard, but enough to sweat. Then you quickly bathed and dressed for the ceremony."

The woman paused, her eyes expectant as she waited for him to tell her she was right. She was studying him, watching him, assessing him. He would have to be very careful with her.

"You've been spying on me?" Jin frowned. If he wasn't mistaken, he saw her mask shift to match his expression.

"Of all the things I saw being dragged into the hall, you did the one thing I could not predict." Her eyes bore into his, probing, searching, seeing. "You claimed me for your bride."

Jin merely nodded, scrutinizing her as closely in turn. Her tone had dipped slightly, giving away her displeasure. Was it displeasure in herself or him? This woman was more than just a little observant. He had to watch what he said around her.

"Why?" she asked, confusion evident in her voice.

He could tell by the way she said the word that she wasn't pleased by the uncertainty his actions caused. Very cautious about every movement, he kept his face blank. "Perhaps it was love."

"At first sight?" she laughed. Jin wasn't sure what to think of her immediate dismissal. "No. I'll wager you're the type of man to love many, not one. I'm not judging you for it. In fact, good for you. Life is a thrill. Why settle? You should take pleasure in it while you have it. But, with all I see of you, I would still know why you claimed me. Is there something to gain by it? Rebellion against your parents, perhaps? Though I don't see you as that type. I bet you always do what is expected of you, don't you, your highness?"

She was trying to bait him into an argument. He kept his wits about him and refused to be provoked.

"Maybe you don't see as clearly as you think." A brow arched on his face and he couldn't help the small sense of satisfaction he felt as her eyelids dropped in annoyance. Still, her body didn't move. "Can you not get up yet? I did not think you would be subdued so long by my touch." Then, just to irritate her, he added, "I must have a greater effect on you than you let on, *bâobèi*."

Instead of answering, she said, "Adventure? Is that why? You see me as an adventure you have yet to try? A man like you would surely get bored here in the palace walls--so pampered and attended. The women here must not prove to be much of a conquest."

Jin wondered if he should be insulted by her assumptions of his character. So what if they were partially true. Is that how he was seen? As a womanizer? A rogue bent on seeking thrills? What man of flesh and blood wasn't like that to an extent?

"Oh, prince!" she mocked, her voice high and airy as she mimicked his people's accent. "You are such a good lover. Yes, I'll do anything for you, princey baby."

He frowned at her sardonic expression.

"There is more to you, prince, than what I determined at

first glance," she admitted. "Pity I won't be around long enough to figure it out."

"We do not execute you for your crimes yet."

"You will never execute me for my crimes. And, if you do, then the fault of it will be mine and I will only have myself to blame." Her eyes narrowed. "I don't deal well with being at fault."

There was such confidence in her, and a touch of recklessness. What was it about her? Did she truly not care? Did she not feel fear?

"I agree," Jin said, lightly touching her side as he ran his finger over her hip. "What happens to you does depend on your actions."

"What? I pleasure you and I get to go free?" she sneered.

So much for seducing the information out of her. Pity. It would have proved to be very enjoyable for the both of them.

"You're very clever, thief," Jin admitted, pulling his hand away. "And you appear very well trained--well enough to know how to bait me into losing my temper. I can only guess your Wushu master was well versed in the art."

Her mask shifted with a smile, but she didn't speak as her jade eyes bore unflinchingly into his.

"Who trained you?" Jin continued, nonplussed. He made a show of leisurely walking about his chambers, gently running his finger over the back edge of a chair. "A student of Master Ming Bo? Of Master Chen Sun?"

"Those men are dead," the woman said. "Killed by your family years ago. Who would be left to learn from them?"

"Killed by their own folly," he corrected.

"Each wave has a different pattern, but in the end it is still a wave," the woman said.

"So you know about the Wushu Uprisings. Evidently your teacher knew something of our history."

"I'm not going to reveal a name for you, prince, so stop probing." She let loose a long sigh. "Now, will you tell me? Why do you wish to marry me?"

Jin didn't know how to answer that. It was clear she didn't know about his grandfather's interference and he didn't feel like explaining to her. It was a delicate game they played and she seemed to enjoy it. How he could tell all this by only seeing her eyes, he wasn't sure. There was just something about her. The puzzle intrigued him, and if he was honest with himself he would admit that it frightened him as well. "I was compelled."

"And I'm compelled to say no to the decree, *ài rén*," she whispered, winking coyly as she said the endearment. "I thank you for the kind offer, but I really must be going."

Jin laughed. Raising his hands to the side, he motioned around him, turning as he looked around his chamber. "And where, *bâobèi*, would you go?"

She didn't answer. Jin completed his slow turn. The smile froze on his face as he looked at the bed. The woman was gone but the perfect imprint of her body was there to ruffle his covers. He glanced around. The door remained closed. There was no way out.

Moving carefully about the room, he looked everywhere she could possibly fit. The woman wasn't on the ceiling or floor and she didn't hide behind the furniture. Slowly crossing to his private bathing room, he frowned. Even the clear waters of the pool were empty. A growl caught in the back of his throat as he spun around to stare at the bed.

His bride had disappeared and he didn't even get her name.

\* \* \* \*

*There are all types of seductions. The seduction of the flesh is the most obvious. The rogue seducing the untried virgin even more so. But there is also the seduction of an object worth having. The seduction of greed, lust, hate. What seduces you, sweet Francesca? What is it you desire most?*

Francesca took a deep breath, remembering the words easily. The prince's light touch along her side had reminded her of the memory. Now, in her mind, she felt another caress--a caress from the past, moving along her naked hip to her breast.

How long since they were spoken and yet even the exact tone of voice that had whispered in her ear was perfectly clear. One didn't forget a day like that--a day above all others.

She closed her eyes. A week ago the answer to that had been simple. What seduced her? Revenge. The Jade Phoenix, an object worth having.

*What seduces you, sweet Francesca?*

Francesca opened her eyes, shaking off the hold the past had over her. So long ago... Too long to dwell on it. And yet she did. She was a prisoner to the past, to her promise, to her loss.

Crouching on the stone ledge, she looked out over the palace gardens. The winged insects that had fluttered above the flowers were gone, and the petals had all shifted with the night until they were one solid form, outlined by the firelight of the torches that lit the paths. It was evening and no one would see her against the moonless sky. Out of all the planets she'd been to, she'd noticed one thing. Night was almost always the same. Sure the color shifted, but there was always darkness and always stars glittering inside that darkness. Just like a vault filled with jewels waiting to be plucked, or a safe with ancient coins, a treasure room buried leagues beneath the sand of a remote planet filled with a dead king's gold. She'd stolen them all, and all was done on nights such as this one.

A cool breeze whipped around her, but she didn't shiver. Instead, she took it in, letting the wind enter her lungs, filling her. Another voice drifted into her head. Prince Zhang Jin. She'd heard his name spoken as she slipped through the halls. The news of his pending marriage was spreading fast through the servants. Every time she heard them say it, the strangeness became all the more real.

*I was compelled.*

Compelled? He was compelled to claim her for a bride? It didn't make sense. A prince would not take a thief as his own, let alone a strange woman who was not of his planet.

Francesca put her head in her hands, rubbing her temples through the mask. No. She'd scanned the room as she screamed at the guards who caught her. She saw everyone, everything.

*Everything.*

"Everything," she whispered. "How did I miss it?"

She had assessed the threats, analyzed the personalities around her. Jin was with his brothers, standing as an arrogant prince stood, surprised by her interruption just as the others were surprised. The screaming had served its purpose. It had taken everyone aback, causing them to react in a way she could easily read.

She was never wrong about someone, not after she looked at them and made up her mind. Prince Jin should not have been a threat. He should not have said a word and he should not have gotten involved with the guards.

But he had.

"Why?" she whispered, as if the night could answer her. "Why did he speak?"

Nothing went as planned. In the event she was captured, she'd imagined she would have been dragged to the prisons and from there she would have eventually escaped. Even though the result was the same--escaping the Zhangs' hold-- the simple fact that he'd managed to surprise her threw her confidence.

*Maybe I'm not ready for this. I needed more practice.*

Then there was the second surprise, even more confounding than the first. Desire. Pure, hot, liquid desire. The kind that made her body ache and her concentration slip. The prince touched her and she desired him. He heated her blood until she couldn't move. The control over her limbs had come back as she waited for him to visit her, but when he touched her that second time, alone in his room, the sensation had made her helpless once again. It wasn't like the first, not a numbing drug that took away all feeling. No, it was more powerful than that. It was the kind of euphoria that rendered her helpless to all but passion.

Francesca took a deep breath, trying to reason through her confusion. She'd been frozen, waiting for him to continue his exploration. Part of her wanted him to pull off the mask, to peel the layers of clothing from her body.

It was something she shouldn't want. The handsome prince was a complication she didn't need. And yet he was the only thing she could think of. It had been so long since anything took her by surprise.

*What seduces you, sweet Francesca? What is it you desire most?*

"The prince," she answered the memory, shamed even as she said it. "At this moment, I desire the prince the most."

\* \* \* \*

"She's gone," Jin said, ashamed as he looked his father in the eye. Every inch of his body was wrought with tension. How could he let her get away? How did she do it? He'd studied martial arts for decades and couldn't dream of being so stealthy.

"Wushu," the empress answered her son's silent questions, nodding sadly. They were in his father's private chambers.

His parents lounged on a low couch with a short wooden back. Smoke from a long pipe rolled over them as the emperor drew short puffs. "It's why the practice was outlawed. Those who studied it became too dangerous, too powerful. There was no one left to patrol them. Master Ming Bo's followers almost ended this empire."

"Yes, Mother, I've read the history of it. Our armies barely defeated them," Jin said. "After that, all practitioners were forced into the mountains to live out their days in solitude in a temple surrounded by guards and ancient Zhang magic so they couldn't escape. Those who refused to comply died."

"No," the emperor answered, his tone gruff as he set the pipe aside. "Master Ming defeated our armies, save but one regiment. It was only by the aid of Master Chen Sun that he was in turn defeated. It was Master Chen who convinced your ancestors that all who followed Master Ming's teachings had to be eliminated for the good of all. He led his band into the mountains where they lived out their days in solitude. Word was sent down when Master Chen died. The art of Wushu died with him."

The empress lightly touched her husband's arm. "We thought it died with him."

"Yes," the emperor agreed. "So we thought. One of Ming Bo's rebels must have gotten away."

"Or Chen Sun's," the empress added. "Not all of his followers were happy with the decision to live in solitude."

"Why didn't you say something earlier about Ming Bo's victory over us?" Jin asked. "The scrolls state clearly that we defeated him. The peasants celebrate the victory with festivals. Is it all a lie?"

"We didn't know the whole truth," the empress said. "And it is not a lie. Ultimately the Wushu Uprisers were defeated. Only, they were defeated by their own kind."

"Grandmother An only now told us of this." The emperor grabbed his pipe and took in a long draw of smoke, only to let it roll slowly from his lips in a white, curling trail. Jin waited, recognizing the gesture. His father was contemplating the situation. "The history scrolls were altered for the sake of public relations."

"History should not be changed," Jin said, frowning. "How are we to learn from past mistakes if it is?"

"You do not have the burden of emperor, Zhang Jin," his

mother scolded, frowning at him. "There are many considerations."

"Are you saying you've changed our history?" he demanded.

Neither of them answered for a long time.

"Father?" Jin insisted.

"No, but had I been emperor in the time of the Wushu Uprising, I would have. The way history remembers the deeds gives everyday people hope that they can survive against great odds. Why should they know the truth of it? That their beloved Wushu masters, who they respected and trusted, nearly killed their empire? It was bad enough that they tried." The emperor paused for effect. "Or that Emperor Song's ancestors would've taken over their half of the planet? Is it not better that they believe their Imperial Guard the victors? That it was their ancestors, ordinary people, who overthrew the Wushu? Do you know the hope that belief gives to people?"

"No one gains by lies," Jin insisted.

"You will mind your place!" the emperor yelled, shooting to his feet. "Unless the gods will it, you will never know the burden of ultimate rule. There are things that must be done to ensure the family line and to ensure peace. Not everything can be as neat as you wish it to be. Not everything is noble and good. The galaxies are a hard place. Would you have outsiders invading our planet? Spreading their filth? Do you wish to see Líntiān become another space port? Torn apart by other cultures until ours no longer exists? Our paradise sucked dry by greed until all we have left is a barren wasteland? That is what would happen if the people are not kept together, joined in one belief. That is why we must protect the public opinion of this empire and of this family. The scrolls were changed to protect our world."

His mother was slower to rise during the emperor's tirade. She placed a hand on her husband's arm. "Jin, you have an honest and noble heart, but you are not meant to rule Líntiān. There are things in this you will never understand. Considerations of which you will never be told. Your place is as a prince, brother to the future emperor. Your sound judgment will help to guide Haun and for that reason we would not have you jaded by such things as these. You have been raised in the traditions for that reason. That is the gift that was chosen for you."

"But how can I help guide if I don't know the truth of our past?" Jin did his best to remain calm, but it was hard. He was taken aback by his mother's blunt words. Raised in the traditions for a reason? Groomed, not to think for himself but to help guide his brother? He'd always known he would never be emperor, but to find out that he was shielded from things just so his judgment in the old traditions would not be clouded with doubt?

"You are only told of it now because of this woman, your chosen bride," his mother said, by way of an answer. It wasn't much of a response.

Jin couldn't speak as thoughts whirled in his head--thoughts of marriage, tradition and deceit.

"My life has been a lie?" Jin knew he said the words aloud, but he could barely hear them.

"A lie?" the empress repeated. "No, my loved son, not a lie. Your life has great purpose. When your mind calms you will see it. The Jade Phoenix blessed you with your path for a reason."

"Your duty calls to you, my son," the emperor put forth, preventing any coddling the empress might have in mind. "You must find your bride. We have decided not to put her on trial, as it might make her even harder to read. Haun agrees that the engagement should go on as planned. We'll spread word through the guards that she was picked up for trespassing on palace grounds and that she was merely lost."

*More lies.*

"Tomorrow, the astrologers will be here to read your future together. Perhaps they will have some insight into your grandfather's actions," his mother said. "Now go, find your bride and do not lose her again."

"I have a feeling we'll find her," the emperor said. "Why don't you go rest, Jin, and await word that she is found."

It wasn't a request. Jin placed his fist to palm and bowed to his parents. His life was spinning in circles around him and he couldn't seem to catch his breath. In one day everything had slipped from his control. He was engaged against his will, told that his life was tailored only to help Haun rule and now he had to try and figure out the plot to protect an empire he wasn't sure he knew.

How much of their history was a lie? How many scrolls

had been altered? The questions he now asked himself shook the very foundation of his soul.

Without another word, he left them in their bedchamber. What could he say anyway? His father was right. Regardless of how he felt about it, he had his duty to perform. Only, somehow, duty didn't sound as noble as it once had.

## Chapter Three

*Fucking Space Balls!*

"Why can't any of you fuck-nuts face me like a man? One on one? Two on one? Bravon's fire! I'll take you all on." Francesca bucked against the guard, screaming at the top of her lungs as they dragged her from the Sacred Chamber hidden within the walls of the Hall of Infinite Wisdom. There were at least a dozen of them and she was irate that they stopped her again from stealing the artifact.

*How in the star blazes do they keep doing that? I was so careful this time!*

The Sacred Chamber was an ornate, yet barren room. Gold lined the walls in intricate carvings. There was a basin etched with a phoenix, a low offering table and, behind a plate of glass, the Jade Phoenix surrounded by smaller pieces of the precious green stone. The phoenix had been cut from old bronze long ago. Its delicate feathers worked in such a way that they should've been impossible to make. Jewels inlaid into the bronze, but none were as stunning as the big green stone on the bird's chest.

She needed that damned bird!

"You're all a bunch of cowards! *Cào nî zûxiān shí bâ dai*!" Francesca screamed in frustration. How in the Solar galaxy did they keep catching her?! "Let go of me and face me in a fair fight. I'll take you all on, you sons of whores! Let go of me, *chùsheng xai-jiao de xiang huo*!"

Francesca meant every word of it too. They were all animal fornicating bastards! How could these inept guards have caught her? She'd slipped by them so easily in the courtyard.

Moaning in frustration, she kicked harder. She had been so close to the prize. Her hand had literally been mere inches away from reaching the bronze feathers before the guards stormed in, pooling into the room like a handful of beads falling on the floor. She fought them, but there were too many. Just as soon as she laid one out with a kick there were three others to replace him. Unfortunately, in the Sacred

Chamber there wasn't any room to maneuver about as they'd crowded her in, overtaking her with the crush of their bodies.

Francesca had no choice but to get caught. Tasting blood in her mouth where they had struck her, she spit it at one of the guards. The man flinched, but only painfully tightened his hold in response.

*Don't do it, Francesca,* she told herself as she continued to scream obscenities at the men. *Don't you dare say anything you'll regret.*

"*Chùsheng xai-jiao de xiang huo!*" she screamed. There, that was good. "Come on, you no-good, mama's boys!"

The hands only tightened, cutting off circulation to her limbs. She felt something stab her leg and looked down in time to see a golden feather dart. The man who jabbed her with it was reaching toward his belt to grab another. Jerking, she tried to stop him, but he hit her again. As he reached for the third, she began to panic. Whatever drug they were tipped with could only be fought for so long. If he kept it up, she'd be knocked insensible.

*Don't say it, Francesca. Don't say it.*

"What?!" she demanded, knowing she was going to say it. "The future princess can't look at the family possessions?"

*Ah, Space Balls! I said it.*

The statement received the reaction she imagined it would. The grips on her body lightened and her legs were lowered cautiously to the ground. Attentive, dark eyes watched her and they refused to let go of her completely.

"Then you have accepted our joined fate."

Francesca's eyes ripped over the men only to land on Prince Jin. He stood in the doorway, his face stern if not a little irritated. The man was hardly the picture of a happy bridegroom. It was fitting. She wasn't exactly an ecstatic bride.

Francesca wasn't above using deceit to get her way. She was a thief after all. But, she didn't like using this particular deceit for some reason. Maybe it was her attraction to the prince that made her hesitate. Or, perhaps, it was the idea of marriage itself. It left a bad taste in her mouth to think of the archaic tradition. People were better off without such attachments.

"It would seem I have," she grumbled, trying to rip her arm

from a guard. The man held tight so she couldn't get free. Others surrounded her so even if she did get away from them, she'd still be in for a fight.

Of course she'd thought of the possibility of being Jin's bride before trying a second time at stealing the phoenix. The second attempt plan had been simple. She did it because no one would expect her to try again so soon. They would expect her to run away scared.

But maybe they did expect her. Had she underestimated Jin again? Francesca bit back a curse, though why she did so now she had no idea. She had no problem spouting foul curses at the guards for all to hear, daring them to do something about it. Death and pain didn't frighten her in the least. In fact, few things did frighten her. For some reason, Prince Jin was fast becoming one of those things.

As Prince Jin's bride, she would have access to all parts of the castle. She'd be watched, but if she laid low and waited, she'd also eventually be trusted. Then, all she would have to do would be to sit back and wait for her chance. The plan would take longer to execute than she would like, but she had waited so long to get a chance at the phoenix, what was a little more time? Besides, it wasn't like the whole 'sneaking in and stealing it' idea was working out for her.

She snorted. Princess Zhang Francesca it was. Even the voice in her head sounded mocking of the title.

Lowering her chin, she looked at Jin and smiled. She knew he couldn't see her face beneath her mask, but that didn't matter. He would see the shifting of her lips, the sparkling in her eyes. Male vanity would fill in the rest. She almost felt sorry for the guy. When she put her mind to doing something, she went all the way. Prince Jin didn't stand a chance.

* * * *

Jin couldn't believe it. Here the woman was again trying to steal from his family. That had to be a record--twice in one day. For years not a single person had tried to sneak into the Sacred Chamber and then it had only been a servant wanting a peek at their people's history. The woman had been properly punished for trespassing, but she had meant no harm.

Then why was this thief, his bride, determined to take it? Was it merely for the challenge? For Emperor Song? What?

Jin wasn't fooled by her sudden acquiescence to the idea of marriage. She'd been caught at her game twice and would be trying another angle. It looked like he was the new angle.

*Wonderful.* The thought rang sarcastically in his head.

The woman set her gaze boldly on him and smiled. The way the lights from above hit the mask, he could see her lips moving. Her eyes sparkled mischievously. Jin gulped, his gut tightened with sudden intrigue and desire. There was no denying this *qin ài de* did something to him. She stirred his blood, making him want to make love to her and punish her at the same time. How close the emotions of desire and anger could be!

Jin didn't move as he waited to see what she would do next. He had a feeling that having her around would never bore him, though he might die of aggravation if forced to endure her for a lifetime. She was like a drug, luring him in and driving him mad.

Then why in the galaxies was he stepping closer to the *Ch'ang Shih*?

The woman continued to look at him, her eyes sparkling with their jade mischief. Every ounce of him wished they'd met under different circumstances, that she was a woman and he a man and this a court celebration. In his daydream, he'd ask her to dance, to walk and eventually they'd end up kissing on the stone bridge that arched over the Enchanted River, or perhaps on a boat floating over the small river that wound through the palace. In his mind, he'd make love to her on the gently undulating water. But, in reality, he was faced with a coldhearted thief who could very well make his life a living *di yu.*

Jin found himself lifting his hand to the guards, motioning for them to let her go. They did, stepping back, even as their eyes stayed suspiciously trained on her. He couldn't blame them. If he was smart, Jin would order the guards to bind her and throw her in the Enchanted River until she drowned.

"Why?" Jin asked her, eyeing her mask as he watched for any detectable changes in her expressions. She slowly pulled a black glove off one hand and then the other, exposing her small hands. Her eyes darted around, taking in the guards before falling back on him.

Lifting her hand to the top of her head, she pulled. Jin's heart stopped. She lifted the mask from her face. It was slow torture. First, her tanned neck was exposed then her full lips, straight nose and finally her jade gaze. A long dark stripe ran from one temple to the other, passing right over the bridge of her nose to encircle both eyes. It was the dark shadow he'd seen beneath the mask.

She was gorgeous.

Lifting a finger, she grabbed a pin on the top of her head. Shaking slightly, curls spilled over her shoulders in dark brown waves. Her hair was messy, but adorably so. She smiled, a slow, seductive smile meant to drive men wild. It worked. Jin's body came to instant attention as the blood rushed from his head right into his very interested crotch.

"Why?" he repeated, his voice suddenly hoarse.

"Love?" She wrinkled her nose playfully.

"At first sight?" Jin didn't move. She was teasing him, enflaming his blood on purpose like a siren sent to do him in.

"Perhaps I was compelled." She glanced back to the guards meaningfully.

"Ah." His tone dropped as she stopped in front of him. Her mask and gloves were clutched in her hands. She petted them, running her fist over them in a leisurely movement. Jin swallowed as he watched. The way her fist drew over the ends made him very aware of how close her hands were to his arousal. He lifted his eyes to the guards, not moving to touch her. Only their presence kept him back. At the moment, he welcomed their eyes on him. Their gazes would keep him steadfast in his determination to stay away from her. If he was to give in to his desires, it could very well be the last thing he ever did. Bedding the woman would be like bedding a poisonous *duchee jyr-juh,* a small forest dwelling spider that breathed toxic gas to subdue its victims before devouring them whole. Trying to remain calm, he said, "It can very well be compelling, can it not?"

The woman laughed and stepped to the side, impishly tilting her head as she moved around him. Jin watched her ass as she walked away, turning to follow. He heard the guards stirring and lifted his hand to stop them without waiting to see if they obeyed.

*So much for them bearing witness and saving me from myself. So much for me not doing the foolish thing.*

She passed through the doors to the outside and began the descent down the long row of stone steps that led to the walkway below. Guards stood at attention next to the columns that lined the outside of the Hall of Infinite Wisdom. Jin ignored them, hurrying to catch up to the woman. He grabbed her arm, stopping her. His bride blinked, staring forward into the surrounding garden.

"It's not proper for you to walk before me," he said quietly. "If you truly mean to be my bride, you must act with decorum. Lest I'll think you don't really wish to be married to me."

"You just try and keep up with me, your highness." She chuckled. Her green eyes cut to him, reminding him who she was and what she was after. The thought sobered him some. "And remember, *you* chose me. I didn't agree to play meek and mild lady for you."

"Do not remind me." Jin offered his arm. "If we're keeping score, then I would say I'm ahead by two. You've been caught twice, *duchee jyr-juh*."

She stiffened, hesitating before taking his arm. The woman didn't take kindly to the reminder. Jin hid his smile. Pride would be her downfall.

"Ah, but you offered to marry me. I'd say that's a point for me. You're up by one, your highness." The woman smiled sweetly. He wasn't fooled.

"*Duchee jyr-juh?*" she asked.

"I believe the translation is heart of many sweets." He gave her an innocent smile.

"Huh, because I thought the translation was poisonous, gas spewing spider."

"Or maybe that," he answered without missing a beat.

"How romantic of you," she muttered.

"Tell me your real name and we'll call the score even," he said.

"Deal." She started walking again, moving through the gardens. He couldn't help but notice she walked toward the royal family's private quarters, toward his room. "Francesca La Rosa."

"Rosa," he repeated. "Do I call you Rosa or La Rosa?"

"Francesca," she corrected.

"You wish for me to be formal with you until the marriage?"

Francesca laughed. "My name is Francesca La Rosa. La Rosa is my family name, just like Zhang is yours. You can call me Francesca."

"Ah, I see. I vaguely remember studying such backward customs as putting the individual before the family name."

"Yes, we foreigners are very strange creatures," she teased. "You had better beware. I might steal more than just precious gold from you."

Jin laughed. "You know, Francesca. If you weren't trying to steal from my family we might get along very well."

Francesca shifted her grip, threading her fingers around his bicep. "I don't know about all that. I think we can still get on rather well. If you can forget I'm a thief, I'll forget you're a spoiled prince."

"I don't think that's possible." He grinned. What was it about her that made him want to kiss and strangle her at the same time?

"Mm, pity. Guess I'll just have to make you forget it."

Before he knew what was happening, she was spinning around him in one graceful movement. He tensed, ready for an attack. But the attack that came wasn't what he expected. Her warm lips pressed tightly to his followed by a soft, feminine moan of passion.

Jin gasped in surprise and she slipped her tongue instantly inside. Her boldness excited him, as did the sense of danger he felt in her. Everything about her was different than the women he knew--from her features and the color of her skin, to the way she spoke, the way she kissed him. For a moment, he didn't move, as duty and desire warred within him. Why was he fighting her? Yes, she was a thief, but he had every right to be with her. She was his bride. No matter what happened tomorrow, tonight she was his bride.

Groaning, he grabbed her arms, pulling her to him. His body pressed into hers, so tight his arousal ground into her warm, accepting body. He felt her smile against his lips before pulling back.

"See. There's no reason we can't get along, your highness," she whispered. "We just don't have to trust each other while we do it."

\* \* \* \*

Maybe sleeping with the prince wasn't her most brilliant idea, but what else was Francesca going to do to pass the time until she got another chance at the Jade Phoenix? In truth, she was damned lucky they hadn't locked her up--not that bars would keep her. Besides, opportunity rarely presented itself for anything more than a one time romp. The prince was sexy. He was in shape and he intrigued her. What more was there to consider?

Jin was taller than her and his body was lean with muscle. She wasn't scared of his strength. Power and strength never frightened her.

The prince lightly thrust his hips into her, letting her feel the length of his erection through their clothing. There was no mistaking his desire for her. A slow, catlike grin spread over his face. She tried to read him, but found that she didn't trust her own judgment completely. Now, that scared her-- uncertainty.

Logic again told her to leave. She was so close to obtaining her goal and Prince Jin was more complication than she needed right now, and definitely more distraction.

*I'm just using him.*

Francesca grabbed his face and kissed him hard, as if trying to convince herself that she could feel nothing beyond lust and that any man in his place would do. The night air was cool and fresh, tinged with the faint scent of smoke from the garden torches and the subtle perfume of his skin. Her senses were sharpened. She'd memorized his smell the first time he touched her and now it became reinforced by the taste of his kiss. This man was in her head now.

Francesca ran her fingers into his soft hair, grazing his mouth with her teeth as she bit at his firm lower lip. His fingers kneaded against her arms, but didn't move to caress her as she would have him do. As each second passed and all he did was lightly thrust his arousal against her, she became more aggressive.

She pushed at him and he took a step back. Their bodies parted. His chest rose and fell like a wild Huthin ready to pounce. Francesca knew the feeling. Desire raged within her until she shook with it. His hands rose to the side and he smiled. It took her a moment through her passion, but she recognized the challenge. She arched a brow, returning his provocative look.

*It's all foreplay, ài rén.*

Jin sidestepped, the action measured and slow. Francesca positioned her body and mimicked his movements as they circled each other. He took five steps to the side before switching direction to take five steps back. His feet landed lightly on the ground, making no sound as he walked. Francesca knew there were Imperial guards within the garden, possibly watching them, though they would not come forward and show themselves unless the prince demanded it. She didn't care.

Firelight danced over Jin's strong features. The orange glow caressed his dark, smooth skin. It reflected in his eyes and traveled seductively over his parted lips. A halo of light silhouetted his hair, shining on the silky locks. He moved like the light--graceful, silent, perfect.

Francesca's heart beat hard in her chest. A man with sex appeal and the ability to fight, could there be anything more arousing?

Each step was like a dance as they continued to size up the other's skill. Francesca knew that, being a man, he'd let her take the first attack. She wouldn't disappoint.

Testing him, she punched. It was a mild assault, not nearly as skilled as she could perform. He blocked it easily. Francesca charged him a few more times, each time adding another combination. He blocked her every time. Withdrawing, she continued the circle they formed. He nodded in approval. She returned the look. Jin smirked at her arrogance.

With a grunt, she shot forward, rigorously kicking and punching in a fury of movement. Abrupt sounds of the fight surrounded them as they moved. They took in deep breaths only to exhale with sudden shouts of energy and power. Some of her blows landed, most were blocked. Jin's body was limber, as if he was well used to training exercise.

Francesca refused to turn the full force of her talent on him. It wouldn't do to beat up the man she would later take to her bed. If he was going to be worth anything between the sheets, she would have to leave him with some ego intact.

"You have strong hands," he said, smiling. By the way he moved, she could tell he was used to training in wide, open areas. The gymnastic quality to his kicks caused them to spread in long, sweeping arches and his punches were just as beautifully executed. She adjusted her style to accommodate his.

Open area or small enclosure, it didn't matter. Francesca could fight under almost any condition. The only weakness she had was when she was up against multiple opponents in a small area, like when the guards pooled in around her. So long as she had room to maneuver, she did all right.

"Thank you," Francesca paused, striking out in a combination of punches. "I spent a year driving them into containers of sand to strengthen their blows."

"And yet they are still so soft to the touch," he answered.

Francesca was taken slightly aback by the low words and missed her aim by a millimeter. It was enough of a mistake to irritate her, even if Jin didn't notice.

Angered that he could make her lose focus, she fiercely cried out and hit the back of her fist to his head, following it with a sweeping kick to his side. He doubled over with a grunt.

Though, afterward, he stood a little too quickly. Suspicious, she did it again, this time more predictably. Again he doubled over. Suddenly, she stopped, dropping her arms to her side.

Frowning, she said, "You are absorbing my punches."

"I didn't want to hurt your feelings. You seemed to be enjoying yourself." Jin's smile remained intact.

"Do not patronize me," she ordered. "I can handle myself in a fight."

"Of that I have no doubt." His expression didn't change.

"Then why do you hold back? Are you afraid to hit a girl?"

"Actually, I wanted to ask you the same thing. Why do you hold back? Are you afraid?"

Francesca grinned at that and nodded. He was right. She had been holding back. It would seem her restraint was as insulting to his talent as his was to hers. "Shall we go again, *ài rén?*"

"If you think you can handle yourself, *bâobèi.*" He shifted direction, raising one fist up by his shoulder as the other angled toward the ground.

"I believe we both know the answer to that." Francesca mimicked his pose. They stopped walking. Tension rippled over her flesh.

"Wushu," he said quietly.

Francesca knew in that moment the real reason why he wanted to fight her. He wanted to see her style, to see if she was what they said. She couldn't do it for she didn't consider him a worthy opponent.

Wushu had developed over the many centuries, starting in the old Earth traditions long, long ago when humans had yet to evolve into what they were now, when Earthlings didn't even know of other aliens' existences.

It was possible that she was one of the few, if not the only one, left who knew the art. Francesca was saddened to think that her knowledge of the ancient military fighting art was all that was left. She had a few scrolls, translated so she could understand them, but she had a feeling there was so much more to be learned. Only, there was no one left to teach her.

Wushu was no longer just a sport of dance-like grace like it had been in the Earth days. It still utilized the spear, sword and unarmed combat routines, but now it was so much more than that. Wushu Masters combined all the strengths of the old cultures--the Ninjutsu's stealth and ability to become invisible, Thai boxing, the kicking of Tang Soo Do, the swordplay of Kendo. They took traits from Karate, Kung Fu, Judo, Aikido, even Iaido and Kobudo which utilized ancient farm implements in battle. The best of all skills were blended into the perfect art form.

*That* was something she would never show him. She wasn't sure why, but she didn't want to use it on him. Even if she had wanted to, she couldn't. Light sparring was one thing, but to bare her talent in such a way….

Francesca refused to move and shook her head. She knew how precious a gift she possessed and she hoarded her knowledge. Only if she found someone who could possibly appreciate the knowledge she had would she pass it on. A Zhang prince could never be that man. He didn't deserve to see the full range of her skills.

The moment her decision to stop their demonstration hit him, she saw it. His eyes narrowed and he charged forward in anger. Jin struck out his fist, aiming for her face. She didn't move, not even to flinch as it came for her jaw. She stared directly into his dark gaze, wishing he'd hit her. What had started as foreplay had become something else, something dark and twisted.

His fist stopped just short of her cheek. She felt the warmth of it as he let it hover a hairsbreadth away from her flesh. Slowly, she turned her face into his hard fist. Her cheek brushed over his naked hand in a small caress. Her body tingled where they touched, running a rampant course through her stirred blood only to settle in her nipples before working down to her moist pussy. She wanted him inside her, wanted to feel his flesh, his strength, wanted to feel the contact that only intimacy could bring.

How long had it been? She honestly couldn't remember. So long since the fire erupted in her stomach, so long since time had stood still for a single moment, a single person.

*What seduces you, sweet Francesca? What is it you desire most?*

Francesca closed her eyes, turning away from his hand. Her body protested, down to the last nerve and an ache fell upon her heart, squeezing it. The denial stung, but she knew she must embrace it, bear it. If she could walk away now, she could walk away later. Turning her back on the royal sleeping chambers, she did just that. She walked away.

Jin didn't follow. She would've heard him if he did. Her ears strained. After some time, she turned. His dark body was silhouetted by the torchlight as he watched her. Slowly, his hand lifted and the guards moved from the shadows toward her.

*What seduces you, sweet Francesca? What is it you desire most?*

"The prince," she whispered as the guards took up her arms. She didn't resist them and they seemed almost glad for it. Jin didn't move and she imagined she could still see his dark eyes looking at her, boring into her with their soul-piercing sharpness. She turned her back on him, letting the guards haul her away.

\* \* \* \*

Jin stood rigid, watching as the guards walked Francesca from him toward the barracks. It was the only place within the palace walls where she could be kept under lock and key.

He took a deep breath. Her insult stung. She didn't think him worthy enough to spar with using the full range of her skills. It was a blow to his manhood, which at the moment had a mind of its own. His hard shaft didn't seem to be taking the blow as badly as his head was. In fact, it was more than willing to forgive her, so long as she came back into his arms and continued her aggressive kisses. Maybe it was because most women feared his power, but no one had ever dared kiss him like that, like she needed him to sustain her own life.

*She only wants something from me. She wants to steal from my family. There is no giving in her, only taking. She is a thief.*

The words did little to calm the fierceness of his desire, even if they did strengthen his resolve. Too bad he couldn't take another to his bed. To do so would be insulting to his honor. He'd just declared a bride.

Why had they started sparring when it had been clear their bodies needed much more than a fight? Maybe it had been the look in her eyes, the need to control him when she kissed him. Or was that punishment in her kiss? Even as she embraced him, she warred with him. Her mouth fought his, their tongues twining in endless circles as she tried to subdue him. Then she had pushed him in the chest, knocking him away when he didn't give her the intimate battle of the wills she wanted. Francesca wanted to be in charge of their situation. Jin had dealt with warriors before. After years of practicing, fighting became comforting to them, familiar. It was no wonder lovemaking would be like war to her. When he would be gentle and exploring, she wanted it rough and emotionless. Was it just another defense? A way to ensure nothing ever touched her heart?

Jin sighed, believing to understand more than he wanted to about his bride. Understanding allowed him to feel sorry for her, to pity her. Mercy was the last thing he needed with someone who wished to destroy all he held dear--someone who wouldn't hesitate to destroy him.

Francesca disappeared from sight, led toward the barracks. The guards would take her to a locked room there and watch over her. If she didn't sleep in his quarters, she'd sleep in the prison hold until they were told otherwise. Orders from the emperor were to keep a constant eye on her. Unfortunately, it was easier said than done. It was Zhang An and another ancestor who had alerted them to her second attempt at the Jade Phoenix.

A woman like Francesca would suspect the guards and it was proven she could get around them. What she didn't know was that their ancestors also watched her. He just hoped it was enough to keep her from her goal. Without the Jade Phoenix, there was no Muntong Empire, no Zhang Dynasty. Without the Jade Phoenix, his family's power would cease to exist.

Jin looked down at his stiff erection. And, more pressingly, without a willing bride to take to his bed, there would be no sweet release for him this night.

## Chapter Four

Francesca lay on the silk-covered mat, staring at the ceiling. The bed was oddly comfortable for a prison, but she decided that maybe she was afforded nicer quarters due to her 'position' as Jin's future princess. Tapping her toes in frustration--both sexual and mental--she sighed heavily. If Jin wasn't going to sleep with her, maybe she should have beaten him until his insides spilled out of his body and he no longer had to suffer. Or until he was too weak to protest her advances.

Francesca smiled. That idea had merit.

The room she was kept in was sparse, but relaxing. A pitcher full of water was on a low table. The blue markings on a white background depicted some sort of fruit. At least she assumed it was a fruit by its plump, round shape. There was a matching cup with a wide rim. A decontaminator unit was in the corner, not fancy as it was exposed to the main part of the room. It worked and that's all that mattered. She'd needed the quick decontamination and it felt good to get clean.

Two guards stood on duty outside her locked door, but she knew she could escape. The men would be easy to subdue. Turning on her side, she didn't make a move to leave. Why should she? The bed was comfortable and they would most likely feed her in the morning. Funny how some people always felt the need to take care of the enemy. It would make more sense to execute her and save the expense of food and board. Come to think about it, she had stayed in a few places that adopted the 'don't waste anything on the prisoner' mentality, though it had usually been bounty hunters in space.

Sleep wouldn't come no matter how hard she tried to relax. That was nothing new. Francesca was used to staying awake, plotting and scheming. With her eyes closed, she tried to picture the last time she was happy. Though it had been long ago, it was easy to recall the exact moment.

The sensation of a hand brushing over her hip tingled her

flesh. She loved those hands, so strong and confident. They were hands that could touch with kindness and kill with precision. Those hands had struck her in training, held her in passion. The man was older than her, but that didn't matter. He looked young for his age and she was wise well beyond her years. When they came together it was out of a mutual sorrow. His was the sorrow of having lost everything he held dear and hers was the sorrow of never having anything to hold dear. No one cared about her growing up. She was fed, schooled, even given small measures of dutiful affection, but never loved.

*If you have nothing to fear, you have nothing to lose. We are all motivated by our desires. There are all types of seductions ... the seduction of an object worth having. The seduction of greed, lust, hate. What seduces you, sweet Francesca? What is it you desire most?*

She had tried to live by those words, tried to eliminate all fear from her life. Death no longer frightened her, neither did physical pain. But, tonight had proved to her that she hadn't succeeded in erasing all emotion. She was scared of Jin, terrified that she could feel passion for him. Him, a Zhang prince, of all people! It was the worst possible choice her body could have made. Why a Zhang prince? Why that line? She'd much rather marry a Liphobian sea slug than feel anything beyond disgust for a Zhang.

Francesca curled on her side, hugging her waist. She missed the sensation of being held as she fell asleep. She had never felt safe as she did when held by those hands and she hadn't felt safe since losing them. Funny how she missed the little things the most--his hands, the feel of breath against the back of her neck, the silence of meditating in the same room as another person, feeling their energy mingling with her own.

*If you have nothing to fear, you have nothing to lose.*

She had something to lose back then and she'd lost it. The pain was something she never wanted to risk again. She thought of the prince, tasting him as if he were right there. There was something about him, his eyes, that reminded her of her dead lover. But that was all, just a look. Otherwise they were different and she would not confuse the two in her mind.

*Do not be ruled by fear!* she ordered herself.

The needs of the body were just a part of being alive, she reasoned. Just like she needed to eat or breathe, so did she need to fulfill lust. There was no shame in it. Taking another to her bed would not tarnish the memories she held.

"Prince Zhang Jin is what I desire," she whispered, giving a small self-deprecating laugh. Her body was tight with longing for him. She thought walking away would cure her of it, but it didn't. The longer she stayed away from him, the more her desires grew. At this rate, it would affect her concentration.

*Maybe I'm going about this all wrong. Maybe I need to work him out of my system, not practice self-denial. Maybe I need to prove to myself that he's not worth the thought I give him.*

"Sounds good to me," Francesca said, rolling back as she kicked her legs into the air only to land on her feet. All this contemplation was only going to make her sad. She did much better if she had a plan of action. Glancing briefly at the colorful silk tunic and pants that were left for her to wear, she decided to stick with her black clothing.

She ran her fingernail down the side of her pant leg to open a hidden seam. Carefully taking out two discs, she placed one in each palm and cupped them gently.

"*Zhùzuĭ,*" she hissed, knowing the guards would hear her. She wanted them to. Let them think she argued with someone in her room. "*Zhè bìng bù huài!*"

Watching the bottom edge of the door, she saw the light shift as a shadow fell over it. She scuffed her heel across the floor, knowing the guards listened closely.

"I said shut up. It's not that bad! I have a plan that will…." Francesca hissed, before scuffing her foot again. She crept across the floor, placing her feet so they made no sound.

It wasn't long before the door was pushed open. The guards never knew what hit them, as she lunged at them only to slap them with the discs--one on the cheek, the other on the naked arm. A wave of nausea washed over her as the mild poison cracked, oozing liquid. She gagged, trying not to throw up as she quickly got over the effects. The guards weren't so lucky. They collapsed on the floor, unmoving. Francesca swallowed, taking several deep breaths. It had taken many nights of dosing herself with the drug to get to the point that she could tolerate it. It served them right, trying to drug her with the dart as they had.

No harm would come to the men. They'd sleep through the night and wake up confused. In a few days they'd be themselves. The confusion came in handy when she needed her captors to forget what they saw until she could get far away. It was a shame to waste two of the discs on her need to get laid, but she could always buy more on Torgan.

Sighing, she shook her head. "Too easy. You guys really are pathetic excuses for warriors. If you were my guards I'd have you flogged within an inch of your life for letting a little thing like me escape."

The only answer they gave her was a soft snore.

"Pathetic," she muttered, shaking her head.

The hallway was lined with giant gold medallions over the dark red walls. Odd blue trees were in pots along the sides, set upon low rectangular tables, and looking very much like a row of miniature circular steps that led to nowhere. Overhead, there were stone arches. The see-through carvings were some of the most intricate she'd ever laid eyes on. Yet all the furniture she'd seen around the palace had simple lines and was made from natural materials like wood and stone. Combined, it had a strong, aesthetically pleasing appeal.

Slipping into the gardens proved to be just as easy. Líntiān had no moons but stars sparkled over the dark sky. It left the fragrant gardens dim, even with the torchlights left burning along the paths. The pink flower blooms had closed. She ran her hand over them and, as she touched them, they opened anew. Walking along, the blooming flowers were like a sign, marking that she had passed.

As she moved to go into the royal chambers, two guards stepped in her way from behind two posts. Francesca lifted a brow. "I'm going to have sex with my fiancé. Is that all right with you?"

"Is Prince Jin expecting you?" one of them asked.

"It's a surprise." She arched a brow. "Why? Did he find someone else to fill the need? If so, kindly let me pass. I'd like to get a look at the wench."

"Prince Jin is alone," the man said sternly in Líntiānese, clearly not amused by her accusation.

"Wonderful, then you won't mind me going to check, will you?" Francesca smiled sweetly, batting her lashes in a way that mocked them.

The men glanced at each other and one nodded. Frowning, one of the guards motioned her to follow and led her inside. Francesca winked at the man left behind. His face remained impassive so she blew him a kiss. He turned away, his lip curling in disgust.

"You guys are just a barrel of laughs, aren't you?" she asked her chaperone. He didn't answer. *"Nǐ bù dǒng ma?"*

"I understand you perfectly, as do we all," the guard said, turning a corner. "The emperor bid us all to upload your language so that we may listen and speak should the need arise."

Francesca made a face behind his back. Did they all have to be so stoic and proper?

*You'd do well to follow their example,* her inner voice said. Francesca rolled her eyes at herself.

The guard stopped at Jin's chamber door. He knocked once before stepping back to let her be seen when the prince opened his door. Under his breath, he added, "However, many will choose not to hear the numerous perversities you seem to enjoy speaking."

His words were stunted and heavily accented by his birth language, but the reprimand was clear. He was saying she wasn't a lady.

*You got that right, Space Cadet.*

"Oh, poor baby, naughty words hurting your sensitive big boy ears?" she teased, giving a pretend pout.

He sniffed, not dignifying her with a response. She couldn't really blame him because she was acting childish. Somehow, the idea that all the people of Muntong thought of her as a foul-mouthed commoner hurt. Why should she care what the Líntiānese thought of her?

*I don't care.*

A little voice in her head, one she chose not to listen to often, laughed at her lie.

The door slid open a crack and a sleepy Jin peeked out. The room behind him was dark, lit only by the barest trace of an orange glow as if from a single candle. His chest was naked, but he wore a loose pair of silk pants. Francesca pushed the door all the way open, rushing forward as she joined her lips to his in an instant kiss. Her mouth drowned anything he might have said at her presence, as she smothered his gruff sound of surprise.

Jin stepped back, letting her in. His arm lifted and she heard him sliding the door shut behind her. Somewhere in the back of her mind, she heard the guard leaving them alone.

Francesca moaned, nearly giggling with excitement. The sensation took her by surprise and she tried to pull back. Jin held her tighter, like he knew she was trying to get away from him. He delved his tongue into her mouth, taking over the kiss, exploring and probing. Logic and reason dissolved, until all she could focus on was the feel of his body against hers. The mindlessness only lasted a brief second, but it was a glorious second.

A small part of her held back, as she listened to their surroundings, constantly alert to any danger. Jin ran his hands over her body, urgently seeking the feel of her skin. Francesca was just as eager as he was. She caressed his naked chest, making her way easily in the dim light. The brief flash of his naked torso when he had answered the door without his tunic was emblazoned on her mind--so smooth, tanned, gorgeous. She touched every inch of his upper body, liking the feel of his firm muscles beneath her fingers.

"*Wo nén ... qin ni ... tiào,*" he tried to say between thrusts of her tongue, "*wu ma...?*

"Shut up," she ordered, not understanding the meaning of his words and beyond trying to translate all of them. All she caught was the word 'pleasure'. "*Zhùzuî*! I'll give you pleasure, lots of pleasure, just shut up and kiss me."

Jin nodded, not stopping in his desperate pursuit of her length. "Fine."

Francesca pulled her mouth from his, slowly kissing down his chest to his nipples, causing them to pucker between her lips. A shiver worked over him, as she moved around his body, caressing him with her mouth and hands until she was next to his back. Boldly, she licked his spine, stroking upward with her tongue. Her fingers dipped down into his loose-fitting pants. She squeezed his tight ass, kneading the hard mounds of flesh. Everything about him was so tight and firm.

Francesca stroked the backs of his thighs, only to drag her nails up over his skin as she pulled out from beneath the silk. The coolness of the material contrasted with his fiery heat.

Instantly, she thrust her fingers back in, liking how hot his body was. She grazed her fingernails over his hips, continuing to lick his back with short flicks of her tongue. He tasted salty yet sweet. Gripping his hips, she felt him flex as a moan escaped his throat. A fierce heat radiated from his powerful erection but she denied touching it. There was an urgency in both of them, but she refused to hurry as she tormented them both, drawing out the anticipation of the flesh.

Francesca nipped the hard planes of his tight skin. His hands hung at his sides, balled into tight fists. Giving the front of his thighs the same stinging torture with her fingernails that she had given the back, she drew her hands up along his hipbone. The waistband of his pants caught on his erection as she tried to pull them off. Leaning against him, she rubbed her clothed breasts up and down, breathing hard as jolts of pleasure stung her aching nipples.

Francesca had to lift his waistband over his arousal to free him of them. The silk whispered to the floor. Kissing down his back, she kneeled, nipping at his firm ass cheek. She bit the tender flesh along the bottom curve. Jin growled in approval so she did it again, harder.

Suddenly, he turned and his arousal was in her face. Passion hummed all around them and she paused, meeting his gaze in silent understanding. They both knew what this was. It wasn't love. There could never be love without trust and that was something she would never do. Prince Jin was the enemy, albeit a sexy one, but an enemy nonetheless. Necessity made her accept the engagement, but she would never go through with the marriage.

Jin had to understand this as well. He didn't trust her either. No, love had nothing to do with what they were about. This was sex. It was passion and lust and carnal instincts needing to be fulfilled.

But it also went beyond that. It was a test, a test of her willpower, her resolve to do what she must. Already Prince Jin filled too many of her thoughts in ways that had nothing to do with her plans for stealing the Jade Phoenix. If she could make love to him and leave him without looking back in anything more than pride at a job well done, she would prove herself a true warrior. Francesca felt no remorse for her actions. It was the actions of Jin's people that had caused her heart to harden. A flash of memories strengthened her resolve. She would not feel anything tender for him. This was sex. Pure sex.

Yes, she would use and then discard him, like he undoubtedly did to so many others.

Francesca wasn't shy as she leaned in to kiss the tip of his erection. She rolled his shaft into her mouth and lightly sucked. Clawing his hips as she gave him pleasure, she pushed back and forth on his cock. Jin moaned, lifting his hands into her hair. He pulled her forward, thrusting against her mouth.

Oral sex was nice and all, but she wasn't a selfless person. Francesca wanted more. She wanted her own pleasure. Pulling off, she didn't dip forward when he tried to thrust between her lips. He groaned in frustration, slipping his hands to her shoulders as he lightly urged her to come forward once more. She refused, closing her mouth as the tip of him pressed tightly for entrance. Jin rocked his hips back and forth, running his shaft along the seam of her mouth.

Francesca wiggled out from under his hold and laughed. Passion ruled his features, but he did not make a move to force her as she reached to pull off her tight, black shirt. The candlelight flickered, caressing his flesh with dim light. She tossed her shirt aside, her breasts bare as she wore nothing but the tight, low-waisted pants and ground shoes. The light glinted off her flesh, giving the barest outline of her erect nipples. Looking down, she touched herself, pulling at her breasts in self-pleasure. His breathing hitched. It was a soft sound, but she heard it easily in the silent chamber.

Francesca boldly met his eyes. Standing, she kicked off her shoes. Jin grabbed her waist, roughly pulling her forward before she could free herself from her pants. Her body crushed into his chest. Her nipples ground hard against him, so sensitive that they shot pleasure all over her body. The sensations centered in her lower stomach, making her wet and ready to accept him.

Who was she kidding? She'd been ready to accept him since he first claimed her in the hall, the arrogant look upon his face. Francesca liked his arrogance, his confidence, his tight, muscled body.

His shaft pushed into her stomach, rubbing along the part of her abdomen that was exposed. Jin slid his hands down the back of her pants, squeezing her ass tight as he lifted her up. She wrapped her legs around his waist as he thrust against her. Her hands found hold in his soft hair, pulling in her urgency to find completion.

Francesca frantically rubbed her hips against him. Maybe all the foreplay had been too much. She was desperate for completion, to feel the tremendous orgasm that built between her thighs. Kissing him hard, she took him in--his breath, his scent, the soft sounds he made. The rubbing felt nice and she did it harder and faster, riding him as he held her up. She cursed her pants for being in the way of their flesh, but didn't have the presence of mind to stop and take them off. Her head fell back until her curls tickled her spine as she moved.

Jin's hot mouth found hold on her breast, sucking the globe deep into its scorching, wet depths. He didn't just lick at her nipple, he devoured a mouthful, sucking and biting and moaning as she rocked. Her body began to tense and she ground her pussy against his shaft until it felt as if they would start a fire from the friction. His fingers clawed into her, hurting in a way that was oh-so-good and right.

Francesca's body clamped down on itself, her clit stimulated beyond belief. She trembled, the orgasm racking through her as she came against him. Jin grunted, but she didn't stop riding him. Her movements became jerky as she milked her body of all its pleasure.

Jin gasped, shaking. His hands loosened their hold for a brief second, and then a hot liquid squirted over her stomach as he came, meeting his release.

Francesca's heart pounded hard in her chest. The candle had blown out, but she didn't remember it doing so. Jin was breathing heavily, the harsh sound mingling with her own. She was glad it was darker in the room for she didn't want to see his face in this moment. It was a memory she was best left without.

"Too fast," he whispered, setting her on the floor. He brushed back her hair from her face. His finger trailed over her cheek in a tender caress.

Francesca didn't like the intimacy of tenderness. She pulled away. Breathing hard, she paused as she sucked in a lungful of air. Then, pushing her pants off her hips, laughed. "Don't worry. You can make it up to me in round two."

"Perhaps we should consider what we are doing," he said. "There is much to be talked about."

"What?" Francesca bit back a laugh. "Are you telling me a man like you can't go another round?"

"It's not the body that I speak of. It's the mind. We should talk."

A wave of utter disbelief washed over her. He had to be the first man in history to have doubts about no commitment, consensual sex. Walking five and a half paces, she reached the bed and crawled on. She didn't need the light to navigate the room because she had the layout memorized.

Francesca flipped over on her back and lifted her hands over her head. She waited for him to join her. When he didn't move, she said, "Are you really tired of playing? I bet a strong guy like you can go all night. You're not scared of a little woman like me, are you? Come on, *ài rén*. I'll even let you be on top. I'll let you be in control. Would you like that? To have the upper hand?"

A long sigh followed by a short laugh was her answer. She knew he was torn between exasperation and lust. Francesca inspired that reaction in men a lot. Love and hate. It was all just emotions and she inspired both in people. Mostly hate though. But, what could she expect? She did steal from most of the people she met.

"Mm, come on. Don't leave a girl waiting," she said, bending her knees and letting them fall open a little. The cool air felt nice against her skin, but she didn't want the cool. She wanted more heat. Her body was greedy for it, starved for attention.

"The astrologers come tomorrow." Jin paced as he talked. She couldn't see him, but she could hear his steps. Her ears trained on the sound, listening to him go back and forth. "They will read our future together. It will be a very long day for us both. You should get some sleep."

"I don't believe in foretelling the future," Francesca said, closing her legs and rolling up to sit on the bed. "It can always be changed by sheer will. Besides, sometimes it's better not to know what lies ahead."

"Regardless of what you think, it is custom and we must participate." Jin moved and she heard the faint whisper of material being pulled over his legs. "If you don't want to draw more notice to yourself, I would advise you to go along with the ceremony."

"You mean the wedding," she whispered, not moving.

"Pre-wedding," he corrected. "It is tradition and we take our traditions very seriously."

"Well, I'm not Líntiānese. What do I care about tradition? Now come here and let me make you forget all about your troubles and traditions."

"I wonder, *bǎobèi*...." Jin stopped moving as his voice trailed off thoughtfully.

"What's that?" she said, purposefully coy.

"How many star systems would like to get their hands on you, my master thief? Or perhaps the Federation Military? Human Intelligence Agency? They wouldn't happen to be looking for you, would they?"

Francesca knew a threat when she heard one. Unfortunately, his was a good one. The Human Intelligence Agency would love to get their hands on her and the Federation Military would gladly fight them for the honor of bringing her in. It didn't matter which group got to her first. Either way, there wouldn't be a trial. And, if they didn't want her, there were at least two dozen empires, kingdoms or planetary governments who would gladly welcome her back ... *into their prisons*.

"You sure do know how to kill the mood, don't you, Jin? Okay, fine, I give up. Just how much tradition are we talking here?" She resigned herself to meeting the astrologers and participating in the barbaric fortunetelling nonsense.

Jin chuckled at the question. The sound was light, so light she barely heard it. She balled her fist, ready to strike the smugness out of his tone.

"The six etiquettes," he said. "They date back to ancient times, though they have changed some. First, I claim a bride in public. Second, we consult the astrologers and they read our future together. If they find all is well, we go to the third etiquette. The information from our reading will be used to set a date for the wedding."

"And if all is not well?"

"Is that hope in your voice?"

Francesca chuckled, refusing to let him know his threat about turning her over to the Federation and HIA had gotten to her.

*Not that they could hold me,* she assured herself.

Before she could respond, he continued. "If it is found that the joining will bring disaster upon our families, then the marriage will be stopped."

"Oh, I get it." Francesca smiled, believing to have figured it out. "You claimed me to avoid someone else and tomorrow the astrologers will declare this wedding unfit." She laughed as relief washed over her. "Why didn't you just say you were rigging it? I would've gone along with the plan. Don't worry. Just tell me what to say and I'll take care of it. Tomorrow you will be a free man. Trust me, I'll make it so no one in their right mind would put me with you."

"I'm afraid you're mistaken," Jin said, his tone hard. "I've made no such plan."

*What?* Francesca frowned, the relief leaving her as quickly as it came. "What?"

"I said I haven't made any plans to overthrow the wedding. The astrologers will give their true reading."

Was this man insane? Why in the galactic hellfires of Bravon did he want to marry her? Self-punishment? Did she look like the kind of woman who would settle down and be a princess wife? Was he insane?

"Third and fourth etiquettes usually entails our families exchanging gifts."

"I have no family," Francesca interrupted. A hard knot formed in her stomach at the reminder.

"None at all?" He sounded surprised. "I am sorry to hear that."

Francesca didn't say a word. Her lip curled in bitterness, but she knew he couldn't see her as he continued to speak with the same tone as before.

"Hmm, as I was saying, the fifth is the wedding day being set and the sixth is the wedding itself."

"You know, I don't think you need to explain all this to me." Francesca tried to keep her voice from sounding too tight, but it was hard. "I doubt we make it past step two. I am clearly not Líntiānese royal material. No doubt the astrologers will be persuaded to see that, no matter what I tell them. Any idiot could."

"They wouldn't dare lie," Jin said. "They will read our future and speak only of what they see. The decision has little to do with what you tell them, except information about when you were born. It's not like an interview where you have to get the questions right. It's more of a science and an art."

"Everyone lies, Jin. Are you telling me that every match the astrologers predict as being happy has turned out wonderful? Come on, even you know that's impossible." Francesca tried to suppress her disdain, but it was hard. Her body shook for a fight. If he wouldn't give her passion, she'd gladly take the next best thing. She wanted to punch something, and keep punching it until she couldn't lift her arm. She wanted to run through the night, slipping undetected until she was off this horrible planet and away from these deranged people.

"There is no divorce, if that is what you ask."

"That isn't what I asked," she said wryly. "Plenty of people stay together in misery."

"Your outlook on marriage is bleak, *bâobèi.*"

"That doesn't answer the question, *ài rén.*"

"Yes, most of the married couples are happy."

"Most." She gave a short, depreciating laugh. "But not all. Good to know the astrologers aren't perfect. I would hate to have my future decided by an exact science."

"Astrologers predict the potential for happiness, not the complete future. There are circumstances which make happiness hard for anyone--the loss of a child, serious illnesses, war, death."

Francesca could tell by his tone that she was in danger of provoking his temper. She quickly changed the subject, not wanting to venture into an argument with him about his people's marital well being. Undoubtedly that would lead to an hour long lecture on how superior the Zhang Dynasty was compared to the rest of the galaxy. "You've never told me why you did it. Why save me? You don't know me. You don't owe me anything."

Francesca moved to stand, her mind forgetting her libido and her desire for a fight as she waited for his answer. She found herself *needing* to know.

"I did tell you already," he said.

She tried, but she couldn't read him. The man was a mystery to her. "Why, Jin?"

"I was compelled."

Francesca closed her eyes and gave a small laugh. "Compelled. Do you always act so rashly with your future?

Can you honestly not see how horrific a match this is? Do you really want to be married to a thief?"

"You rest here. I'll sleep in the other room. In the morning you can use the decontaminator and I'll order an appropriate gown brought for you to wear. You cannot keep running about in black as if you wish to do us mischief."

"Wait," Francesca insisted. "One more thing."

"Yes?"

"If you have the technology for a decontaminator, why do you use torches and candlelight?"

"Because it's pretty."

The sound of a door sliding open kept her from saying more. From the direction of the sound, she knew he went into one of the other rooms. She fell back, staring into the darkness of the chamber.

Francesca stared at where the candle had been lit. Oddly, she hadn't noticed the exact moment it had burnt out. She usually took in every detail and to miss even the smallest thing was strange. First she misjudged Jin in the hall and now she missed the candle burning out. What next? The instances might seem small, but they weren't. She was slipping.

*Don't lose focus, Francesca,* she scolded herself. *You're here for a reason.*

Turning on her side, she closed her eyes. Sleeping wasn't what she'd planned on, but why not try? It looked like she was going to have to play the accepting bride if she was to get another chance at the Jade Phoenix.

## Chapter Five

Francesca waited, trying to appear indifferent as the old woman looked her over. In truth, she was a little nervous. The Hall of Infinite Wisdom was filled with guards and what Francesca guessed were Líntiānese noble families by the richness of their clothing. They had all come to witness the astrologers' readings. As far as she could see, there were no children.

The women in the crowd had intricate hairdos, as if they spent hours in front of a mirror just to get ready for the day. Silver and gold combs stuck out at all angles. Some had feathers, others gemstones and long sticks with tassels. Their gowns ranged from long, slender tunics with raised necklines, to billowy gowns that draped off the arms in long sleeves.

The men were just as well dressed, though their hair styles were more subdued. Most had longer hair lengths, pulled high in a top knot with the bulk flowing down the back. A few had shorter hair like Jin and his brothers. Most of those men were the younger ones in the crowd.

"Mmm," Madame Eng, the old woman before her murmured thoughtfully. She was one of the five astrologers sent to read her future potential with Prince Jin. As far as Francesca could tell, Madame Eng was the leader of the band of old cronies that trailed dutifully after her--Madame Bing, Madame Kel, Madame Chaim and Madame Cong. They all wore long, green silk dresses that hung loose to the floor, hiding what little figures they had left. The gowns had long sleeves that hid their hands from view and their varying shades of gray hair were coiled high on top of their heads. Madame Bing was round, the only contrast among the thinner ladies. They were all short and shuffled when they walked. Francesca couldn't tell if it was habit or age that made them do it.

"Mmm," the old astrologer hummed again.

Madame Eng squinted her eyes in disapproval as her wrinkled hand gestured from beneath her overlong sleeves.

She waved at Francesca in irritation, much like she'd been doing since they started questioning her about her past. The woman's yellowed nails were quickly hidden by the green silk as she again lowered her arm.

Finally, Madame Eng turned to her fellow band of astrologers. She slowly walked over to them and they started to whisper to themselves, gesturing to her in irritation. As Francesca waited for the women to confer, she glanced to her side.

The emperor and his wife stood next to Jin, who in turn was by her side. They were on a stage like area before the thrones so all could see. For someone who liked lurking in the shadows, Francesca wasn't too fond of being in public view--especially without her mask. She felt the witnesses' eyes on her face, staring at her, memorizing her. This mistake might just land her under a Medical Alliance surgeon's knife. If any likeness of her survived, her thieving days would be over. She would be compromised. Painful surgery to change her looks would be the only option. Francesca tried to think of something else. Her eyes landed on Jin.

Prince Zhang Jin was handsome in the ceremonial garb he wore. The red chinoiserie jacket had what he called frog fastenings and a Mandarin collar. The buttons were undone, and beneath the jacket was a white buttoned shirt of matching design. Soft drawstring pants covered his legs. According to him, it was traditional garb, brought with his people from the planet Earth long ago. She had no idea why he thought she would care, but it didn't stop him from talking. It was almost like he wanted her to appreciate his culture as much as he obviously did. She wasn't stupid enough to fall for that ploy--making her fall in love with the country so she would feel too guilty stealing from it. If Jin thought that would actually work, he'd sorely underestimated her.

Francesca was less impressed with her ensemble. The red dress was made of a silky brocade fabric, embroidered with a bright floral pattern. The long skirt was fitted down her legs, making kicking nearly impossible. It was also what Jin called the Mandarin style. If she didn't know better, she would've thought he picked the dress to keep her from trying to escape the day's events, though if danger presented itself she'd have no problem shedding it and taking on the whole Zhang Imperial Guard naked. However, seeing the Zhang princess in a similar gown, she knew that wasn't the case.

Princess Fen was pretty with long straight dark hair and eyes. She looked like her brothers, only more feminine and meek. The Zhang men stood protectively at her sides. They too came to bear witness to the readings. Only problem was, the astrologers weren't getting what they wanted from her.

By keeping her ears opened, she now knew the royal family by name and even that one of the Princesses, Mei, was married and off with her foreign prince husband. There were six children total. Haun was the one who tried to interrogate her the first night only to storm off mad. He still glared in her direction and it was hard not to laugh at him. The other men she remembered seeing, but had yet to form a solid impression of them. After misjudging Jin, she was hesitant to draw conclusions about the others. Shen seemed thoughtful and guarded. Lian was graceful when he moved, like a dancer.

"Emperor," Madame Eng said, bowing in respect.

Francesca listened closely to the Líntiānese language, picking up more and more as she heard it. The woman again helplessly lifted her hands and then dropped them.

"As you know," Madame Eng said, speaking so those who watched from below couldn't hear, "what we do is highly complex."

"There are many factors," Madame Cong added, nodding smartly, as she too kept her voice soft.

"We cannot get a clear reading without the necessary information," said Madame Chaim, just as quiet as the others. She shook her head and clicked her tongue to emphasize her meaning.

"It is impossible to determine her chart if we don't have her hour and date of birth," Madame Bing inserted, gesturing quickly forward and then pulling back behind her peers.

"We cannot determine her sign or her element," Madame Kel said.

"These elements cannot be merely guessed at," Madame Eng finished with a wide gesture. "She has none of these things."

Francesca suppressed a yawn. She couldn't really care less

about getting her future told by some star doctor type. Her future would be her own doing and she highly doubted fate was going to take an interest in her after a lifetime of indifference.

"Why do you not answer?"

The question drew Francesca's eyes up. It was the empress addressing her. She glanced to the floor, doing her best to appear like she was respectful of the lady's position. In truth, she felt it was none of their business about her past. "I don't have them. I don't know when I was born, let alone what hour or where."

It wasn't a lie. She didn't know anything about her birth. In fact, she knew little about her parents.

*I can't even tell you what my parents called me.*

"Then you must use all your talents, Madames," the empress said, ever majestic. "We look to your wisdom and your guidance and bid you to consider my son's future very carefully."

Madame Eng looked like she wanted to protest. She pressed her lips tightly together, glaring openly at Francesca. Finally, she gave a curt nod and turned to the others. Francesca wondered why the royal family didn't just declare her an unfit match due to lack of information. It would save them the trouble of having to continue the pretense of accepting their crazy son's decision. Certainly they couldn't actually want her in the family.

After a long, whispered discussion, Madame Eng turned back. Loudly, she said so the hall could hear, "This is a very difficult reading and we must consult the scrolls. We will have an answer tonight, after the banquet."

A low murmur sounded over the hall. The empress bowed her head, smiling politely. The women returned the look, but none of them seemed happy about it. They shuffled in a straight line down the platform, through the part in the crowd. Those they passed nodded in respect and the hall was deadly quiet as the old women left.

Very regally, the empress put her hand on her husband's outstretched one. He led her down an aisle formed between the standing crowd. The onlookers bowed lower than they had for the astrologers. Princes Haun and Shen followed directly behind and Lian escorted his sister. Finally, Jin offered her his hand. Francesca slipped hers over his.

Touching him only made their unfinished lovemaking come back to mind. The night before wasn't nearly enough. She wanted more.

With effort, she pushed thoughts of tackling Jin to the ground from her mind as he led her behind the others. Once they were through the front doors, Francesca glanced over her shoulder. Those inside were forming a procession to follow them.

"Where are we going?" she asked Jin. "You said I just had to show up at this thing and we were done."

"We're going to a banquet while we wait for 'this thing' to finish." His chin was lifted and he didn't turn to her. The chiseled planes of his face were hard, regal to the point of being stoic. It was the same emotionless look she noticed on all the royal family's faces. "Is it true what you said? Your people kept no record of your birth. Were they from a primitive planet?"

"Do you mean were my parents animals? Yes, and I'm a baby gorilla from the conservatory on Earth. Just call me monkey girl."

"What girl?"

"Monkey, it's a creature that Earthlings used to believe were the beginning of ... never mind. It's an animal that throws dung."

"Why do you always insist on believing everything I say to be an insult or an attack? Can't you have a conversation? A real conversation?"

"I was abandoned as a baby. There was no one to keep a record," she answered dryly. "No day of birth to even celebrate. I was raised in an orphanage."

He lifted a brow slightly.

"Orphanage. It's a place for unwanted children, or those with no family and, actually, it was technically called a monastery and was run by a religious sect who took pity on those less fortunate and gave us a place to stay in exchange for manual labor and piety." She had no idea why she was telling him so much. "Gee, isn't this fun? All this lovely *conversation.*"

"Keep talking," he ordered. "And drop the sarcasm. You might find you actually like being polite."

Francesca bit back her immediate retort and instead continued as he suggested, "I was both--unwanted and without family. As I grew up, I simply had the tag Human Girl Two Six Nine. It wasn't until I was five that I was given the chance to pick my own name. I was reading an old book on the orphanage's handheld at the time, called 'Francesca the Red Rose of Italy'. The girl in the pictures looked like she could've been my mother so I became Francesca La Rosa, Francesca the Rose."

"I am sorry you had it so rough, Francesca." His words sounded sincere.

"It is hardly yours to be sorry for." Francesca followed his example, keeping her eyes on Princess Fen's head. The woman's hair was really shiny, like the silk of her clothing. "It is possible you weren't even born at the time."

Jin let loose a long laugh. "How long ago was it?"

"Thirty years."

He chuckled. "I was nearly your age when it happened. I am fifty five years."

Francesca tried not to lose step as she considered his words.

The procession turned and she let Jin lead her along the path that went along the side of the Hall of Infinite Wisdom. Looking around, it was hard to remember that she hated this place and wanted to leave it. The pretty flower blossoms of the courtyard were opened but the winged creatures were gone. The day was warm, the air sweet and clean. Long, thin torches were unlit as the sun beat down upon the earth. Líntiān had one sun, but it was huge compared to other planets she had seen. Amazingly though, the temperatures always seemed to be moderate. According to the modestly informed conversation she'd had with a cyberpedia some years back, except for a few rains, the planet was as close to paradise as any other in the known galaxies.

In the distance all she saw were the palace walls, a stark gray line against the pale blue of the cloudless sky. She knew that outside the walls was a village and trees. Beyond that were rolling hills with blades of yellow-blue grasses and more villages, their short thatched rooftops clustered together along parts the countryside like a picture out of an old Faerian children's tale. Large farms surrounded the villages filled with a low to the ground crop of giant red flowers. It was beautiful beyond the walls, simplistic. She wondered why the family chose to shut it out.

"Then what they say is true," she said at length. "You do have the power of immortality."

"Immortality?" Jin chuckled. "I would not say that."

"But, you don't look a day over twenty-five," Francesca said. "You're human like me. You come from Earth, or at least your people did at one time. You said it yourself."

"We do come from Earth and we are human. But our kind has evolved with time. We take care of our bodies, eat right--"

"And you have a secret you are refusing to tell me," she broke in.

"We both have our secrets, Francesca. Are you ready to reveal all of yours so that I may share mine?" She looked at him just in time to see his brief smile. "I thought not. Now, quit staring at me. Keep your eyes forward. It is--"

"Tradition," she finished dryly. Everything with these people was tradition.

"Yes. Tradition."

"Well then," she said wryly, "let's hope I haven't forgotten the tradition of how to properly dine at a table. It has been awhile since I've used utensils."

Francesca tried not to laugh as Jin missed a step.

* * * *

Francesca stared at the two ivory sticks they gave her to eat with. She'd seen them before, but had never gotten used to eating with them. When she implied that she might not remember how to eat at a table, she meant it as a joke. However, she was fast learning that there was a lot she didn't know about Líntiānese dining culture. On the run, she usually ate whenever she could, whatever she could. The plates were made of handcrafted pottery, painted with delicate blue swirls on white, and the cups were shallow bowls that they cupped with two hands. Setting the sticks down, she reached for the small bowl and took a drink of the sweet liquor.

*Thank the gods they have alcohol!*

They sat on a cushion on the floor, next to a round table. It was low to the ground, but she didn't mind. What she did mind was the fact that she was seated with the royal family. The other tables had polite conversation, laughter even, but theirs was dead silent. The Zhangs all stared at her, refusing to talk but ever watchful of her every move. She imagined the princes to be counting her every sip of the wine, as if she took one too many she would prove herself unworthy of their presence. Even Jin didn't have anything to say.

Francesca guessed she couldn't blame the royal family. She was a trying to steal from them after all. It struck her that maybe Jin's declaration was a way to keep their enemy close. For the life of her, she couldn't reason it any other way.

Servants brought the food, placing it on the table. The serving dishes matched the plates, their blue swirls larger on the white backgrounds, but still the same design. After the servants left, the empress served the meal and Princess Fen refilled the drinks. Everything was done with such precision and decorum, yet with a practiced ease that made it look like the most simplistic of rituals.

Francesca didn't recognize most of the cuisine set out for them. The large red flowers she'd seen in the farmlands beyond the palace were the first course. The petals were steamed until their texture was like silk. They tasted sweet as they practically dissolved in her mouth. Next a giant sea creature was presented on a bed of dark green spiny leaves mixed with purple plant shoots and round yellow pebble-like dots. Francesca could only guess that the sea creature came from the giant river that divided the planet. When the waiter placed it in front of her, he angled the dish so that a large single eye was facing her direction. She stared at the large green pupil, instantly losing her appetite. The long tentacles grew out from its round, pink head toward the emperor. The empress deftly severed one of the limbs with an ivory handled knife and put it on her husband's dish on top of a bed of the spiny plant life salad.

After the emperor had been served and the empress had distributed the spiny plants among those at the table, the children helped themselves to the fish. Francesca didn't move. Each person took a tentacle, leaving her with the round head and giant green eye.

Francesca glanced at Jin's plate. He had the skin of the tentacle with one pair of eating sticks and the meat of it with another. The food came apart and he dropped the skin by his plate. He then set the extra pair of sticks down. The dark red tentacle meat was gelatinous in appearance, but fell apart as they lifted it to eat. Never one to have a weak stomach,

Francesca gagged. She managed to cover up her distaste by taking a quick drink of the wine, but the nausea did not pass.

She stared at the green, round eyeball and took another drink, only to discover her glass was empty. What had happened to the mushy pink flower soup? That wasn't so bad. Surely, they didn't expect her to eat the eyeball thing? She glanced up, suddenly noticing everyone at the table had stopped eating and was looking at her. Francesca knew her face had to be pale. She lifted her hand as if reaching to move the head to her plate only to draw her arm back.

"Please, allow me to serve you, Francesca. It would be my honor," Jin said quietly. To her horror, he lifted the head and put it on the spiny bed of plants on her dish.

*Oh yeah, big help there,* she thought sarcastically. *Thanks a lot. That's so much better up close.*

The creature was now right under her nose and she got a whiff of its fishy, sea life smell. Now that it was nearer, she discovered that the creature wasn't baked.

*Raw?!*

*The expected her to eat a raw sea creature?*

The empress took a slow bite, but no one else moved. Francesca stiffened her resolve and grabbed her sticks. She poked lightly at the head. The eyeball popped out and rolled down on the plate. Gagging visibly, she dropped the sticks and closed her eyes.

*I can't do it.* She took a deep breath, trying not to get sick all over the disgusting head. *I can't do it.*

"Francesca?" Jin asked softly. She felt his touch at her elbow, squeezing gently.

Francesca shook her head slightly. Leaning into him, she refused to open her eyes, as she whispered quietly, "I can't eat that."

"But, why? It's a delicacy, served in your honor," he whispered back. "Do not feel uncomfortable, the choicest cut is meant for you. Please, eat. You are the guest of honor."

"I...." Her mouth worked, but she couldn't make the sound come out. Uncomfortable? He thought she was embarrassed to eat the 'choicest cut'? Ugh! Gag! "I can't eat it, Jin. That thing is looking at me."

Jin chuckled. "It is only food."

"Jin?" the empress asked.

"*Méi guānxi*," he answered. "It's all right."

Jin leaned back and lifted his hand. A server came forward. Francesca heard him whispering, but his Líntiānese was so fast she couldn't keep up with it. When he'd finished, he lifted his hand to his family. The gesture kept them from questioning as the server took her plate. Appreciative, she looked at Jin. If he wasn't technically her enemy, she would have kissed him.

"I explained that your religious practices do not allow you to eat meat," he said, loud enough so the others at the table could hear. "That you are a… *sù shí zhe*. It means, vegetable eater."

Francesca loved meat--normal meat. Though, at the moment, she was only too happy to give it up for the ways of a vegetarian. Suddenly, more waiters came forward and she saw that a few of the other tables were refusing to eat, or finish eating, their heads as well. Most of them were older noblewomen.

The server came back with a plate of fried vegetables-- yellow Grog peppers, bean discs, more of the pink flowers, root sprouts and a few others she didn't recognize. So long as they didn't have eyes, Francesca wasn't about to complain. She sighed in relief and was glad when the smell of raw sea creature no longer invaded her nostrils.

The meal continued in silence. After the main dishes, Princess Fen poured tea for the table and a bowl of warm linens was passed around so they could clean their hands. She wondered if every Líntiānese dining experience was like this. In truth, she'd much prefer to eat on the run, away from the witnessing eyes. She felt every bite she took was gauged. Seeing Prince Shen staring at her, she nodded. He returned the gesture and turned his eyes down.

"Will you honor the word of the astrologers if they say this is a good match?" the emperor asked. All eyes at the table turned to him in surprise at the direct question, only to immediately move to her.

Francesca, slowly lowered her sticks mid-scoop and closed her mouth. Putting her hands in her lap, she didn't answer. What could she say? They wouldn't like the truth.

"I see," he said, not giving her a lot time to respond. The emperor stood, reaching for his wife to help her up. Without another word, he led her from the table. Instantly, everyone stopped dining and moved to stand. The princes and their sister walked behind their parents. Jin looked at her, but didn't offer to help her up. Francesca glanced at her food, wanting to take a few more bites before they left. Out of the corner of her eye she saw Jin move and hurried to join him as he walked out of the banquet hall.

"Please tell me this is about over," she grumbled when they were again outside. Francesca had about as much ceremony as she could endure.

Jin took a deep breath, not bothering to hide his scowl. "You should learn tolerance of other cultures. There is no reason to be rude to my family. They are showing you hospitality despite your transgressions against them and you repay them by disrespecting their ways."

"What? I--"

*I wasn't that bad.*

"Your manners are an embarrassment, your tongue insolent and your expressions offensive. You strut around here no better than common space trash." Jin walked faster and she fell behind for a moment before rushing to keep up. "You scoff at every gesture of goodwill. I had hoped that you had just been given a hard life and that underneath what you did for a living, you were a good person. I can see after tonight, that's not so."

*That's a little harsh. It was just dinner.*

"I never asked to be here. If I'm such an offensive embarrassment, you should have locked me in the prisons for my crimes. No one asked you to do all this. I only agreed so I could get another chance at stealing the Jade Phoenix."

Jin quit walking. The procession stopped several feet behind them, but the royal family kept going. He took a deep breath. "You won't give it up, will you? If you were smart, you would realize you should demand my hand in marriage as is your right to do. You would push for it. Then you could live here in this palace, attended by servants for the rest of your days. You'd be rich enough to buy whatever you desired, not to mention you'd be powerful and protected. There would be no need for you to steal for a living."

"Now I'm stupid?" Francesca lifted her jaw. "Stupidity is picking a gilded prison and convincing yourself you are free. Can you not conceive that everyone doesn't want to be like you? You and your people hide out on this world like you're too special to mingle with the rest of us foreign space trash. Maybe it's our ways that are too special to mingle with yours. Besides, if I'm so horrible, why do you want me?"

Her eyes bore into his dark ones. He looked like he wanted to strangle her. The defiance turned her on and she thought of the night before, desperate to finish what they started. Her body pulsed, wanting to know what it would feel like to make wild, passionate love to him just one time. Her pussy ached to know the intimate contact of his claiming touch.

"My life is not a prison," he growled.

"Sure thing," she quipped. "That's why you're following all this tradition when it's clear you don't want to be married to me, that you made a mistake in saying you did. It was a rash act that should have been disclaimed immediately. That's why you refuse to send me, your chosen bride, to the prisons right now. It's because you are held prisoner by the will of tradition. You are more prisoner than I have ever been, *ài rén*. I've been locked in some of the galaxy's most horrific jails and still I was freer than you could ever imagine. And you hate that. You hate that a lowly little piece of space trash like me could be happy without your treasured ways."

"I do what must be done out of honor." He gritted his teeth.

"You do so because you are a prisoner. What you don't get about people like me is that we would rather be free or dead, Jin. You can't conceive of me not wanting your precious, overly pampered life."

*Time to regroup, Francesca,* she told herself. *Know when to cut your losses and run. Next time, you'll be more prepared.*

She bit the inside of her lip. Next time? Francesca had never run out on a job.

*I'm not running out,* she reasoned. *I'm regrouping.*

He moved as if to grab her, only to stop and glance back. She followed his gaze and chuckled. The people waited for them to walk and his family was no longer in sight. He instantly began to move, heading down the walkway back to the Hall of Infinite Wisdom.

"You are an ignorant foreigner."

Now was not the time to run. There were too many witnesses and her dress was too tight. Flippantly, she responded, "And you are a pompous, ridiculous prince."

He snorted, walking faster. "Let's just get this over with. If luck is with us, the match will be denounced and this will all be over. You'll get your prison bed by night's end and I'll be done with you forever."

\* \* \* \*

"The match is well made. The wedding date should be set to occur by the end of six moons at the latest. "

Jin stared at Madame Eng, waiting for the buzzing in his head to stop. Six moons? That couldn't be right. No one got married within six moons. The old astrologer couldn't have meant that. Francesca was possibly the worst choice he could've made.

*I didn't make the choice. Grandfather did.*

*Then why was I fighting so hard to convince her that this was a nice life?* his inner thoughts argued. Wonderful. Now he was unstable, talking to himself like a poor lost soul. He gritted his teeth, as his own words to Francesca rolled in his head. *If you were smart, you would realize you should demand my hand in marriage as is your right to do. You would push for it. Then you could live here in this palace, attended by servants for the rest of your days. You'd be rich enough to buy whatever you desired, not to mention you'd be powerful and protected. There would be no need for you to steal for a living.*

Jin pressed his lips tightly together. That settled it. He was a fool.

Taking a deep breath, he was unable to even look at Francesca. She didn't know what she was talking about. He was not a prisoner in a gilded cage. He was responsible. He was tradition.

*I am tradition.*

His ears buzzed and he felt a thin bead of sweat drip down the back of his neck. It became hard to breathe. The hall spun around him, pressing in on him as he became dizzy.

The empress' words to him filled his head, adding to his torment. *Jin, you have an honest and noble heart, but you are not meant to rule Líntiān. There are things in this you will never understand. Considerations you will never be told of. Your place is as a prince, brother to the future emperor. Your sound judgment will help to guide Haun and for that reason we would not have you jaded by such things as these. You have been raised in the traditions for that reason.*

Jin was tradition. He was shielded from things just so his judgment in the old traditions would not be clouded with doubt.

*I am tradition.*

He kept his eyes on Madame Eng. A lump formed in his throat. He didn't want to look at Francesca, didn't want to hear her words swirling with the words of his mother. In fifty-five years he'd never been uncertain about his life, his place, his country and traditions. That Francesca could undo his sanity and make him doubt his place made him hate her. The buzzing in his head continued and he realized it was the onlookers murmuring in excitement. His heart beat harder, pounding uncontrollably until he felt lightheaded.

Out of the corner of his eye, he saw his father lift a hand. The hall quieted. Madame Eng nodded slowly, as if answering the unasked question of the entire hall. "Yes, within six moons. The signs were very clear on that point. It must be within six moons or discord will fall upon them."

"We are certain," Madame Chaim said. "Though we could not consult her birth chart, there are other ways."

"More difficult ways," Madame Cong put forth, smiling wide as she nodded. She looked more at the watching crowd than the royal family.

"We asked the ancestors for guidance," Madame Kel added. Jin saw his mother's eye turn down slightly at that.

"We consulted the bones." Madame Bing shyly started to step forward but drew back behind the others at the last second. Her lips pressed tightly and she didn't say anything else.

"*Chien Tung,*" Madame Eng added. The bamboo sticks were her favorite, but the other ladies didn't seem to put much stock in them.

"Shells from the Satlyun." Madame Kel nodded smartly.

Unable to resist, Jin glanced at Francesca. Her usually tanned face was pale but her eyes were blank. He watched her breathing. It was shallow and even, like she was completely unaffected by what happened around her. That's when he realized she wasn't even listening to what the old women said. Her pupils twitched slightly. She was scanning the room, taking in what was happening beyond the astrologers. Part of him was insulted. This was their future the women talked about and she couldn't care less.

*Our future?* Jin thought in dismay. *There is no future for us. Her actions prove that. She doesn't care what happens here.*

She'd struck a nerve with her words. Yes, he thought the Líntiānese way was superior. They didn't have the problems that other planets had. They'd preserved their way of life for centuries. They didn't fight, their countries didn't change hands and their people flourished. Wasn't that proof of their superiority? That their way was better?

It's what he'd been raised to believe--that tradition, the Zhang Dynasty was better. But were the things he was raised to believe a lie? Or, if not so harsh as a lie, a distortion of what was? Was he really just a sheltered prince with no concept of the galaxies? Suddenly, he wished he was with Mei, flying about space and learning about other cultures for the sake of the family. He did not envy her path when she left her home, but maybe there was something to fate choosing a prince who was also a space captain for his sister. The things Mei learned in her journeys with her husband would only help their understanding of the universes. Why couldn't he have asked to go with her?

Jin stared at Francesca, but she didn't look at him. What game did fate have in mind for him? Or was this merely the meddling of a bored ancestor? Was his grandfather watching even now? Laughing hysterically at the turmoil he'd caused? Or was this just fate's way of making the past right again? Was that to be his purpose, his siblings' purpose? To make the past right again?

His head spun, plagued with too many thoughts at once. Confusion set in, leading to desperation and anger.

Francesca's eyes continued their tiny movements as she looked around the room. He imagined she was frantically searching for a fight, a way out so she could run. In that moment, he wouldn't stop her. He hated that she made him doubt his place, his world, his traditions. Before her, life had been perfect. He knew his place in the world and had been happy in his ignorance. Such a strange turn a couple of days could make.

The astrologers were still talking, listing off the many ways they predicted his future. He didn't want to know the future, didn't want to be told by his ancestors and elders what to do, what to feel, what to be. He was fifty-five years old and just now figuring out that life was more than an imperial palace on Líntiān. If fate was laid out for them, then let fate show them in their own time. Why did they have to rush to know everything? What would happen if they stopped looking at the signs and just let life happen?

His hands began to shake. Jin didn't move as he pierced Francesca with his gaze until her image blurred. He blamed her for this.

"The match is well made. Fate has blessed this union!" Madame Eng said loudly. The hall burst into commotion, though none really seemed happy about the declaration. Jin knew the nobles would have issues with him taking a foreign bride--one who they knew nothing about, one whose family they knew nothing about. The fear of outsiders ran deep and some would fear that his taking a foreign bride would open their ports to others like her. To them, it was bad enough that one of the royal children had married off planet. The commoners on the other hand might have an opinion, but it was doubtful they'd do or say anything about it.

"No!" Jin said loudly. It took him a moment to realize that he'd spoken the word so all could hear. He took a deep breath, not caring at the moment. Francesca's eyes turned toward him. Their jade depths were confused and surprised at the same time. "This union is not blessed. It is forced. I care not what the ancestors told you. She will not be my bride."

Francesca gasped. Jin bowed, giving her a self-depreciating smile, saying, "It's as you wish, *bâobèi,*" before turning to walk out.

"Zhang Jin!" his father called, angry.

"Jin!" his mother yelled.

Jin ignored their calls. The walls of the palace were caving in on him. He stormed through the crowd, breathing hard and barely seeing them as they hurried to get out of his way.

*If this is fate, I defy you! I defy her!* He didn't look back as he hurried from the Hall of Infinite Wisdom. *Zài-jiàn, Francesca, you are free to go. I don't care anymore. Just leave and never come back!*

## Chapter Six

Francesca stood in the hall, all eyes on her, as she stared after Jin. She couldn't believe he did this to her! First, he claims her rashly against her will, now he dumps her and leaves her to suffer the embarrassment--against her will. Where did he get off? By all means, she didn't plan on marrying him, but to discard her publicly, as if she were nothing?! Did this man honestly believe he could do whatever he wanted to people and not have to pay the price? Did he think he was so much better than her that he could treat her like Liger dung and not have to face the consequences of his actions?

*"Shénme?"* she demanded, pretending to be stunned past logical words when in fact she knew exactly what she was doing. "What did he say? *Shénme?"*

With revenge in mind, Francesca sobbed so loud it echoed over the bewildered hall. She didn't care that she was making a spectacle of herself as she carried on, crying out like Jin had just broken her heart into a million bits of star dust. Falling to her knees, she put her head in her hands and began rubbing her eyes, hard and frantic until they teared in irritation and were red from the friction. She was about to put on the performance of a lifetime.

*"Shénme? Shénme?"* she cried. "What did he say? What? I don't understand."

"Francesca?" It was Princess Fen's voice.

Francesca felt someone touching her shoulder. She glanced up, blinking back tears that weren't there. Fen knelt beside her. The woman's face was stricken and she looked like she wanted to comfort her, but didn't know how.

*"Shénme?"* Francesca whispered, gasping and wrinkling her nose. "He couldn't have said that. Last night, when...." She paused, gulping erratically for breath. "He said that love made him choose me. He said he was compelled. And now? After he had me, he...? Does his word mean nothing?"

The entire royal family hung on to her every word. They appeared shocked, as they glanced at one another. With the

way the Líntiānese prized their family honor, her words
would strike a devastating blow. It worked just as planned.

Haun stepped forward, waving his hand at the crowd.
"Leave us!"

The emperor blinked at his son's command but nodded
before turning to his wife. They spoke in low tones, so low
she couldn't catch more than the words, 'dishonor', 'family'
and 'Jin'.

"He is scared," Fen said softly, nodding frantically as she
continued to pat Francesca's back. "He does not mean this.
Jin would not tell you of his love unless it was true."

Francesca almost felt guilty for the agony she caused the
royal family--*almost*.

"My son will honor you, Francesca," the emperor decreed
loudly, though only the royal family was left in the hall to
hear his words. "You will be married to Jin or he will be
exiled from his home and his family."

Now she was really starting to feel bad. Exiled? From his
home? Francesca only meant to teach him a lesson about
treating others like they were expendable pawns to his every
whim. She never meant to get him kicked out of his home.
Her mouth fell slack and she couldn't speak, as she
remembered what it was like not to have a family. How
could she do that to him?

Shaking herself from feeling sorry for him, she reasoned
that if he was exiled, it would be the ultimate lesson. He
would have to pay for every arrogantly callous thing he'd
done in his fifty-five princely years. Surely she wasn't the
first person he used for a diversion.

*Arrogant bastard!*

"Francesca La Rosa," the empress said. "I am sorry for
your pain. We had no idea that you carried such love in your
heart for our son."

Francesca looked at the woman. The empress said one
thing, but her face said another--that she didn't believe
Francesca. The woman smiled knowingly. Francesca
sniffed, not giving up her act.

"You will go rest now," the emperor decreed.

"Fen," the empress insisted, motioning her hand.

Fen nodded, leaning to take Francesca under the arm.
"Come, Francesca, *zhè bìng bù huài*. It is not that bad, you
will see. *Zhè bìng bù huài*."

Francesca let herself be pulled to her feet. The princess urged her to walk with her toward the door, repeatedly saying that everything wasn't as bad as it seemed and that everything would be all right.

"Jin will make it right by you, Francesca," Fen said confidently. "You will see."

\* \* \* \*

Francesca stared at Jin's chamber, well, actually it was hers now. His family had kicked him out--unofficially--and he was not allowed back into his room until he publicly apologized and she forgave him.

Francesca grinned. Making him grovel was going to be fun.

She lay on the bed, her cheek pressed against the mattress as she looked at her surroundings. The room was filled with baskets of fruit and decorative pots of flowers. There were even a few small trees. The presents were all for her, as if suddenly, thirty birthdays had happened at once. It was hard not to be seduced by all the material objects, by the lavish lifestyle of the royal family. The outpouring of gifts was hard to ignore, but she did her best to keep her resolve strong.

Able to explore Jin's home at leisure, she found that one of the interior doors led to his decontaminator and the other to a small living room area. The living room area was more like a sitting room and closet combined. A button on the wall released a long pole upon which hung his clothing. In the middle of the room was a low couch with two golden dragons holding the sides up. The statues' backs humped up to form the arms of the furniture. They were fierce, snakelike creatures with round eyes and long mustaches. One held a ball under his foot and the other shielded a baby dragon.

A series of long, narrow windows were on one wall, but they were so slender, it was hardly worth looking out of them. When she looked, she'd seen a sliver of the walking path beyond, but that was it. Most likely, they were constructed for the outside light they offered more than for showing a view.

Until her presents started to arrive, Jin's living area had been nearly empty. Now it was packed full of her gifts. They had trickled out of the bedchamber into his sitting room. She'd left the door between the rooms open so she could see all her presents easily from the bed. They formed a curving path over the floor, so she could weave among them.

One common theme ran through the presents--the phoenix. Some were carved on pots, others were sculpted, one transparent phoenix hung from a potted tree and one was carved into the tree's bark, scarring the plant with the design. Staring at a silk painting of one bright depiction, she took a moment to appreciate the beauty of the creature. In all her desire to steal the Jade Phoenix, she never really looked at the bird it represented. Was this a real creature? She'd never seen anything like it. The bird was beautiful, so bright and vibrant with colors, with long feathers especially at the tail. Its head was small with a short beak and it had an oblong body with long, thin legs.

The animal was undoubtedly an object of great celebration to the Líntiānese people because it was incorporated into everything, almost as much as the dragon was. Regardless of what it meant, it didn't change anything. Francesca was sorry she was going to have to leave all the gifts behind when she left, but she'd come to Líntiān for revenge and she would not forget her promise to steal the Jade Phoenix.

The gaze of the frozen birds stared at her, almost condemning in their silent disapproval of what she was doing, what she would do. Francesca closed her eyes.

The Zhang family had taken her in after her little scene in the hall. It was almost too easy and she couldn't help but think of them as trusting fools. Even if the empress didn't believe she loved Jin, she acted as though it were possible.

However, her assessment of the royal family wouldn't make her lower her guard. She knew she was being watched, listened to. Every word had to be carefully planned, every look, every sigh, every blink of the eye had to paint the picture of the hurt lover. Only Jin would know that truth, but after his actions in the hall, his family would be wary of his reasoning. Such an outburst would have to be an embarrassment to them.

Where was Jin at anyway? Did he have to stay in the prisons? Outside?

*And why in the galaxies do I care?*

"Francesca?" Fen's voice called. The woman tapped lightly on the door.

Francesca looked at the entryway as it slid open. She sat up on the bed, pushing her hair back from her face. The locks fell in long, curly waves over her shoulders. For some reason, Jin's decontaminator tended to make her hair curlier than usual. She didn't mind it, only it was harder to manage.

"I have come to see if you are better," Fen said, closing the door behind her as she entered the room. The princess looked around at the gifts. "I see you are already being welcomed by the people."

"The people sent all of this?" Francesca asked, surprised. "But, I thought...."

Fen paused and waited, smiling expectantly for her to continue.

"I thought your family had sent them," she finished weakly.

Fen shook her head, "No. Family presents will come later. These are from the noble households, welcoming you into the royal family. They wish to show their support of Jin's choice in a bride."

The households? She'd thought them bribes from the royal family to tempt her into their lifestyle.

"But, didn't Jin un-choose me?" Francesca asked, purposefully lowering her eyes. Right after the words were out, she wanted to punch herself in the head. She could not care what Jin thought of her. She couldn't! Her stomach tensed at the thought and she suddenly felt bad.

*It's not like I actually care. Do I?*

*Blessed Stars! No. I don't care about him!*

*I don't. I don't. I don't....*

"I wasn't going to mention that," Fen said, "but since you brought it up, I can tell you that many of the people were moved by your heartache, especially the young women. They are very supportive of you."

"Even if he does not support his choice?" Francesca asked, doing her best to keep the disbelief out of her tone. The Líntiānese people actually supported her? Her inner voice laughed in response. The sound was mocking and she refused to acknowledge it.

"I wish I knew what Jin was thinking, but I do not. I can only say that I am sorry for your pain. It is clear to us that you have had a hard life, one that has forced you into thievery, but you are here now in your new home. And fate has brought you to us for a reason."

Yes, perhaps fate had brought her, but Francesca knew it wasn't for the reason Fen suspected. Regardless, Francesca was astonished by the woman's show of blind faith. Goodness radiated off of her, shining brilliantly out of her kind eyes. The woman trusted fate, trusted those things that she couldn't see. She had beliefs that Francesca couldn't begin to understand.

Francesca had always believed in herself, in what she saw, touched, stole. Her life was in her hands, as was her future. If she was captured, it wasn't because fate intervened but because she'd failed, because she wasn't good enough.

"You believe in fate, don't you? I mean, really believe." Francesca stared at her, wishing she could share some sort of conviction. But the truth was, she'd seen too much of the darker side of life to believe in Faerian tales.

"Yes, of course," Fen answered. "We all do. Without fate, where would we be?"

"How do you know what fate wants? How can you be sure that's why I'm here?"

"The spirits of our ancestors guide us to see it," Fen said thoughtfully. "There are signs as well, you just have to know how to look."

So that is why they just accepted her presence as easily as they did. Francesca bit her lip. She'd wondered at the almost lax way they let her into their lives. For a thief, she had really been treated rather well--almost too well. Not that she could really complain about being treated nicely, but it was odd.

*Poor trusting fools.*

"Oh, this is lovely," Fen exclaimed, lifting a red silk gown with golden flowers interwoven with long dragons. "It must be from Lady Hsin. Her family produces some of the finest silks in the entire planet. They brought the worms with them when our kind migrated from Earth. The breed she uses is still from that original bloodline."

"Worms make this?" Francesca asked, touching the silk on the bed. She wasn't sure whether to be grossed out or not.

"Yes." Fen nodded, smiling brightly as she fingered the silk. "It's actually quite interesting. The baby worms only eat mulberry. It's a plant bush Lady Hsin's ancestors brought with the worms. You feed it to them in large amounts as they grow. The more they eat, the more silk they produce. She has many workers feeding the silkworms and even more tending the mulberry. Her farm is one of the largest in Muntong."

"And you string the little worms together to make material?" Francesca asked. The one-eyed sea creature buffet popped into her head.

"No, they grow and form a transformation cocoon around themselves. When they emerge as the 'flying silk', the silk material itself is collected from the remaining cocoon. The substance taken from the silk threads is used in our hair rinses and some other products." Fen lifted her smooth, shiny locks, letting it fall slowly from her fingers to show how pretty it was. "The silk is then spun into a lightweight yarn, processed, and eventually made into what you see here. After the flying silk comes from the cocoon, they are taken to a garden where they mate, lay eggs and live out their short lives. Those eggs are hatched and the process starts all over again."

Francesca didn't say a word. She wasn't sure what she could say. Normal, everyday conversation really was beyond her realm of expertise. She could make small talk in a bar, but there was nothing friendly about it. Or, she could spar with words, avoid a conversation, use a conversation to get the information she needed out of someone. Only, she didn't need anything from Fen and, from what she could tell, Fen didn't need anything from her. What was the woman doing there anyway--talking of silk and worms and making thread? Undoubtedly, it was interesting, but ... why?

It was almost as if the woman was trying to be her friend.

"If you like, after the wedding, I can arrange a trip to Lady Hsin's, if you would like to see." Fen set the silk gown down, her expression full of hope. "Mei often would take trips with me, but now that she is gone, I have no one to keep me company."

"There isn't going to be a wedding, Fen," Francesca answered honestly. What else could she do? The woman was comparing her to a sister. It made her uncomfortable and it just felt plain wrong.

"Oh, no, shhh." Fen shook her head, coming forward to place her hand on Francesca's shoulder. "Don't think like that. Jin is a man and they are moody creatures. Leave him to his own troubles and he will come around. In the meantime, stay here, relax, do what you must to prepare for the wedding celebration. When the time is right, he will come begging your forgiveness and all will be well."

Again she couldn't help but note how Fen talked of life as if it were a Faerian children's tale--so perfect and neat with a happy ending. The princess was an idealist that was for sure. Francesca didn't want to argue with an idealist and found herself not wanting to ruin Fen's picture of a happy life. So many things in the universes were dark and ugly, why take away such a picture of good?

"What's with all the phoenixes?" Francesca asked, changing the subject.

Fen's smile brightened even more and she sat on the bed, running her fingers through Francesca's hair to smooth the messy curls. "The phoenix is from Earth as well. As you can tell, many of our customs have come from the old ways. I always tell Jin that we Líntiānese don't like to let a perfectly good tradition, or symbol, go to waste--jokingly of course. But we do tend to decorate everything with the same pattern over and over again, if you haven't noticed. I tried to get the emperor to let me redesign the gardens, but he says they're fine as they are."

Francesca didn't say a word.

"But I digress. The phoenix was an ancient bird, though none I know of have survived. I think they died out before our ancestors even conceived they would leave the planet."

"That's too bad," Francesca answered.

Fen nodded. "Yes, but the virtues they represent still hold true."

"And what are those?" It was strange being touched in friendship, but she didn't stop Fen from combing her long hair. The personal contact felt nice. She'd never had a sister before and had barely had female friends. Even then it had been at the monastery and she could barely remember the girls' names as it had been so long ago.

"The virtues of courage, valor," Fen said. "But also chastity. It is doing what is right and not doing what is wrong. It's making good decisions, living a good life. The phoenix also symbolizes rare talents, or sometimes matrimonial happiness and peace."

Francesca hummed softly to indicate she listened. "Mm-hmm."

"I see a lot of the phoenix in you. I think that is why you

are drawn to take it," Fen said. "You are the phoenix--brave and strong, a fighter, and yet you long for marriage with my brother. You are rare, Francesca, rare to my people because of your differences, rare because you know Wushu when the art is said to be dead. I do wish you'd tell me how you learned, for I am very curious...."

*Ah-ha! There it is. She does want something from me. Her family sent her to get the information from me. Very sneaky.*

"I hesitate to say that for fear you think that's why I'm here. I assure you it's not. I don't care if you never tell me, so long as you allow us to be friends."

That was too much. Francesca quickly stood. "I'm hardly a phoenix, Fen. I'm just a woman in an awkward position."

What was it about Fen that made her *want* to be the woman's friend? She couldn't make friends with the woman. To do so would make leaving so much harder than it already was. Why did these people have to be so nice?

"If it helps, our people celebrate the phoenix. You will be forgiven, if you seek to be." Fen smiled and walked to the door. "Forgiveness is a virtue as well, Francesca. Our people know that."

"*Our* people?" Francesca said, before she could stop herself.

"Yes, you are one of us now. We accepted you into our family. When the ceremony is done, it will be official. You will be Líntiānese. We will be your family."

Francesca couldn't move. As a child, all she wanted was a family and here one was being offered to her. But as an adult, she didn't care about such things, did she?

*What seduces you, sweet Francesca? What is it you desire most?*

*A family.*

"By the way, Jin is also Líntiānese." Fen grinned. "He too enjoys celebrating the phoenix."

Francesca frowned. Did Fen just try to tell her that Jin wanted to celebrate her? Whatever did that mean? The woman left her alone, shutting the door behind her.

Francesca fell back on the bed, her arms spread. "That decides it. These people are crazy--every last one of them."

*Only crazy people would welcome me into their home.*

\* \* \* \*

"Zhang Jin! What have you done?"

Jin blinked, looking up from his solitary hideout, where he sat leaning against the Hall for Worshiping Ancestors. He wasn't surprised to see his grandfather Manchu standing before him. Glaring at the spirit for a short time, he blinked once and looked away. His lips pressed tightly together and he refused to answer.

"Zhang Jin!" Zhang Manchu insisted.

Jin again looked up at the transparent figure, his eyes hard. He blamed the ancestor for his problems with Francesca. The woman was a foreigner. She didn't understand or appreciate his culture or his life. All she cared about was taking. How could his grandfather have done this to him?

"Fine, do not speak to me, but listen," the old spirit said. "If you lose her, you lose your heart."

Jin narrowed his eyes. "Who are you to tell me my fate with such certainty? What do you know or care about my heart? It is your fault I'm in the state I'm in."

"You will watch your insolent tongue." His grandfather's form shimmered in anger. "And you will show me respect."

Jin snorted. Reaching behind his back, he grabbed a cylinder of *pò bai* and unscrewed the metal top. He was well on his way to a drunken stupor and wasn't about to let the old man disrupt that. The plan was to keep drinking until he passed out.

"You must make amends with her," his grandfather insisted.

"What do you care? It is my life we're talking about here. Perhaps I am not looking for a wife or marital love." Jin snorted again before taking a quick drink. The thick brown liquor burned its way down his throat, but he didn't care. He welcomed the numbness it would bring. "I have been satisfied without them so far."

"That may very well be, but she is for you. It is time." He turned in a circle. *"Nî bù dông ma?* Don't you understand? It is time. I don't speak only of marital love, but your love of your people and country. You will do what you must, Zhang Jin. You will do your duty."

"Time to do what, old man? You speak in riddles." Jin snarled, lifting the cylinder to his lips. "I have no time for riddles. Take them and be gone. I want no more of this conversation. I want no more of you."

Zhang Manchu blew forward on a gust of wind. It hit Jin

hard, throwing him back against the stone building as it whipped his hair into his face. He dropped the cylinder on impact. When he came to his senses, his grandfather had the liquor in his hand and the cylinder was as transparent as he was. Jin would not be getting it back.

Frowning, Jin tried to push to his feet. Manchu called the wind, blowing in warning. Jin fell back to the ground. Crossing his arms like a pouting child, he stared up at the sky, refusing to move.

"Leave me be," Jin protested. "She does not want me. I do not want her. Only *you* seem to want this marriage."

"You must marry her, Jin," his grandfather said quietly, leaning over him.

"Let me guess, by six moons? Was it you who told the astrologers that this was my fate?"

"I did."

"In six moons?" Jin laughed. It felt as if the ground spun under his back. His head swam, but he was too far gone to care. "Six moons?! Weddings are not planned in so short a time. Why so soon? If you want this marriage, why push so hard? If fate truly favored our being together, it would have happened. No, fate wants no part of this. This is your doing, Grandfather, yours alone. You want this match. You are bored and you have nothing better to do. I know not what offense I've committed against you. Perhaps I brought the wrong wine. Or gave too much to another ancestor in offering and made you jealous. Regardless of what I did, I will not play your game any longer. It's over, *lâotou*. There will be no wedding in six moons. There will be no wedding in a million of them. I have ended it. It is done."

"You are drunk," his grandfather spat.

"Yes, and I'd be unconscious by now if you'd kindly hand me the *pò bai*." Jin lifted his hand, waiting for the liquor to be handed back and knowing all along that it wouldn't be.

"If you do not marry our way of life will end. The Zhang Dynasty will end. Do you not understand? It is time. A sacrifice must be made. One of our own must marry. You Jin. You are the one. And it must happen quickly."

Jin blinked, his mind slowed by liquor. "What do you mean? Tell me what is happening or I swear on twenty generations of you dead, meddling ancestors that I will never marry--anyone."

Manchu sighed, closing his eyes. Jin saw movement in the background and lifted his head. He blinked heavily, trying to focus his blurry vision as he caught glimpses of more spirits, some he didn't recognize, more than he'd ever seen gathered before him in his life. Some were clearly ancestors by the dragons on their clothing, others merely spirits. It was common understanding that the dead stayed on, living in the in-between, gaining knowledge and guiding the future generations before moving on to the next plane.

Jin pushed himself to sitting and rubbed his eyes, but the spirits did not fade. If anything, they doubled their numbers until a crowd of thirty surrounded him. His eyes round with apprehension and awe, he didn't move, didn't speak.

"Our curse," a woman said. By the look of her spirit, he couldn't tell her age when she died. She looked young, but carried herself with the dignity of many years. Her thick, black hair was pulled high on her head and wrapped into a ponytail that fell a long way down her back. She wore the clothing of a fighter and had a sheath with no sword. "When Chen Sun went into the mountains to live out his days, he was betrayed by those who feared the Wushu would once again rise up against the empire. Those who practiced Wushu were killed, only one man escaped."

Jin studied the woman. Her eyes were sad. He tried to stand, overwhelmed with the insane urge to comfort her. The spirits behind her didn't move, didn't speak, merely stared at him. Their eyes were pleading, yet somehow demanding him to do his duty.

"Who escaped?" Jin asked.

The woman with long black hair looked away.

"Master Chen Sun," Manchu answered, glancing at the woman.

The woman continued, "Master Chen fought valiantly by the sides of his followers. They killed all those who betrayed them, but for one young warrior who was left wounded. It would be Master Chen's one mistake, for that one would tell others and they would go on to hunt him down."

"I thought Master Chen led his band into the mountains where they lived out their days in solitude. Word was sent down when Master Chen died and the art of Wushu died with him." Jin thought of his parents words, told to them by Zhang An. Why now was he being told that Master Chen escaped?

*Was their no end to the lies? Did no one know the whole truth of it?*

"Some believe that. But I was there," the woman said. "I know the truth."

"You are the one Master Chen left alive?" Jin asked to the woman, surprised. Now he might be getting somewhere. Finally. An eye witness.

She nodded once. "The Wushu were too strong. Their ways had to be stopped. My family line ended with the Uprising, as did many others. It was my honor to destroy the last of them."

"And the curse?" Jin asked.

"Years later, Master Chen was found and killed by those whose mission it became to avenge those killed by the Wushu masters."

"Except it was Master Ming who defeated the Zhang armies," Jin said. He tried to reason through the fog over his brain, but it was hard. Though, if any topic was going to sober him, this was it.

"These things are never easily explained. The stories can be told, but to be understood you must be there to live them," the black-haired woman said.

"What is your name?" Jin asked.

"Guan-yin," she answered.

Jin was shocked. *The* Guan-yin? He didn't have to even ask for she nodded once in silent answer to his question.

Guan-yin was said to be a great warrior, one of the best. She showed herself a hero during the Wushu Uprising. Children's songs were sung in her honor and she was greatly celebrated every year at festivals. Looking at her spirit now, he saw the distinction in her.

"But, you don't look like your carvings," Jin said. Guan-yin looked to the ground before glancing back up.

"Jin, it is because of what was done to Master Chen that you must marry," his grandfather said. "When he died, he promised that one would come to destroy the Zhang Empire and all they hold dear unless they gave her something more powerful than the wrong done to him."

"More powerful?" Jin repeated. He laughed, drunkenly tossing back his head as he pointed at himself. "Me."

"Love," his grandfather said. "Love is more powerful than

death."

"So," Jin paused, grunting as he stumbled to his feet, "you think Francesca La Rosa is here to avenge Master Chen's death and unless I marry her, she will destroy us."

"She seeks the Jade Phoenix," Manchu said. "Master Chen must have trained her. She practices Wushu. She is the one Master Chen has sent for vengeance."

"It's only a matter of time until she succeeds," Guan-yin said. "In your lifetime, you never had to face warriors like these. She must be stopped."

"Why not just kill her?" he suggested.

"That was discussed," Guan-yin stated bluntly. Jin's stomach tightened with knots. He hadn't been serious.

"We decided against it," his grandfather interrupted. "The curse was brought about by death. Who knows what will happen if we kill the last known practitioner of Wushu?"

"It will be over," Guan-yin said.

"We don't know that!" Manchu argued. They glared at each other, obviously at wit's ends with the other, even though they fought for the same cause. A ripple flowed over the spirits behind them, waving their transparent figures. Still, the silent ones in back did not speak, only watched.

"There is only one problem with your plan, Grandfather." Jin shook his head, chuckling lightly because he didn't know what else to do. The situation was too surreal. "I may marry her, but that doesn't mean there will be love in the marriage. You can fool the astrologers into misreading signs, but you can't force what isn't there."

"You want her," Manchu charged. "Try and deny it."

"Lust," Jin stated. "Not love. I lust for her. But I am a man and I lust for many things that intrigue me."

"The wind has whispered its secrets to us," his grandfather insisted. "It told me that you were the one. You are connected to the past. You can make it right. The Jade Phoenix has given you that gift. You must use it to find the answer."

Jin laughed, a loud and mocking sound. He didn't want to hear anymore of their curses and changed history. Who knew what the truth was anymore? Memories, over time, distorted what had been as did vanity and pride. Confusion spread over him. Everyone around him had their secrets, their angles, their faulty memories and motivations. Guan-yin was bitter about the war and about one escaping. His grandfather still thought he was emperor, though his time had passed.

The spirits watched him as he backed away. Stumbling, Jin's hand fell through a couple of them like air. Holding out his arms to the side, he bowed slightly and said, "And yet, the wind says nothing to me."

"Zhang Jin!" Manchu yelled. "You will do your duty."

Jin spun on his heel, holding up his hand in dismissal as he stumbled drunkenly away. He needed to find a place to lie down--a place far away from meddling ancestors and thieves who threatened everything he held dear.

"Keep the *pò bai*, Grandfather," he yelled. "I'll find more!"

## Chapter Seven

Francesca stared at the intricate latticework hanging above the Exalted Hall. The afternoon weather was nice, just like it always was in Honorable City. The heat was cooled by the temperate breeze. Depictions of Gods were on each of the two panels on the doors, swords drawn as they stood ready for combat. Fen had told her that the carving was for protection from evil spirits. Actually, Fen had told her a lot of things--so much that Francesca was considering hiding from the woman. It was as if the princess was desperate to make Francesca love the Muntong Empire and its culture as much as she did.

It had been three days and Jin had not come to her. Three very long days. She was curious about where he was, but told herself she didn't really care. The royal family had given her Jin's room, and she was technically in 'solitude' so she didn't have to eat with the family. Unfortunately, since Jin had said she was a vegetarian, all she was given to eat was vegetables and fruits. She was getting desperate for a thick, juicy piece of meat--so long as it didn't have eyes and didn't come with legs still attached.

*Mm, a giant slab of unrecognizable, unnamable meat. Perfect.*

The Líntiānese culture was rich and interesting, Francesca would give them that, but she wasn't Líntiānese. She didn't worship her dead ancestors. In fact, she didn't even know of any ancestors--living or dead. She didn't believe in fate making decisions for her life. *She* made decisions for her life. Things like honor and tradition didn't bind her every movement and she couldn't understand a system that would force a believer to marry a person like her.

Were these people just plain foolish? They actually wanted Jin to be married to her? If they were hard up for some new bloodlines, didn't they realize they could pay corporations like Galaxy Brides to furnish willing women eager to get married? From what she understood, the corporation would even ship the brides to them and let them have a pick, just like they were shopping for bolts of material and other trade goods. Francesca would have told them about Galaxy Brides if the plan didn't work against her goal of stealing the Jade Phoenix and destroying the Zhang family for revenge.

Francesca was pretty sure she'd abandoned the high road long ago, the day she stole her first box of what she thought was food. It turned out it was adhesive. Though she was starving, it had been fun to watch all the Gittan dignitaries as they stuck to the floor in their expensive, gem-studded shoes. The blue creatures were a vain lot from the tops of their pointy ears to the tips of their four toeless feet. Afterward, she'd been caught, reprimanded and expelled from the space dock. Lucky for her, Gittans had no use for humans. If it had been any other species, she might not have gotten off so easily.

The hairs on the back of her neck stood on end and Francesca froze. She was being watched, she could feel it. Everywhere she went within the city walls, she was followed. Only, she never saw who watched her. The guards often hid behind posts and columns, but there weren't any in direct view of where she was standing.

*Maybe I'm just getting paranoid.*

Francesca had no doubt that she could escape the eyes of others if she really wanted to, but instead she bided her time, waiting for the perfect moment. At present, the royal guards were on edge, too suspicious--as they had a right to be. She had tried to steal the Jade Phoenix twice already.

Most of the time, she avoided all company, pretending to be in a solitary mood. Fen was convinced it was because she pined for Prince Jin. Francesca let the woman believe what she wanted.

Honorable City was a beautiful place, with attention paid to every detail--from the curved roofs that pointed up toward the heavens to the mosaic pathways that led to a few of the sacred buildings to the position of each flower blossom. She'd seen the many gardeners tending the plant life within the walls. The Imperial Garden was the most fantastic, located behind the emperor's sleeping quarters. Larger versions of the blue trees she'd seen in the prisons grew in the corners, so strong she could step up on one's branches, following its stair step pattern around until she reached the top. From there, she could just see over the palace walls. Fen had showed her the trick. The princess said that the guards often climbed the trees at night like watchtowers to keep a vigilant eye over the emperor's private chambers.

The sensation of being watched intensified. Francesca stiffened, no longer seeing the two doors leading to the Exalted Hall where she was to be married to Jin. After forty minutes of standing before it, it was clear she couldn't force herself to look inside anyway.

She was dressed in an orange silk floor-length tunic, edged with the pattern of puffy circular waves and embroidered with flowers and stylized insects. Its loose folds fell around her figure, with wide sleeves that reached past her hands, hiding them from view. Underneath she wore loose pants. They too were silk.

Someone tapped her shoulder as the wind stirred behind her. Francesca turned, her mouth opened, ready to speak. No one was there. She frowned, glancing around the palace grounds. Rubbing her shoulder, she could have sworn someone had touched her.

Seeing a wisp of material fluttering around the far corner of the Exalted Hall, Francesca moved to follow it. Was someone messing with her? A guard perhaps? Jin? One of the princes? Every turn she took seemed to be timed perfectly with the person she was following taking another corner. Each time, she just saw wisps of clothing before the person disappeared. Whoever it was stayed one step ahead of her.

Francesca moved faster, determined to catch the person and see what they were doing spying on her. If anything, the short run was good for a diversion. Walking around the palace had left her a little bored. Sure it was beautiful, but she was too scared to exercise for fear of being studied or worse, questioned. She'd gone on runs a few times, but there were only so many places a person could run to inside a confined space. The Honorable City was nearly a half of a mile by three quarters of a mile long, but to her it felt like she was living in a box.

As she wove past the entry to the Imperial Gardens, she hurried by the royal chambers. Suddenly, she tripped, flying forward to land face first on the path. She glanced up, as a loud groan sounded behind her. The figure she followed was gone. Irritated, she looked to see what was in her way.

Jin stared at her from where he sat on the ground. His legs were sprawled out in front of him and his eyes were bloodshot with dark circles beneath their stormy depths. For a moment, she couldn't breathe. She'd spent the last days telling herself that she felt nothing for him, but as she looked at his worn, tired face, she knew it was a lie. She desired him. Every nerve in her body reached out to him. She wanted to touch him, be touched by him. Francesca didn't move as she stared at his eyes. They were beautiful, dark and seductive, slanted in such a dramatic way to draw attention to their serious depths. Full lips beckoned her with the memory of their kisses.

"Jin," she said, as if in a trance, her voice soft. Francesca wished she could draw the word back into her throat, but it was too late.

"They can't stop meddling, can they?" he chuckled. "No, they have to lead you before me, hoping I'll be tempted by you."

Francesca frowned, glancing around. No one was there. Did he mean the person she'd followed before tripping over him? Pushing to her feet, she brushed off her long tunic. "Who? The guards? Your family?"

"The costume does not hide the fact that you are not one of us," he said, his words slurred. "My family may want you, but I am not fooled. You are here for only one reason. To destroy us. To destroy me."

"You're drunk," Francesca said, frowning in disappointment.

"Yes, very much so," he laughed, pointing at her, "but I'm still right."

Francesca nodded. "Yes, you are right. I'm not one of you. I don't want to be."

Jin laughed again as he ambled to his feet. He swayed slightly. "Tell me, is it because you don't think me worthy of true combat that I make an unfit husband in your eyes? If I beat you up, would that make me worthier, *bǎobèi?*"

"Come on, you need to sober up." She made a move to grab his arm, but he jerked away from her.

"Don't tell me what to do." Jin lifted his hands, readying for a fight. "Or do you not fight me because you are scared that I will win? Are you frightened that you will have to submit to me? Are you scared that I can best you?"

"I fear nothing," she stated. Okay, that was a lie. She feared feeling anything for the people she'd vowed to destroy. She feared the strength of desire she felt even now, looking at the rumpled, unbathed version of the noble prince swaying before her. How far he had fallen since meeting her. No longer was he arrogant and self-assured. Now he was broken, drunk and preoccupied. Had she done this to him?

He snorted. "I have tried to figure out what your game is, Francesca. You deny marriage to me, and then agree to it unwillingly. Then when I let you go as you demanded, you cry and carry on, telling everyone that I promised to love you. Why? What do you want from me?"

Francesca froze. She had said that to Fen in the hall and had no idea how many had heard her say it. Possibly, the entire royal family had heard her words. Well, it was too late. She couldn't take them back now. Lifting her jaw, she didn't answer.

"You said you wanted to marry me, to be my wife." His eyes narrowed. "You told my family I said I loved you. Did you think I said that? When I said love, did you think I meant to love you?"

"No. I knew you didn't mean it. You don't love me." She lowered her eyes to the ground, unable to meet his.

"Then why did you say it to them? My father is threatening to exile me for this."

Francesca swallowed. A tremor worked over her body and she tried to harden herself to him, but couldn't. She blinked back a tear.

"Well?" he demanded. "Did you say it? Did you?"

Francesca nodded once, whispering, "Yes."

"Why, woman?!" Jin yelled. Francesca jolted at the harshness of his tone. "Do you see what you have done with your lies? There is no escape for you now, for either of us. I have to marry you or I will be turned out from my home, my family. I will be stripped of my title. They won't let you run, Francesca. They will hunt you down. *I* will hunt you down until you go through with the vows. There is no stopping it now. A promise of love is a word that cannot be broken."

Her stomach tightened, not because she was afraid of being hunted, but because she was hurt by how unappealing he thought marriage to her would be. She didn't plan on being a wife, but the rejection hurt nonetheless.

"I never told you I loved you," he whispered.

"No," she answered, her tone dead. Numbness curled from the pain in her stomach and she welcomed the sensation. "No, you didn't. I'll tell them the truth. I'll take the words back. Don't worry. They'll believe them. One look at us and they'll know the truth, if they don't suspect it already."

"It will do no good," he whispered. Before she could answer, he growled, waving his hand at her erratically. "It doesn't matter. It's too late. It's too late. The date will be set soon. It is too late."

Francesca tried to ask him if there was any way out of the marriage. She tried to speak, to mock him, to yell and scream at him for treating her as unworthy. Instead, she kept her calm. Emotionlessly, she said, "You are the one who claimed me, your highness."

"I told you I was compelled."

"Compelled? Compelled! What does that even mean? You saw me, got frisky and suddenly it's my problem? I have news for you, prince, it is your fault that we are in this situation."

He growled, charging her. Francesca swept to the side, grabbing his arm and tossing him to the ground as she avoided his sloppy attack.

Breathing hard, he stood. "Will you marry me? Will you honor what has been done?"

"No," she stated, anger filling her. "And you need to sober up. You're not thinking rationally. Come talk to me when you're not drunk."

He charged her again, yelling as he came at her face with a balled fist. Francesca didn't move as she waited for him to hurt her. She wanted him to hurt her, as he obviously desired to strike her to end his own frustration. His fist stopped inches from her face.

"Do you feel nothing!" he cried, his face in hers. "Does your face never show emotion of any kind? I can't bear to look at your eyes, always looking at me so cool, so blank."

Francesca would have laughed if she could find the strength. She thought the exact same thing about him. He was always so stoical when he looked at her, thoughtful and hidden.

"Say something!" he demanded. "It is like there is no soul in you, Francesca. You're so dead inside, it pains me to see it. Looking at you is like looking into a void."

"I'll marry you." The words surprised even her. She didn't take them back though. "So long as you stop yelling at me, get yourself sobered up and, by all the stars, bathe. You smell like a starship full of cheap, sweaty whores."

Okay, it was a horrible analogy, but he'd said some pretty harsh things.

"Did you just say you would marry me?" he asked suspiciously.

"Don't make me repeat it."

"Why?"

"I'm compelled," she answered, motioning to her rich clothing. "Being a princess has its perks. I'm a thief. You know that. Why wouldn't I want to live in riches?"

"I don't trust you," he said.

"I don't trust you," she answered.

"I don't love you." Jin stepped closer, his hand lifting to cup her cheek.

"And I don't love you." Francesca followed his example, moving closer.

"So long as we're clear on that," he said.

"We're clear."

"Yes. Clear." His voice dipped and he looked at her lips as if he would kiss her.

Francesca shook her head and stepped back.

"But we have passion," he inserted, looking again at her mouth. "You can't deny that we have passion between us. That is something, isn't it?"

"Yes, we have that." Francesca didn't want him to kiss her, not until he cleaned up. She was thankful that he needed to bathe, otherwise she wouldn't be able to control herself. She'd have him naked right there on the pathway for all to see.

"Francesca--" he began, his voice husky with desire.

She held up her hand.

"What now?!" he demanded. "*Wode tìan*! I swear you torment me on purpose!"

"Everything that happens in this marriage is your doing. You started this. You chose me, not the other way around." Francesca's body shook and she fought to control it. "Remember that, prince."

*You deserve what you'll get, Jin. This changes nothing.*

"I marry you for the money and power. You marry me because you are a fool," she said. It was only half a lie. He was a fool, but she would marry him because Fen had let it slip, in not so many words, that Francesca would have access to all family possessions after the ceremony-- including the Sacred Chamber and the Jade Phoenix.

He laughed. "Yes. A fool who has no choice."

"Good. It is settled. Go bathe and then we will do whatever must be done to right your stupidity in the hall."

"My stupidity?" he grumbled in irritation. "You are the one who cried about how I'd made you promises of love."

"It's your fault, Jin," Francesca reminded him, turning to go inside the royal chambers. "Not mine. You started this, *ài rén.*"

"Whatever you have to tell yourself, *bâobèi.* Though, don't forget, I didn't bring you to my planet. You did that all on your own."

\* \* \* \*

Francesca swallowed. Her mouth was suddenly dry as she watched the green lasers of the decontaminator hitting along Jin's tight flesh. He'd dropped his clothing and stepped into the unit without bothering to shut the door for privacy. She attributed it to him being drunk, but the more she looked at the way his body moved within the unit, she couldn't help but imagine that he purposefully gave her a show.

Purposeful or not, she was watching. And she liked what she saw. Very much.

Her engagement presents were lined up against the wall. She wasn't sure what to do with them, so she'd just pushed them out of the way. Jin had glanced over the gifts when he walked in, snorted softly to himself but said nothing as he'd gone to the decontaminator to bathe.

Looking at him now, she shivered. The decontaminator was in a separate small room that had just enough space to undress before stepping inside. The way the unit was angled gave her a full view of the inside. Moisture built between her thighs and she spread her legs slightly as she sat on his bed. The action didn't help cool her ardor. If anything, the seductive pose made her all the more aroused.

The attraction she felt wasn't surprising. He was a sexy man with a well formed physique. When he wasn't drunk and stumbling, the prince carried himself well and moved with the grace of a fighter. Since the first moment she had seen him, she couldn't help but stare in complete fascination. He was in her mind, enchanting her with the very thought of him.

The lasers worked over his dark, thick hair. A thick lock fell over his brow and he pushed it back. Francesca licked her lips. The motion gave her a clear view of his profile. His bent thigh was raised just enough to hide his cock from her, while adding to the curve of his buttocks. She clenched her hands into fists, remembering the feel and heat of his flesh against her palms. Her legs fell open even more, as if by their own accord.

Jin turned, arms raised as they crossed over his head. His strong, muscled back was to her. Her eyes followed the beam of light as it roamed over the delicious curve of his spine, the perfection of his hips and thighs. He might be a spoiled prince, but there was no way he spent all his time on that firm ass of his. This was a man who worked out and took care of what he had.

A low moan sounded and his biceps flexed, rippling muscles from his arms, down his shoulders and back. Again he slowly turned as the lasers dipped over every last inch of his gorgeous flesh. His thighs parted and the light hit between them, causing an eerie glow over his balls and the bottom of his half erect shaft. The way the light caressed it made his cock come to life, spotlighting it for her complete perusal.

Francesca let loose a long breath. She wiggled her hips in a slow circle as heat spread over her. Her nipples ached for attention as did the rest of her. Jin's hand glided down his tight stomach. His head was down and he didn't look at her as he reached between his thighs. Locks of his dark hair hid part of his face from view and his thick, dark lashes fanned over his cheeks. Touching himself lightly, he stroked his shaft in his strong hand. He moaned again, the sound hoarse and low in his throat.

The erotic sight made her shiver and she rocked her hips even as she edged to the end of the bed. Her pussy was soaked with need. She wanted to force him to his knees before her. She wanted to turn around and demand he take her. Thoughts flew through her mind, fueled by desire and a wicked imagination. He had never entered her body during their previous intimate encounter. She ached for him to do so now. Francesca needed to feel him inside her, she needed the release he could bring.

Tension built within her until she was stiff with the demands of her arousal. His fist pumped again, as it swallowed the full length of his growing arousal. Francesca slowly unbuttoned the front of her tunic. Jin's eyes turned instantly to her, as if he somehow knew what she was doing.

When his eyes met hers she felt a spark of fire ignite between them. She willed him to come to her on the bed. When he didn't move, just stood staring at her, she smiled. Francesca got to her feet, pushing the long tunic so that it slithered to the floor. Her breasts tingled and ached for attention. Jin watched, his hand moving up and down over his now extremely stiff length, as she took her hands to her hips and slowly pushed the silk pants down her legs. When she stood, she was completely naked.

His eyes dipped over her form and he moved his hand faster over himself. He devoured her with the heat in his gaze. Unable to deny her own body's needs, she cupped her breasts, massaging them gently. Keeping one hand against a nipple, she reached between her thighs, parting the wet folds so she could run the tip of her finger along her swollen sex.

Francesca waited for him to make the first move, to cross the distance and toss her on the bed. He stayed in the decontaminator, just on the other side of the opened sliding door. The lights continued, as lasers cleaned his perfect body. He took his hand off his shaft and placed it on the wall, leaning into it. The way he looked at her, his lids heavy over his eyes, the come hither purse of his lips, made her forget who they were.

Francesca was the first to give in and she moved anxiously toward the decontaminator. There was plenty of room for both of them and he moved over as she stepped inside. The lasers hit her from every direction, their warmth sending tingles over her flesh. She gasped at how sensitive her body was. Jin looked at her breasts and lightly reached for her hip. The caress was light, but it was enough to weaken her knees.

"I didn't invite you in," he said, his voice low.

"Why bother acting coy, *ài rén*?" Francesca gravitated closer, drawn by the sexy tone in his voice and the heat of his flesh. "We both know the only thing we have is passion."

"Don't you think we might have more? Perhaps in time?" His expression was shaded.

Francesca shook her head, even as her stomach flipped around inside her. *No, ài rén, there will be no time for us. We are not forever.*

"Mm," he moaned thoughtfully in the back of his throat, but he didn't appear upset by her silence. Pulling her closer, he slipped his hand around to her lower back, massaging her body into his. His arousal brushed her skin, so thick and hot. She longed to feel its firm texture inside her. "I'm sorry I said you had no soul. I didn't mean it. And I didn't mean whatever else I said to you."

Her breath caught as his mouth came for her, cutting off any response. It was for the best. She didn't have a response to give.

Lasers caressed their skin, the green lights running over her sensitive flesh like a million fingers. She softly moaned as his lips met hers. They were firm, confident and they definitely knew how to move against her in such a way as to heat her already hot body. Jin's lips moved impatiently against hers. She liked knowing he wanted her as much as she wanted him. Her mind tried to hold onto her surroundings, but the more he kissed her, the more she let go of herself.

His hand tightened on her hip as he turned to press her into the wall. She lifted her thigh along his leg, opening her body to him. This was insane, but she couldn't stop and think beyond the feeling of his body next to hers. His kiss was intoxicating, and his mouth was clean, not tasting like liquor as she suspected it would have moments before. Her thighs tightened as her heart lurched in her chest. She'd never been so aroused in her life and she felt like she was losing control.

"Is this what you want, *bâobèi?*" Jin rocked his hips into hers, letting her feel his naked erection against her.

"Yes," she gasped, the words breathy. "Oh, yes. Very much so."

Groaning, he kissed her neck, nipping playfully at her flesh. Animalistic sounds washed over her as their bodies meshed together in a sweet melody of passion. His hands roamed her body, grabbing her breasts, exploring her stomach, teasingly going around her aching sex.

Francesca spread her thighs, shifting her leg to the side in the hope that he would find his way between them. Jin kissed her nipples, sticking out his tongue to playfully circle the erect buds until they ached in torment. She grabbed his head, forcing him roughly onto her breast. He sucked hard and pleasure racked her body at the forceful gesture.

The more she responded to the force of his passion, the bolder he became, until their lovemaking became almost like a battle. Each fought for control as they explored the other, grabbing and biting and pinching as they hit new heights of arousal. Francesca's back hit hard against the decontaminator wall as Jin pressed her against it. There was something surreal about sleeping with the opposition, knowing that she had secrets he'd love to hear.

Jin eagerly moved from her chest down over her stomach, flicking his tongue against her navel as he passed. Every thought fled as she gripped his head and forcibly pulled him forward so that his mouth found her ready sex. Her pussy was wet for him when he kissed her. The lasers ran over his lips, drying his kisses even as he moved over her flesh. The sensation was too much, warmth and pressure combined with the tingling of the lasers.

Jin moaned, his lips instantly parting to drink her in. Francesca arched against the wall, riding his tongue as he licked her. His dark hair tickled her stomach and she stared at him between her thighs. Her foot slipped, but he held her up against the hard wall. The man looked like a god, worshiping at her feet. The lasers hit her flesh, drying her sweat as soon as it appeared. She grabbed her chest, rolling her breasts roughly in her hands as he worked his mouth in long strokes.

Jin kneaded her ass, pulling the cheeks apart as he rocked her into his mouth. The smothered sounds of his pleasure vibrated against her clit. Aggressively, he latched on, pulling the tender bud between his teeth. The sounds he made only aroused her more. Pleasurable sensations overwhelmed her and she jerked hard. He didn't let go as he forced her to take what he gave her. She did so willingly, shaking and panting as sweat beaded over her body. He expertly kept her on the brink of climax, building her up, letting her fall, building her up again. It was wondrous torture.

Release was near and she welcomed it, needed it, cried out incoherently for it. "Jin, yes. Yes. Yes!"

Her orgasm hit her like a comet, incinerating her in its tremendous wake. She stiffened, too far gone to cry out as her mouth opened in a silent scream. Her sex clenched and she was forced to hit his shoulder to get him to pull back. The sensations were too much. Jin looked up at her, his lips wet with her body's moisture. He licked them slowly, his eyes narrowed in heady pleasure.

With the swiftness of a phaser blast, he stood up and captured her lips. He stole her breath as he let her taste her own cream on his mouth. It was wonderfully seductive and she sucked his tongue between her lips. Lazily, she kissed him, still breathless from her release. Jin's body pressed insistently into hers, rubbing up and down along her stomach. He still sought his release and she wanted to give it to him.

"Why do you deny us both?" she asked.

He arched brow in question and glanced down, obviously confused. "Deny?"

"You don't actually come inside me. Is it against your beliefs or something?" she asked, breathing heavily as his hips moved against her.

"So impatient," he whispered, nipping at her neck and earlobe.

"Impatient?" She gave a weak laugh.

"Pleasure is to be drawn out," he paused, kissing her, "enjoyed--"

"Mm, but--"

"Not rushed through like some unpleasant task you must get over quickly."

Francesca giggled. "How many days have we known each other? I would say we aren't rushing anything."

Okay, to some a few days wasn't a long time, but when she wasn't used to having the same person around for more than a few hours, it was a lifetime.

Jin grinned in response. Taking her hand, he pulled her out of the decontaminator and led her toward the bed. He walked backward, staring at her the entire time. With a firm tug, he pulled her forward, stepping out of her way so she landed with her hands on the bed.

Francesca wanted to stand, but the truth was she was still shaky from her first release so she was forced to crawl onto the bed. Jin was instantly behind her, caressing up the length of her back. His fingers traced her spine, sending delicious chills over her. She fell down on the bed and his body brushed closely against hers.

Her body was relaxed as he pushed her hair aside to kiss the place where her neck met with her shoulder. His heavy erection rubbed along her ass from behind, so firm and hot. She'd never seen a man practice such self-control in the bedroom, especially when he was so ready. Moisture gathered in her sex. Jin put his legs between her thighs, parting them as he boldly slid his knees apart.

Hands on her hips, he sat back on his legs, dragging her up with him. Her body was opened, exposed. He pulled her back so she was straddling his lap, facing away. Jin reached around her, guiding his cock toward her opening. He slid it back and forth in her cream, only to press up into her as he found what he'd been looking for. Boldly, he thrust his hard shaft inside her, prying her apart with the heavy length.

Francesca moaned as he filled her. He used the position to advantage, reaching around to grab her breasts. Grasping them vigorously, he massaged the tender globes in his palms, running his fingers over her nipples.

She rocked her hips, working him in shallow strokes. He angled his hips toward her, letting his hands slide to her hips. Jin groaned passionately, as he made animalistic sounds of pleasure. He lifted her up only to bring her down hard. Francesca cried softly, biting her lip. Jin did it again, harder than before.

It clearly wasn't enough, for he pushed her forward onto her hands and knees. His body parted from her for a brief instant before he was kneeling behind her, hips finding their way to her pussy once more. Again he thrust into her, going deeper than before. Jin groaned, becoming wild as he rocked back and forth. His thumb pressed along her clit. Tremors racked her, jarring her body with pleasure. He thrust harder, faster, deeper. Suddenly, he grunted, shivering as he came.

Francesca collapsed on the bed, completely sated. A soft moan left her lips and she mumbled incoherently, not even sure what it was she was trying to say to him. All she knew was that she felt good--better than she'd felt in a very long time. The bed shifted as Jin lay down next to her. He cradled her in his arms.

Feeling Jin's body cradled next to hers, she stiffened. What had just happened? Well, she knew what happened, but how? How had she gotten to the point that she forgot everything? She forgot to listen past Jin for danger. She forgot to keep up her guard. She forgot to monitor her actions to make sure she didn't screw anything up. As he kissed her temple, she pulled away and rolled to sitting.

*What have I done?*

"Francesca?" Jin asked.

"Hum?" She stretched her arms over her head, doing her best to feign relaxed indifference.

"Lay back down. We'll fight more tomorrow." When she didn't move, he sighed heavily. "I promise."

"It's early yet," Francesca said, getting up. "I think I'm going to go exercise."

"More exercise than this?" The words were teasing, but there was no merriment in his hard expression when she glanced at him.

She pulled on her pants and grabbed the orange tunic. As she slipped it over her shoulders, she said, "Don't read more into this than there is, Jin. It is what it is and it definitely isn't love. Save the cuddling. I don't need it."

Francesca walked out. Every bit of her wanted to turn back around and slide into his arms. She wanted to be held by him and that scared her.

*There are all types of seductions. What seduces you, sweet Francesca? What is it you desire most?*

"A home," she whispered to the memory, hating herself because it was true. "And I want a family I can never have."

*I'm disappointed in you, my sweet,* she imagined the voice from her past to answer, *so incredibly disappointed.*

*I'm sorry, Chen Sun. I never meant to betray you. I'll do better. I'll keep my word. You will be avenged.*

\* \* \* \*

*"Don't read more into this than there is, Jin. It is what it is and it definitely isn't love. Save the cuddling. I don't need it."*

Jin frowned as Francesca left him. Her words stung. Part of him waited for her to come back, to admit that what they'd shared was special. He knew it, so didn't that mean she had to know it as well?

When she didn't come and he was left staring at the door, he whispered, "Maybe it is I who needed to hold you, *bâobèi,* even if you have no use for me."

## Chapter Eight

The gifts kept coming. Francesca still wasn't sure what to do with them all. It had been less than a week since she'd pulled her 'crying fit' over Jin's coldness and she was already tired of getting presents. In fact, it was just making her uncomfortable. What was she supposed to do with baskets of vegetables and fruit from the local farmers? The gesture was nice, she supposed, but she'd rather they just kept the presents. Each time she received them, she felt bad. Taking from the rich nobles was one thing, taking from the working class farmers was another altogether. The rich could well afford a few trinkets, poorer farmers could not.

Slowly lowering her body, she extended her arms out to the side. Francesca kept her movements deliberate, each one fluidly moving into the next in practiced order. She breathed in and out, trying to stay relaxed as she focused her mind. Simple breathing was one of the first things she'd learned when she started her training. Sun had insisted she learn that much without the aid of uploads before she crammed years of knowledge into her head. The uploads only took her so far and then the rest had been up to her. They'd spent hours training together, always with him riding her to do better, to be more.

Francesca shoved her palm out as she struck a pose and paused before moving to the next fluid motion. She'd done this very same exercise with Sun, every night before bed. Never once did he let her slack.

*I didn't save you to let you fail yourself, my sweet.*

Jin had insisted on sharing her bed the night before. Francesca couldn't resist him when he looked at her with his half closed eyes. She was like a baboian fly drawn to the icy crags of Sintaz--mesmerized by him to the point she couldn't see anything else until it was too late. Sex was fine, but he had slept next to her trying to hold her afterward. Cuddling was too intimate and made her uncomfortable. She wanted to keep their affair on a strictly professional basis. But who was she fooling? It was getting personal. Very personal.

About an hour before dawn, she'd slipped from his embrace, still awake from the night before and had gone for a run around Honorable City. She must have traveled over every single pathway before stopping, including the waterway paths and bridges that went over the Enchanted River, a small stream inside the palace walls. By her estimation, the city was about a half of a mile long by three quarters of a mile wide from the longest points which meant for about three miles worth of useable running paths. By the time she had gotten back to Jin's chambers to cool down and clean up, he was gone.

Her arms swooped around to the side as she lifted her leg. Balance was the second thing she had learned to master under Sun's strict guidance.

"Francesca! He's done it! My brother has done it!"

Francesca frowned, wavering slightly at Fen's happy tone. There was something in it that caught her off guard, a true happiness and excitement. The woman's unassuming friendship always took her by surprise and she kept expecting it to fade away as common sense returned to Fen.

*Apparently, she has no common sense,* Francesca mused. But even as she thought it, she knew she didn't mean it. She truly liked the woman. *This job is just getting more complicated every second.*

"Francesca!" The door slid open and the excited princess came in. "Jin loves you."

Francesca stumbled over her own feet, tripping herself. She fell forward, catching her weight with her hands in a lopsided pushup only to thrust her weight off the floor and quickly stand upright.

*Huh?* She was too stunned to speak, so she merely stared, wide-eyed with her mouth hanging open.

"Didn't you hear me, Fran?"

"Francesca," she corrected absently. *Huh?*

"Sorry, I forgot. Fran-*cesca*, didn't you hear what I said?"

*Huh? Jin loves who?*

"Jin has done it. He's offered his apology to you." Fen looked her over and clicked her tongue in disapproval. "*Tiānna!* You're all sweaty. We have to get you changed. Those clothes will never do! Oh, please hurry. *Tian xiâo de!* The crowd is starting to gather and...."

Francesca didn't move as Fen became a whirlwind of activity around her. She blinked, feeling as if she moved in slow motion.

"...get dressed after you bathe," Fen continued. The princess grabbed Francesca's hand and pulled her toward the decontaminator only to let go as she saw the gown amongst the presents. "Oh, here, you'll wear the gown from Lady Hsin. *Ni hao ma? Hâo?* Yes, it will be perfect and I'll do your hair and paint your face...."

Francesca heard a buzzing in her head, making it impossible for her to translate the princess each time she slipped into Líntiānese, which became more frequent as she tried to rush Francesca across the chamber.

"*Tian xiâo de! Zhè bìng bù huài....*"

Francesca's clothing was tugged back and she blinked in surprise, coming to her senses, as Fen tried to help her undress. She'd never had another woman try to get her into a bath before, though she knew many women used servants. Fen's features were so preoccupied, she didn't notice as Francesca artfully escaped her helping grasp.

"*Wode tìan! Ti--*"

Francesca quickly disrobed and stepped into the decontaminator. She closed the door to the unit.

"Fen," Francesca broke in carefully. When the woman didn't stop, she said more firmly, "Fen!"

The woman stopped talking. "*Shénme?* Yes?"

"What did you mean when you said that Jin...." Pausing before she said, 'when you said that Jin said he loved me?' she changed her mind and finished, "had done it? What did he do?"

"What?!" Fen called. She sounded far away. "I'm sorry, I didn't hear you."

"What did Jin do?" Francesca yelled louder. The green lasers washed over her and she lifted her arms so that they could clean over her entire length.

"Oh," Fen said, her voice muffled, "he is publicly apologizing to you for his actions when the astrologers were here doing your reading."

*I know that!* Francesca rolled her eyes. "How?"

"*Duìbùqî?!*"

"How?" Francesca asked louder.

"What?!"

"How is he apologizing?" Francesca didn't move, listening carefully.

"Oh ... it ... he ... *lìngrén jìngyì* ... and.... " The words were choppy, as if the princess was digging around Jin's chambers. "*Wode tian!* Never mind, I got it!"

*Okay, was Fen being elusive on purpose?*

Francesca quickly ran her fingers through her hair, lifting the heavy locks so that the lasers hit them. When she finished, she peeked out of the decontaminator. Fen was there, smiling brightly as she held up the red gown with the flowers and snakelike dragons Lady Hsin had given to her.

Wiggling the beautiful dress back and forth, Fen said, "I think this will look perfect on you!"

\* \* \* \*

For someone who had insisted they hurry, Fen took her time in getting Francesca ready. She didn't know why she submitted to the princess' administering hands, but she did. By the time Fen led her out of Jin's private chambers, Francesca was all done up in Líntiānese finery. The red silk gown fell to mid-calf like a tunic shirt. It split up the middle with the Mandarin collar and frog buttons like the outfit she had worn when the astrologers predicted Jin's and her future together.

*Little they know.* Francesca let loose a derisive laugh. *They predicted our future together to be a good one.*

"Francesca?" Fen asked, pausing on her way out of the royal chambers.

"I didn't speak," she answered.

Fen made a soft noise of wonder, but continued walking.

Curiosity boiled inside of Francesca. What was Jin up to? What was this public apology going to consist of? Surely it was just an overly traditional ceremony like everything else on this planet. She was certainly dressed for another ceremony.

Her long hair was elaborately coiled on top of her head, held in place by long straight hairpins. The dark color of the pins blended with her locks so they remained unseen. The coiffure was finished off with an artfully arranged mass of curls decorated with a long, hollow piece of purple jade from the Lin Yao Mines across the Satlyun River in Singhai. The jade hairpiece was held into place by an elaborate gold pin with colorful glass inlay.

It was odd to have live hands do her hair for her. Normally, she twisted it back or hid it under a mask. Whenever a job called for dressing up, she had used a beauty droid. The machines were programmed to do about any style within mere minutes.

Fen had also produced jewelry to go with the hair decorations. A gold necklet wrapped stiffly around her neck, ornamented with symbols of good luck to ward off evil influences. Francesca had to laugh at that. Evil influences? Like the compulsion to try and steal the Jade Phoenix?

A matching gold armlet coiled in a spiral around her wrist, up her forearm to her elbow. Cosmetics were also applied to her complexion, powdering her face, darkening her eyes, adding fake color to her cheeks. Francesca found that odd, since the Líntiānese women she'd seen didn't really wear makeup, except maybe a subtle enhancement here and there.

Suddenly, an idea struck her and she felt nauseous. She reached for Fen, stopping the princess from pushing open the door leading out of the royal chambers. "This isn't a marriage ceremony, is it?"

Fen laughed. "No, no. First he has to apologize and then the wedding can take place. All you really have to do is forgive him."

Francesca relaxed. It was a real possibility that she'd be marrying Jin, but she wasn't ready for that possibility yet. She'd always told herself that she would do whatever it took to get this job done. If she had to get married, then she would. It's not like she'd honor her vows and stay married.

"Sounds easy enough," Francesca answered Fen's expectant look.

"Excellent!" Fen beamed with excitement. "Now come. Jin is waiting."

**\* \* \* \***

Jin waited nervously in the Hall of Infinite Wisdom. Glancing at his brothers who stood on either side of him, he took a deep breath, trying not to make it obvious that he was apprehensive. His brothers were all dressed in black with thick red sashes around their waists. The long floor-length tunics were the exact opposite of Jin's, which was dark red with a black sash that tied on the side and hung down from the waist. Beneath the waistbands, the male gowns flowed freely, allowing movement of the legs. Buttons were fastened all the way down the front of the outfit. At the collars and the end of the long sleeves, bits of white could be seen. The white was the underlining of the male gowns and very soft to the touch.

The brothers stood before their parents who sat regally on their thrones. The emperor and empress also wore red, only their silk brocade was embroidered with the black dragons outlined in gold. The empress wore an elaborate hairdo, complete with fringe that hung before her face in long golden chains. They all waited for Francesca to arrive.

Jin knew his sister had orders to keep Francesca busy until all the noble families arrived to bear witness, but the wait was slowly killing him. The night before it had been hard not to tell her what was going to happen the next day. And that morning, he'd panicked upon finding her gone. The nobles had already been invited to the palace to bear witness. Luckily his brothers had stayed outside the royal bedchamber for the night, watching for a possible escape attempt. When she left for her morning exercise, ancestors were watching her every move.

Fen had been a great help to the family, more so than Francesca could ever realize. His sister had a truly good heart, one that shone in her every word, but she also loved her family and her people above all else. When she talked to Jin's bride, Fen's goodness would shine through. And when she deceived her, it would be believable. People like Francesca made their minds up quickly about people. From what Fen said, she treated the princess just as she intended to be treated.

"This is the only way, Jin."

Jin glanced at his younger brother. Shen was blessed with the ability of foresight. It was this gift, one of the many bestowed upon the royal family with the aid of the Jade Phoenix, that the younger prince saw with now. A deep thinker, Shen well understood the paths people walked. He might not know why, but he could see where they would end up due to their actions. The problem was, as people's action changed, so did their course and nothing was ever certain. The further ahead Shen looked, the more unclear his foresight became. And he couldn't always control what he saw. He claimed most of his knowledge was based on instinct and feelings.

All of the Zhang children were blessed by the Jade Phoenix the day they were born. It was a private ceremony, one the Líntiānese people didn't know about. It was feared that if they did know, others would try and take the Jade Phoenix for themselves. What only those blessed with the Phoenix's power understood was that only the royal family could use its gifts. If everyone used it, the power of the Phoenix would be spread out too thin and no one would profit. It was this power that kept their world safe from outsiders. Without it, Líntiān would become a common space port.

The Jade Phoenix caused a strange balance on Líntiān between the two dynasties. The Songs controlled the jade mines, the main source of intergalactic trade on the planet which helped the entire race to thrive and the Zhang controlled elements that blessed the planet with protection from the outside world. The Zhang also had the most fertile soil, which made for agricultural goods to trade for purple jade. Nevertheless, if one side was to have power over both the purple jade and the Phoenix, they would be the controlling empire and eventually would have all the power on Líntiān.

For the Zhangs to conquer the Songs, they'd have to invade Singhai and seize the mines--a very substantial campaign. But, for the Songs to conquer Jin's family, they only needed to obtain the power of the Jade Phoenix. After that, the Songs would simply bide their time and a generation later, the lands would fall under Song rule for they'd have all the money and power.

So long as the balance of power was equal, both empires were safe. It was a delicate stability, one that they'd kept for centuries. The Zhangs did not wish for ultimate power, but did the Songs? The two royal households did not mingle more than was necessary. There was always a tension between them, as if neither side knew how to bow to the other. Of course, there was respect, but when two authoritative powers of equal standing entered the same room, who became the ultimate authority? The less they saw each other, the less chance there was to fight over petty things. Business stayed business between the two empires and trade went on as usual.

Until now.

After Haun discovered the jade mines were being used to

manufacture chandoo, he'd been honor bound to report it to the Songs. The Songs were upset to have their honor questioned, or at least that was Emperor Song's position on the matter. Since then, relations had been strained and fights were breaking out on the trading docks between the two peoples.

That is why protecting the Jade Phoenix was so important. It's why he needed to marry Francesca to keep the curse from coming true--though he wasn't sure he believed in a wedding breaking the curse. The ancestors seemed positive this course of action would reveal Francesca's secrets to him. And, since he didn't have a clue what he was doing, he found himself here, in the Hall of Infinite Wisdom, not feeling very wise as he waited for his unsuspecting future wife to join him for their wedding.

Jin's stomach tightened. Francesca was being tricked into this because she wanted to steal from him. His family believed that she would try to stay engaged long enough to achieve her goal, but if they were married perhaps she would change her mind, or in the very least Jin would be able to 'keep the enemy close' so to speak.

*I am tired of deceit.*

When Francesca said the words that would bind them for all eternity, would they be real? When she joined her soul to his, would she mean it? The answer came over him like a shout from his soul. No. No. No. Only love could make her mean the words and Francesca did not love him. And how could she mean what she didn't know she was saying, or more importantly doing. There weren't many words in the marriage ceremony, just actions.

Was Francesca sent by the Songs to destroy them? Fen thought not and she was blessed with charm. It was more impressive than it sounded, because with her charm she could control minds to an extent. It was the smooth, sweet quality to her voice and in her captivating expressions that made people want to tell her the truth.

The Phoenix blessed Haun with strength and a warrior's heart. He was brave, sturdy and did what had to be done no matter what. When the time came, he would make a great emperor.

Their baby sister, Mei, was influenced by the elements, mostly the wind. It would whisper in her ear, making her act on instinct. If little Mei felt something should be a certain way, it usually should be. She knew when to strike and when to be the meek, pretty flower. Mastering the art of both was what made her a good negotiator.

Lian was blessed with grace, both in movement and temperament, and with knowledge of the present. He could defuse any situation with logic, to the point that it was irritating. The prince also made one fine dancer.

Jin's gift had always been the past. All his life he'd wondered why his siblings would receive such amazing gifts when all he could do is see and understand his people's history--and not even all of it. It's why he was looked at for keeping traditions. Anyone who wanted to read the scrolls could learn of the past. However, since discovering that the scrolls had been altered, he realized now that he was the only link to the truth of what once was. Unfortunately, it wasn't a clear vision like watching a communicator image or seeing smuggled ancient Earth transmissions, but more like feelings about how things had really been.

The clear visions would have been a lot easier to understand.

Now with tension over the Wushu Uprising surfacing once more and the so-called 'curse' he was meant to save his people from, he needed his gift more than ever. Only problem was that all he knew was a maze of lies that needed to be staggered through. And not everything was exactly a lie, but the memory of someone else--an ancestor or spirit who only saw past events from their point of view. One viewpoint was a narrow vision indeed and memory was often fueled by the person's emotional scars.

"Jin," Shen repeated. Jin glanced at his brother as the man said again, "This is the only way."

Jin nodded once. What else could he do? The family had decided that it was time for him to marry and that is what he would do. Grandfather Manchu believed that marriage would save the family. Jin didn't have the same opinion, but it was too great a thing to risk just for the sake of his own pride. So what if he did not wish to marry Francesca? Or, so what if he did but for a different reason?

*Blessed ancestors, help me. Stop this. Find another way.*

Jin looked around the crowded hall. He saw glimpses of spirits mingling with the live crowd, but it appeared that no one else saw the dead. Were they showing themselves to him as an act of intimidation, to remind him of his duty and to keep him steady? It really wasn't needed. Nothing could make him forget it. Or was it simply they could not longer hide themselves from him anymore?

Ever since the spirits came to him when he was drunk, they hadn't stopped coming. He saw them everywhere, doing practically everything a live person would do. They walked over the paths, exercised in the halls, floated invisible boats on the Enchanted River and danced when there was no music. He'd even walked in on a couple having sex in the Imperial Gardens. Empress Zhang theorized that he could see so many spirits because they were of the past and that was his gift. It made sense, but the sight of them only made the weight on his heart all the heavier. Not only were the living dependent on him, so were the dead. It was a profound burden.

*Why are they just now appearing to me? Why can't they leave me be?*

"This is a happy day, *gē ge*," Lian said. "You shouldn't look so fierce."

"Try to smile," Shen instructed quietly.

"But not too wide," Lian added. "For it is a serious occasion."

"You know, I never got that." Shen leaned forward, looking past Jin to Lian. "It's a wedding. Shouldn't the joining of two lives be a time of complete celebration? Why do we all have to act serious?"

"Huh, I never thought about it," Lian mused, contemplating the question. Jin hid his chuckle. Shen just asked the question to mess with their brother. Lian would be thinking about the logic of being serious at weddings for weeks.

Shen winked at Jin, smirking as Lian's expression clouded in deep thought.

"You are doing what you must, *xiǎo dì dì*." Haun nodded in approval. "You honor us greatly today."

"Happiness for honor," Jin said softly. "I only hope none of you have to make such a trade."

Haun's lips tightened, but he didn't speak. There was nothing he could say.

A murmur rose over the hall. Jin turned to the entranceway

in time to see his sister stepping aside for his bride. His breath caught. Fen had done an amazing job. Francesca actually looked like true Líntiānese woman. A square lace veil covered her head and face, hiding her foreign features from the crowd. It wasn't done on purpose, as the veil was traditional wedding attire. The dark red matched her clothing. When she walked, platform shoes caused her body to sway and her feet to shuffle in small steps.

*Beautiful.*

Jin couldn't breathe. She was beautiful. His heart beat faster, pounding so hard he was sure his brothers could hear the sound. He knew that her presence, that this ceremony was a lie. The knowledge caused an ache to wash over him, so intense he wanted to fall to the ground screaming. Instead he held perfectly still, watching his little thief come closer. He wished that this moment wasn't a lie, that part of her could actually love him.

*Love?*

He bit back a self-depreciating laugh. Love had nothing to do with this, and yet he yearned for it more than anything. He loved her. Part of him had from that first moment he saw her cussing out the guards, so defiant and strong. She was so outspoken compared to the noblewomen he knew. When they came together completely, and he'd released his seed inside of her, he knew for sure. He loved her and that would be his downfall.

*You will destroy me, won't you, bâobèi?*

Thoughts ran rampant in his head. Now that he admitted his feelings to himself, he couldn't stop them. Francesca stepped closer, the embodiment of everything he held dear. Her clothing represented his people, his past and future. He wished for her to share all of it with him. Part of him wanted to cry out, another part wanted to run and another still wanted to bow at her feet and beg for mercy.

*Mercy? She would sooner crush me with my own heart than show me mercy.*

"Time," Lian whispered, as if reading his thoughts. Jin couldn't take his eyes from Francesca. "Time will reveal all. You have little to do but wait for it."

"That is easier said than done," Shen mumbled. "I am truly sorry, Jin."

Francesca stepped up the stairs. Arranged marriages were

supposed to be a thing of the past, but here he was facing a marriage arranged by his ancestors to protect the family. With each passing second, his body tightened with nerves. Maybe he was overly emotional because of what today was. He hadn't been given too much time to prepare for it. In fact, he hadn't known Francesca all that long. Perhaps it would have been different had he known all his life that this decision wouldn't be his. Instead, he'd been led to believe that his bride would be of his choosing.

*But who else could I choose?*

*I am a fool.*

*I can't do this.* Jin took a deep breath, shaking his head slightly. *I can't do this.*

"I can't do this." The words came softly out of him. He tried to step back from the line formed by his brothers, but Haun was suddenly at his side, gripping his arm tight from behind.

"Then you kill us all," Haun hissed into his ear.

"You say that because this isn't your future," Jin whispered.

"If it were me, there would be no debate. The wedding would be done. I know my place, Jin." Haun's grip tightened. "Look around, little brother. If you don't do this, we're all dead. That is my future as well as yours."

Jin did look. He looked at the people of Muntong staring at his bride. He looked at the dead, staring back at him. Then he looked at his parents, watching the whole proceeding expectantly. Finally, his eyes found Francesca. She studied him from beneath the veil. Haun squeezed tight in warning before letting go.

Francesca's round dark gaze drew him to her from beneath the lace veil. She held power over him, even if she didn't know it. Jin stepped forward, passing his brothers. Taking a step down the platform to meet her, he said, "I apologize."

It wasn't the eloquent speech he'd prepared and it wasn't even close to what he wanted to tell her, but it was all he could manage.

"I apologize," he repeated, louder.

Francesca slowly nodded. Her tone questioning, she answered, "I accept?"

Jin studied her. She really had no clue what was going on. He saw movement behind her as servants hurried out the door toward the front of the building.

Fen cleared her throat, the sound oddly loud in the quiet hall. "Ah, Jin?"

Jin bowed to Francesca. The sound of onlookers came over them, as the crowd voiced their approval. It wasn't a wild, happy cheering, but a proper amount of respectful appreciation of his match.

Francesca's brow furrowed as she glanced around without moving her head. She appeared annoyed by the whole ordeal more than anything.

*If she's annoyed now,* he mused wryly, *then she's going to hate what happens next.*

"Come." He offered his arm and she took it without thought. Jin led her through the hall to the door. As they reached outside, she asked, "Where are we going? Is that it? I'm forced to get dressed up, you say you're sorry and we leave?"

"No, there is one more thing we must do today," he answered.

"Ugh, I should've known." Francesca shook her head. Then, with a sound of irritation, she swatted at her face. "What is with this veil anyway? Can I take it off?"

Jin was glad to have something to talk about. "Soon you can take it off. It's an old custom, when men believed a woman's face to be the downfall of self-control. A man wouldn't want his wife to attract others with their beauty. So she, in an effort to please, would wear the veil to show her loyalty to her man."

"You mean 'her husband,' don't you?"

Jin laughed lightly and nodded. "Yes."

Francesca pulled the veil from her head. She shook her hair.

"France--"

"You are not my husband." She handed him the veil. "And I am hardly some meek woman wishing to hide my face for the sake of your self-control." She winked audaciously at him. "In fact, I like when you don't show control. It leads to great things."

"It is also for unmarried women." He tried to give the veil back but Francesca took a step and wobbled. "It's a sign of your virtue."

Francesca laughed, grabbing his arm as she pulled the

platforms from her feet. "My virtue? Need I remind you about how virtuous I am? When I said 'great things' I didn't mean the fighting. Though that is fun too."

She glanced down his body in meaning and Jin felt a stirring between his legs. Francesca slapped a platform into his outstretched hand as he tried to give her back the veil. She leaned over and took off the other shoe, sighing as she set her bare foot back on the ground.

Jin didn't know what to say. His bride was undressing before the wedding in public view. Servants came around the corner, carrying a sedan chair for her. Maybe not telling her what was going on was a mistake.

The sedan was red with enough room inside for one person--the bride. The gold roof was styled like the palace buildings. Red silk covered the walls and hung over the front section to hide the bride from view and there was a window on each side of the sedan so she could peek out.

"Huh, would you look at that." She nodded at the sedan. "What's it for?"

Jin watched the servants lead the sedan to the end of the Hall of Infinite Wisdom's steps. It hovered over the ground, not like the old days when people actually carried the vehicles on their shoulders. Even though the servants didn't do that anymore, there were still four bars sticking out at each corner like the old days. Instead of carrying, the servants led the chair with them.

"It is a sedan. Get in," Jin said.

"What? Inside that? Why?"

"It's.… It's your ride. Just get in. It's tradition that you don't walk."

"Great," she laughed. Then, taking a finger, she touched his sleeve. "You want to go in with me? I promise it would be more fun than this whole apology business. You said sorry, I accepted. Sounds like it's all taken care of."

Jin read the meaning in her beautiful jade eyes and his body desperately wanted to say yes. "I can't. We won't both fit and the others will be coming out soon. They expect to see me walking."

"Fine, but you better not try to sacrifice me in some weird ceremony and this better be over soon." Francesca ignored the servant who offered their hand as she pulled herself up into the sedan.

Jin started to turn to go get the crowd, but stopped and crossed over to her. He pulled the front cover aside and set the shoes and veil on her lap.

She groaned, picking them up. Before he could speak, she mumbled, "I know, I know. It's tradition. Save the lecture, I'll put them back on. Promise."

\* \* \* \*

A feeling that something wasn't right nagged at Francesca as she was led away from the Hall of Infinite Wisdom in the sedan chair. But, since everything the Líntiānese did take a long time and was surrounded by endless tradition and ceremony, she decided she was just on edge. Lying in Jin's bed all night, surrounded by his smell as she fought the longing in her body, had left her tired. Not to mention the morning run and Fen's insistent pampering.

In the hall, he'd looked like his brothers, only he stood out because of the dark red of his gown compared to their black. No, it was more than his clothing. He stood out because he made her heart beat faster when she looked at him. The clothing was like a tease, a seduction of her senses as she imagined slowly undressing him for her pleasure. The fact that everything was soft and silky to the touch only made the sensations all the more erotic. His hard muscled skin would be so firm against the material of their clothing. When they had sex partially dressed, the combination of hard and soft had been extremely fascinating and arousing.

Francesca closed her eyes and leaned her head back against the sedan, doing her best to ignore the fact that she was aroused to such a fiery extent from thoughts of Jin. The ride was smooth, like she rode on a cloud. Hearing a cough outside, she pulled back the silk and peeked out the window. A procession of all the noble witnesses from the Hall of Infinite Wisdom followed her.

*Great, it's a parade.* The voice in her head was heavy with sarcasm. She sat back down and sighed heavily. *Just put up with it. Soon this will be over. I'll be 'officially' engaged to Jin. Their guard will drop and I will get what I came for. This will all be over soon.*

Francesca hummed an absentminded tune. She looked at the shoes on her lap, already regretting that she'd promised to put the torture devices back on. The platforms rested on the red lace veil. Not knowing why she bothered to keep her promise, she slipped the platforms back onto her feet. They were uncomfortable, making her taller, even as they caused her to teeter back and forth since the platform was centered under the middle of the foot and not under the toe and heel.

*Jin owes me for this one,* she thought, eyeing the shoes.

The sedan stopped and she again looked out the window. She was in front of the Exalted Hall. The two doors with the protective gods were opened, held so by a serving man on each side. Francesca didn't move. What were they doing before the Exalted Hall? Could it be? A wedding? No, Fen had said it was just an apology. The woman wouldn't have been able to deceive her.

"Francesca?"

Francesca yelped at the sound of Jin's soft voice and jerked back in her seat. Her heart beat hard in her chest and she couldn't speak.

"What's wrong? You're pale." Jin reached for her.

Francesca looked at the opened doors. "What are we doing here?"

"Apology," he said.

*There, see, just an apology. Not a wedding. Stop overreacting.*

Still, she hesitated before taking his hand. "What do I have to do?"

"Just follow my lead. We'll go in, pay homage to the sky and earth, give offerings to the ancestors so they know the seriousness of our claim, drink some *shui guo chá* and we're done."

"And that's all?"

His eyes dropped and he nodded, not looking at her directly as he looked back at the crowd. "That's all. Then it will all be done."

Francesca nodded, letting him help her down from the sedan as she tugged the lace veil over her head. "All right, then. Let's get this over with."

## Chapter Nine

The apology ceremony was just like Jin said. He escorted her inside the Exalted Hall and they were left alone with the royal family as they did what they must. They paid quick homage to the sky and earth. Jin's part of the ceremony was more elaborate, consisting of a cap that he put on his head and then left on the altar. Francesca really hadn't paid attention to his whispered words. She'd been too busy cursing her horrible shoes and trying not to think of how great Jin looked in his red ceremonial robe. After he was done with his cap, they left a jug of wine and small pastries on a low altar for Jin's ancestors, and finally drank *shui guo chá*, a tea spiced with locally harvested red bavine fruit.

Afterward, Jin led her out of the Exalted Hall. The crowd cheered as he escorted her toward his private chambers. It was slow going because she was forced to take small, shuffling steps in the platforms. She'd never thought her balance training would come in so handy, and in such a bizarre way. The crowd of nobles followed in procession, talking loudly even as the royal family was quiet. Francesca was thankful that they went to the royal sleeping chambers next and even more so when Fen closed the doors, assuring that the crowd didn't enter behind Francesca and the royal family.

Francesca sighed once they were alone in the front entryway. Without stopping to think, she pulled the red veil off her head so she could see in the dimmer light. The princes studied her intently, but said nothing. Fen took the veil, beaming widely. Grabbing Francesca's hand, the princess shook it in excitement.

"It is done," Fen said, smiling wider.

"Yes," Jin interrupted, his voice strained. Fen glanced in his direction, her smile faltering some as she stepped back.

"I'm just happy that I will have a new sister," Fen said quietly by way of excuse.

"As are we all," Haun said, his voice hard. Francesca met the future emperor's eyes. He didn't mean the words at all and didn't even try to pretend he did. Out of all the Zhangs, Francesca understood Haun's temperament the most. He was a warrior, like she was and they shared a mutual distrust.

She could tell from studying the princes that Haun would make the most worthy combatant, but Jin's skill wouldn't be far behind his brother's. Lian and Shen seemed the type to pursue more intellectual interests but she had no doubt they too could hold their own. Fen could go either way. She didn't seem to have the temperament of a fighter, but she did have the grace.

Next, the emperor and empress came to stand before her. The empress patted her cheek, saying nothing as she stepped back. Her expression gave nothing away, but her eyes traveled over Francesca's face as if searching for answers. Francesca kept her features blank and dispassionate. Jin's father merely looked at her, twirling his mustache around his forefinger, before nodding once. He too stepped out of their way. The princes didn't move as they nodded like the emperor had.

Jin motioned that Francesca should go toward his bedchambers. She did so, gladly. The public attention was getting to her and the royal attention wasn't helping matters either. If she decided to stay a thief after she got the Phoenix, she knew she'd really have to change her face. There was no telling how many likenesses of her the Zhangs would have.

When the door shut behind them, she sighed and kicked off the horrible shoes, launching them across the chamber. "I am never wearing those awful things again. Ugh, I swear you only did it to torture me."

Jin laughed, but he sounded distracted. He refused to look directly at her. She couldn't shake the feeling that she was missing something. Maybe he was just upset that they were officially engaged again. The man did seem to change his mind a lot in that regard.

Francesca rose up on her toes, stretching her feet and ankles. Her hair was still pinned into place and she caught a hint of her face in a reflective sculpture of the phoenix. The shiny metal distorted her features, but she saw the hints of makeup still on her skin. Everywhere she looked caused a war within her. More and more she was forgetting her mission in coming to Líntiān, giving it up for the lifestyle offered her. She was being seduced by lavish gifts and a sexy man.

*There are all types of seductions... What seduces you, sweet Francesca? What is it you desire most?*

Her head ached to think about the past, but she forced the memory to stay with her. She was wasting too much time in Honorable City. The longer she stayed, the harder it was going to be to do what she came to do.

"People aren't going to start sending presents again, are they?" she asked.

"No."

Jin stood, studying a tree that had been given to her as an engagement gift. She walked up behind him when he didn't move and lightly ran a finger down the middle of his spine, feeling the silky texture of the red material he wore. She desired him and would have him. It was time to leave and she would taste him once more before she left. Whispering, she let a sultry tone enter her voice, as she said, "We are done with the apology, aren't we? There's no more to do? People aren't going to come rushing in to check on us or anything, are they?"

"No. We are done. My family goes to host a banquet for the guests. We will be left alone for the evening and night. Food will be delivered after the banquet, but other than that we are to be in solitude."

"Mm, well, then how about we…?" She paused, grazing her fingernails over his arms from shoulders to wrists and back up again.

Jin turned to face her, a brow raised on his handsome face.

"…find a way to pass the time before the food gets here?" she finished.

Francesca pulled on her gown, as she walked toward the bed. Stopping, she slowly pushed the material off her shoulders. It caressed her lightly, like a warm breeze along her flesh. She shivered, letting it fall to the floor.

Francesca left her hair pinned on top of her head, liking the almost fantasy effect it gave the foreplay. She was hardly a submissive woman, but the silk, makeup and hair made her feel like a concubine. As a fantasy or game, it was fine, but she couldn't understand what would really make a woman give everything up for a man.

Francesca stepped out of the circle the fallen gown made around her feet and crawled naked onto the mattress. The weather was always nice and it made the use of underclothing unnecessary. There was something seductive about that as well. The Lĭntiānese were very sensual people without even realizing it.

*This is the last night,* she promised herself. *Only one more time and then it's time to go.*

Her body heated anew, cream building between her thighs as she thought of Jin looking at her. Flipping on her back, she pushed up on her elbows, her ankles leisurely crossed. "What do you say, *ài rén*? Want to pass the time?"

Jin answered by pulling on his own clothing. His long fingers pulled on the thick belt, unwinding it from his waist before tossing it on the bed next to her. Then, he slowly pulled at a button under his collar. Francesca never tired of looking at his gorgeous body. The movements of his hands entranced her as he slowly disrobed.

The dark red material flowed to the floor, pooling around his feet. When he moved toward her it was with stealthy grace. Jin crawled to join her on the bed, his hand skimming over the sash. He grabbed it, not stopping in his movement. His eyes pierced her. Coming to her side, he dragged the sash slowly over her flesh, starting at her toes and working along her inner thigh. Francesca shivered, falling back on the bed. The gentleness of his caress made her long for more, even as it sent little shockwaves of energy and passion throughout her blood. Her nipples hardened without being touched and her thighs parted willingly.

"Tell me, *bǎobèi*," he questioned, "who sent you to steal the Jade Phoenix? Who paid you?"

Francesca couldn't believe he was asking her now, as they both were naked on his bed. Her intent couldn't have been any more obvious and he wanted to talk business? Then, again, his intent was becoming exceedingly clear. If he thought that the lack of clothing would stop her from walking out on him so he could question her, he was sorely mistaken. She began to push up, but he stopped her with his stern look.

"Do you really want to talk about this now?" she asked, trying to be coy but failing. She spread her thighs a little more. His eyes glanced down to the soft curls covering her sex before darting back up to hers. When he adjusted his weight, she easily saw how much he wanted her. His cock was hard with need, thickened to the point that she could see the veins straining beneath his taut flesh. Taking the sash, he pulled it between her thighs, letting it caress her as it slid over her pussy.

"Who?" he demanded, ignoring his own arousal.

"No one paid me," she said, shading her eyes under her lashes.

*So this is the game he wants to play?*

Foolish as it was, Francesca was willing to play along. Taking a deep breath, she said, "That is all I'll tell you."

"Was it Emperor Song who sent you?" Jin drew the sash over her chest, tickling her breasts with the whispering stroke.

Francesca put her hands over her head and arched into the silk. Panting, she answered, "No. No one paid me or hired me to come here."

"*Gôu pì!*" he swore, jerking the silk over her neck and pulling it tight. She felt the pressure, but didn't lose the ability to breathe. "Do not lie to me! Why do you seek to destroy us?"

She said nothing and didn't move to fight off the somewhat attack.

"Francesca," he warned. His hips brushed closer to hers and she felt the tip of his cockhead pressing into her thigh. Pushing up he kept the silk over her neck. Francesca knew about a dozen moves that could easily knock him off of her, but she found the forceful side of him highly arousing. She'd been hit enough in the past not to be frightened by a little threat of pain.

"It's a little late for you to ask this, isn't it?" She smirked.

"The time wasn't right before now," he said.

"Why now, *ài rén?*"

Jin's dark gaze bore into hers. The tip of his penis demanded her attention as Jin maneuvered higher on the bed. He pulled the sash up over her face and drew it along her arms, only to stop where her hands rested above her head. His heat surrounded her and his smell entranced her.

Francesca didn't move. Jin stared at her as he worked, tying her hands together at the wrists. When he was done, she was free to lower her arms, but her wrists were shackled together.

"This is not a game!" Jin grabbed the end of the silk and

held it against the bed, keeping her arms trapped. "If you take the Jade Phoenix it will destroy us--all of us. *Dong ma?*! Don't you understand?"

Francesca didn't move. The urge to run washed over her. She'd been idle at the Zhang palace for too long. Jin's body blocked her easiest escape route and he didn't take his eyes off of her. She tested the grip on her wrists. It was secure.

"It is not just some prize to sell on the Torgan black market. Now, tell me who sent you and why. How did they know about the Jade Phoenix? Who taught you Wushu? Was it Master Chen Sun?"

"Don't you dare say his name to me," Francesca swore. She balled her hand into a fist, but couldn't move to strike. "You are not worthy of his name."

"Then it was Chen Sun," Jin whispered, as if he didn't want to believe it. "It's true. You're here to fulfill a curse."

"Curse?" Francesca was confused by his words, but didn't want him to know it. Breathing hard, she let all her anger and frustration show in her gaze. "I curse you, Jin, and your family and your people. I curse this whole planet--each and every snobbish, elitist corner of it! You think you are so superior. I hear your family's arrogance in every word. You talk to me like I'm a child, telling me of your history. Oh, how grand it is! Oh, how perfect you all are! Everything around us has meaning. This flower means peace. This door means protection. This walkway means tranquility and proves how wonderful and powerful the Zhang family all is. But, I know the truth, Jin. I know that you hunt and kill innocent people. I've heard how you slaughtered an entire village of peaceful men and women, people who were sent to the mountains because you were afraid of them, because you didn't understand their ways, because you were jealous of the Wushu art."

The rage was a strange contrast to the desire, which only stirred to greater heights as her emotions soared.

"I did none of these things," he growled. His eyes flashed in anger.

Francesca didn't care. The past welled inside her, needing to get out, needing a voice--her voice. The dead couldn't speak, so she would speak for them. "Your people did. You claim the victories of the past as your own, you who are so steeped in tradition it makes me sick! If you claim the victories, Jin, then you can claim the sins as well. Your family took everything I ever had. That is why I'm here. That is why I curse you."

Francesca made a move to jump off the bed toward the door. Jin grabbed hold of the silk tie and jerked her back down next to him. She opened her mouth to scream, but his lips stopped the sound. He kissed her hard, grinding his teeth with his infuriated passion.

The taste of him was too much. She wanted to have the willpower to pull back, but she couldn't. Her mouth warred with his in a groaning battle of the wills. His teeth cut into her lip and she bit him back, drawing blood. Neither of them cared. She kept kissing him hard as if she could tear him apart with her mouth, as if by doing so she wouldn't have to want him anymore. He was everything she shouldn't desire and yet she couldn't make herself stop touching him.

Passion sizzled between them. Jin's free hand glided hard over her flesh, gripping her tightly, almost painfully. Francesca moaned for more. She lifted her thigh and kicked at his waist to flip him onto his back. He did, still holding her hands captive. Francesca straddled his waist with her thighs as she pinned him down with her weight. Jin didn't let go of the sash and it gripped her wrists tightly. His warm stomach flexed along her sex as he thrust his hips up. The firm length of his member rubbed along her ass, parting her cheeks slightly as she moaned in approval.

Jin let go of her wrists. Francesca left them tied, pulling the material apart just enough so she could run her flat palms over his chest, scratching him as she raked her nails over his tight flesh. Leaning over, she supported her weight awkwardly on her arms as she kissed along his neck, biting and licking the salty taste of his skin. Taking her time, she enjoyed his hot flesh. She bit his nipple only to soothe it with her lapping tongue.

Jin moaned and squirmed for more. He gripped her shoulders, letting go only to do it again. She took her time, enjoying his hot flesh as she played with his small, erect nipples. Then, moving down to his hips, she leaned over his erection, framing it with her elbows and bound wrists. Her breasts skimmed his hot shaft, rubbing along each side of it, up and down, up and down, as she pumped his cock between the mounds.

Jin pushed into her breasts, making small animalistic sounds to show how much he enjoyed fucking them. Their movements were still hard and frantic, as if the battle hadn't ended but only changed course. Francesca pulled back and bit the tip of his shaft.

Jin gasped, jerking away from her mouth. "*Xiâoxin!* Careful! Take it easy, *bâobèi.*"

Francesca looked up his long, muscled body and grinned. A trail of the red sash flowed from her wrists over his chest. Jin groaned at her look. She kept her eyes on his and stuck out her tongue. Reaching down, she licked the red spot her teeth had left on his tender flesh.

Jin reached between his thighs and took his erection in hand. She avoiding touching it as she tormented him with her hard kisses. He pumped his fist over the turgid length several times before angling the tip toward her mouth. Pushing up, he guided his shaft forward, rubbing the tip to her lips. His dark eyes begged her take him into her mouth.

Francesca licked him, lightly flicking her tongue over the tip of his arousal. As she teased him, he pumped his hand over the full length. Jin's breath caught and he thrust up, trying to work himself deeper into her mouth. She moved to the side, kissing along the shaft, bumping his hand with her chin, but she refused to take him between her lips. Instead of sucking him, she twirled her tongue around the tip of his shaft. She nibbled the sides, teasing him to the point of torture.

"*Qíng, bâobèi, qíng,*" he begged. "Please, *bâobèi,* please."

Francesca took pity on him and finally moved her mouth over his shaft. Sucking him in, she worked her mouth up and down over the firm length. He tried to thrust between her lips, but she held back, controlling the situation. Unable to fit him in her mouth, she brought her wrists down to help. She placed his shaft between her bound wrists and continued the tormenting pleasure.

Jin started to grab her hair, but ended up letting her go as she aggressively sucked him. Jin reached for her shoulders, massaging them the best he could in their position. His gorgeous body was tense, flushed with desire as a light sheen of sweat beaded on his skin. She cupped his balls, rolling them in her palm.

"Mm, yes, *bâobèi,*" he cried.

Francesca moaned. His intimate smell excited her. He stopped thrusting and froze. She knew he was on the edge and she pushed him over it with her sucking lips. Jin climaxed, releasing his seed into her mouth and she drank in his taste. When she pulled back, he was breathing hard.

Francesca ran her bound hands up his stomach as she pressed her body against him. She could feel his heart beating wildly beneath her. The world seemed to spin around them. Desire and passion heated her blood, but she didn't move as she lay against his still body.

Jin ran his hands over her back. She closed her eyes, feeling every subtle movement. Suddenly, he flipped her on her back and once again trapped her hands above her head. His lips found hold on her neck. The gentle undulation of his kiss against her pulse told her he planned on taking his time, that he wasn't going to rush what was happening between them. Francesca let him have his way, and in that instant their lovemaking turned from violent to tender.

She tried to feel nothing, tried to fight what was building inside her, but she couldn't. When he touched her with such sweetness, she couldn't breathe. Her mind slipped from everything until all she could do was feel. There was no world outside of the bed, no Jade Phoenix, no revenge or past.

For the first time since before Chen Sun's death, Francesca let go of herself completely.

Moaning, she arched against Jin. At her response, he drew back to look at her in surprise. His lids drooped lazily over his eyes, the dark gaze of them hazy with passion. Capturing her lips, he kissed her, rolling his tongue into her accepting mouth.

Francesca drew her legs along his hips, opening her body to him. A fevered need burned inside of her. It was a need greater than that of the flesh. It was the need for contact, the need to let someone close to her, the need to feel beyond revenge and anger and depression.

She moaned, again and again, unable to vocalize what she was feeling beyond the simple primal sounds. His mouth and hands seemed to be everywhere and their movements became a blur of pure sensation. Jin pulled a nipple between his lips, kissed her throat, ran his hand along her sex. All the time her hands were trapped and she was forced to take every caress. There was something sexy about being bound helpless, unable to fight as the torrent of emotion took over and made her too weak for battle.

Soon, his lips and mouth weren't enough. She needed him inside of her. Francesca grabbed his hips with her legs and pulled him closer. His erection rubbed along her folds and she angled her sex to him, doing her best to make him slip inside.

Jin pressed his forehead against hers, taking her slowly as he thrust into her willing depths. Francesca gasped, shivering at the way he filled her to the brim. He let her kiss him briefly before drawing back so he could look in her eyes.

Francesca turned her head to look away, but he nipped at her jaw to get her attention back on him. Holding his gaze, she took his breath into her lungs. Even with the intimate contact, there was so much between them. Part of her wanted to connect to him, wanted to speak, to yell, to fight for a marriage.

*A marriage?!*

The tension built. It was too much. She couldn't fight her release, and she came hard. Pleasure erupted in her stomach, spreading like a cosmic blast over her entire frame. Jin's grunt joined hers as he stiffened above her. The sash slipped from between his fingers, releasing her from his hold.

With his body deeply embedded, she slowly came down from the cloud of pleasure she floated on. As sanity returned, so did her last thoughts. Marriage? To Jin? Into the family who caused Chen Sun's death? Francesca pushed at his chest with her bound wrists, stunned that such words could ever have filtered through her head.

"Francesca?" he asked, his voice faint against the pounding in her ears. She pushed at him again and he rolled off of her. "Francesca? What is it?"

She sat up, biting at the silk to free herself. The world spun around her and she took a deep breath, and then another.

"Francesca?"

"I want to be married to you," she said, not bothering to stop the words. Hearing them out loud made the guilt she felt worse. The silk loosened and she jerked her arms free.

"*Ni meí shì bà?*" he asked.

"Of course I'm not all right!" she snapped, throwing the wrinkled sash at him. Francesca suddenly realized that the words had been too soft for him to hear. "I said I want to be married to you, Jin. I like it here. I like it in the palace and I even like your hardheaded family some of the time."

She didn't dare look at him, but instead stared at the door. Her legs were weak and she knew she'd never make it.

"You don't know how happy those words make me," he said.

Jin touched her arm and she pulled away. Chancing a glance back, she was surprised to see him smiling. Why was he smiling? This was the worst realization in her life and he was grinning like a fool!

"Your words make me happy, because we are married, Francesca."

"*Nooo*," Francesca moaned, dropping her head in her hands.

"Yes, today. The ceremony made us man and wife. I didn't think you'd go along with it, so I didn't tell you. But it's all worked out, my love...."

*My love? Married?*

Okay, she had to admit that a very small part of her knew what she was doing when she walked into the Exalted Hall, or at least had hoped. She knew what happened in the hall and if she would have allowed herself to seriously consider the possibility, not just dismiss it a few times in passing, she would have realized it was a marriage ceremony. Francesca didn't seriously consider it because she didn't want to have to stop it. Thinking back, she could've seen the lie on Jin's face and heard it in Fen's voice the few times she did ask. No. She wanted to be Princess Zhang Francesca. She wanted to be Jin's wife.

"This can't be happening." Francesca groaned, rocking back and forth as she held her stomach.

*I'm sorry, Sun. I'm sorry. I didn't mean to do this.*

"It is, my love, it is." Jin tried to pull her back into his chest. Francesca jumped up from the bed and spun on her heels to face him. He looked so handsome, sitting back on his legs, his arms reaching as if he would hold her, as a smile spread over his happy features. There was no shame in him when he looked at her.

Francesca shook her head. He might not feel it, but she did. Shame welled inside her. She backed away, whispering, "I love you, Jin."

The words scared her blood cold.

"Francesca…." He made a move to stand and she again shook her head.

"No, don't say anything. Don't do anything. Please, Jin. This … this changes so much. I…."

He opened his mouth to speak.

"No," she demanded. It took all her will not to cry. "Please. Time. I need time."

"I understand," he said to her surprise. Jin dropped his arms.

*I doubt that.*

"You are a warrior and you came here to do a job," he said. "Loving me complicates that and you must come to terms with this decision."

*Okay, perhaps he does understand a little.*

"You will have to come to terms with your decision to stay as my wife. And you will need to gain the courage to tell me why you are here. This does change everything." He nodded in understanding. "I know."

*That is where you're wrong, Jin. This changes nothing. It can't. Don't you see?*

"I love you, too, Francesca."

*I'm sorry, Sun. I'm so sorry. I won't betray your memory. I won't betray you. I will keep my promise.*

Francesca backed away, squeaking out the one word she could. "Time."

"Take your time, my love." Jin stood and picked up her gown. He handed it to her. She took it, snatching it away before he could touch her again. Jin sighed but didn't move to trap her in his quarters.

"Don't…." Francesca slipped the gown over her shoulders, buttoning it. Her eyes stayed fixed on his.

"I won't follow you," he answered, automatically knowing what she was going to say. "You will have your time."

"*Xièxie nĭ,*" she whispered. "Thank you."

"Fate has brought us here, Francesca. It is right that we embrace what has been given us. Nothing else matters. You will see."

She smiled sadly. *Goodbye, my prince. I know you will never forgive me, as I can never forgive your family.*

\* \* \* \*

Jin's heart soared. She'd admitted to what was between

them. She loved him. She loved him! His wife loved him and she wanted to be married to him. The curse was over and he was in love! Nothing else mattered.

The news flowed through him, sweetly nourishing his soul. He wished he could hold her in his arms, make love to her again and again, but he saw her need to be alone. Confusion marred her flushed features. Francesca never thought to love him. The words probably weren't even in her vocabulary, so to speak. The possibility of them would never have entered her mind.

No, she was a warrior. To admit love would be a strange thing for one such as her. Jin didn't care. He could wait. He could give her time.

"She loves me," he whispered, falling back on the bed. A wide smile spread over his face. "Grandfather was right. We are meant to be."

## Chapter Ten

*Free Space, Outside the Black Market planet of Torgan,
Three months later....*

"Grandfather is a foolish, meddling old man. I curse the day he appeared to me and I curse his spirit to the darkest of all afterlives. I hope he rots for an eternity."

Jin rubbed his swollen eyes. His body was weak from the endless nights spent drinking, punctuated by the long days flying through endless space. Francesca was gone, disappeared on their wedding night without so much as a hint that she was leaving.

*Please. Time. I need time. I want to be married to you, Jin. I like it here. I love you, Jin.*

The memory of her words burned him to the soul. The wretched *Ch'ang Shih* had lied to him. She took out his heart and stomped it into a million pebbles. He was a half man since that day, walking and breathing, but not really in the world. Evening had turned to night, night into dawn, and still he'd waited for her. Foolishly, he thought she was walking the grounds, coming to terms with her new life at the palace.

What a fool he was! A lovesick, stupid fool! He waited for her, trusting that their love would keep her steady.

*I want to be married to you, Jin. I like it here. I love you.*

Blessed Ancestors! He'd believed her lies! He believed that she loved him. Even now his heart wanted to hear the words. His brain wished to make excuses as to why she left.

Jin had laid there alone on his wedding night. He hadn't sounded the alarm, hadn't sent the guards to watch her. He'd told himself that he had to show her trust, had to let her know that he wanted a life with her to work. A woman as skilled as Francesca would know when she was being followed. The living and the dead had been at the banquet celebrating his wedding, feasting into the early morning hours only to sleep in late the next morning. During it all, the Sacred Chamber had been left unprotected. It had been the perfect opportunity to strike and she had taken it. And Jin waited like a *chûnrén* as his wife stole the Jade Phoenix right out from under them. She did the one thing no one else had been able to in the whole history of the Zhang Dynasty. And she did it with four simple, magical words.

*I love you, Jin.*

Jin snorted, taking another shot of the stout liquor. Though he had never tried whiskey before this flight, he now wondered how he would ever function without it. He had found the heady alcohol one night while trying the different liquors in the food simulator on Haun's ship. There must have been hundreds to choose from.

Haun's spacecraft, *Míng tian,* was circular in design in the traditional Líntiānese style of spaceship building. The cockpit was on the very top with a rounded area constructed directly beneath it. Living quarters were along the edge of the circle, with viewing screens that opened to show the far depths of space. Jin kept his viewing screen open as he wallowed in self-pity, staring out at the blackness between the twinkling stars, wishing it would suck him up into the inky depths and crush all feeling from his soul.

In the center was the dining hall, communications, engine room and just about everything else the ship required. Jin wasn't much of a flyer, so he hadn't paid too much attention over the years as to how the thing worked. He could fly if he had to, for the emperor demanded they all learn, but it had been a long time. Beneath the living deck was the cargo hold.

*I love you, Jin.*

Jin growled into his drink. What did she know of love? She felt nothing! She knew nothing of the bittersweet emotion that now tore out his heart and soul, leaving him a walking corpse to plague all those around him. He hadn't been whole since the day she left him. Every moment was spent with her in his head, the image bashing his brain until he needed to blur it out forever.

Love was driving him mad. He felt his sanity slipping all around him, leaving him with one burning thought. If he couldn't have her love, then he would kill her. He would kill his pain. He *had to* kill his pain.

"Jin," Haun's voice sounded over the intercom. "We've made contact."

Jin nodded before remembering that he'd disabled the

communicator's camera. He'd grown tired of his brother's disapproving looks and constant check-ins.

"Jìn? Are you awake?" Haun asked. "*Wode tìan*, Jìn! Are you passed out again?"

"No, I'm awake and I heard you," he grunted, taking another long drink. *Unfortunately*.

"Jarek has agreed to meet us at the Torgan docks." Haun paused. "Clean yourself up before Mei sees you. You don't want to give her cause her to worry in her condition. Jarek said she's close to having the baby and in a very delicate state. He's worried that she might try to come along on this. You know Mei, he won't be able to keep her on his ship if she doesn't want to be there."

Haun gave a small laugh. Jin heard the excitement in his brother's voice. Haun missed Mei.

Jin grumbled an answer and took another drink before capping the bottle. Their brother-by-marriage, Jarek, was a good man and his help was appreciated, but Jin didn't want to face Mei. To see his sister so happily married when his own marriage was a farce would be unbearable. But, bear it he must. It had been his duty to watch Francesca and protect the family and he had failed. Now it was his duty to bring her home. He could not fail them again.

The emperor had put out the alert for 'La Rosa', knowing that money would be the easiest way assure whoever captured her wouldn't harm her. It turned out that Jarek was able to find her first, using his connections in space. For that Jin was grateful. The idea of some bounty hunter touching her only made him sick to his stomach.

"Jin? Did you--?" Haun started to say, his voice loud with authority.

"*Hâo!*" Jin yelled, "All right! I hear you. Now, stop bothering me!"

Throwing the bottle against the metal wall, he watched it shatter. Caramel-colored liquor ran down the metal and pooled on the floor. Jin stared at what he had done, only to be disappointed as the ship's cleaning droids came out of the wall and started tidying up his mess.

*I love you, Jin.*

\* \* \* \*

"*Míng tian,*" the computer's monotone voice translated as Torgan Ground answered the Líntiānese ship's request to land. "This is ... Torgan Ground."

One of Haun's crewmen answered the call, pausing as he waited for Torgan Ground's side to translate his answer. It was slow progress when using ship translators, but it was also Líntiănese policy not to reveal they spoke another language. Often arrogance revealed much when people thought they weren't understood.

Jin stared at the viewing screen that curved around the wall of the cockpit. The trade city of Madaga was magnified before him, though they had yet to approach. Torgan was a horrible looking dust ball of a planet. Rings spun around it at unorganized angles, but they hardly added beauty to the brown-gray of the planet's barren surface.

Madaga was the main city, intergalacticly known as a black market trade port. On the surface, it looked like a legitimate trading center, but it was no secret what went on there. However, since the entire planet refused to expel the black market, there was nothing that outside galactic forces could do about it. For those who knew what to look for, it was a virtual smorgasbord of fenced goods and tawdry services. If it was illegal and could be sold, it was on Torgan--from sex slaves to smuggled goods, to drugs and hired guns. Everything could be bought for a price.

*Even wayward wives.*

"You are," the computer translated in slow precision, "clear ... to land. Proceed directly to docking ... platform ten, ten, six and report to Dock Master Metnis."

The crewman answered Torgan Ground once more, agreeing and signing off, before warning everyone on the spacecraft of the likelihood of a turbulent landing.

Jin glanced at his brother. Haun was staring at him, a look of concern on his face. But the expression was also tempered with a barely contained irritation and anger. It had been on his older brother's face since the day Francesca was discovered missing with the Jade Phoenix.

Jin didn't need Haun's look to remind him of how he'd failed or of what was happening on their home planet. The empress was sick with worry and the last time he'd seen Fen, her eyes had been puffy and red. Zhang An's spirit gloated over them all and Grandfather Manchu refused to show himself.

*Coward,* Jin grumbled to himself, thinking of the old man.

The emperor didn't have to say he was disappointed in him. Jin saw the truth plain enough on his father's face. Lian and Shen tried to offer condolences and support, but their understanding was about as bad as the emperor's and Haun's disappointment and Fen and his mother's constant sorrow.

Jin tried not to concentrate on the past, nor did he think of the present. He focused on the day he would meet Francesca, of what he would say to her, of how he would punish her. He was sure her actions killed anything he felt for her.

*I love you, Jin.*

No, he was wrong. He still felt every bit of the heartache as the words played in his head, running like a broken circuit he couldn't stop.

*I love you, Jin. I love you, Jin. I love you, Jin....*

Jin didn't believe those words. How could he? How could she love him and then ruin everything he held dear? She'd run out on him. She'd embarrassed him, insulted his family honor, stolen, lied. The list of her crimes was endless.

*I love you, Jin.*

*More lies,* he thought. *So many lies.*

Her voice in his head wouldn't stop, no matter how he tried to drown it out. The words kept going, repeating over and over to torment him. Finally, he gave up fighting and let them have his soul. The more he hurt the more resolve he would have against her. Curse her jade, lying eyes and her black, unfeeling heart!

*I love you, Jin. I love you....*

\* \* \* \*

Jin didn't smile as he looked dispassionately around the open clearing of the docking platform. Hard, smooth rock stretched over the area. Rows of alien ships were docked in marked squares, packed together snugly to maximize the use of the docking lot. Between the ships were walkways, just wide enough to haul cargo loads toward the main trade area. The place was packed full of every shape and color of spaceship imaginable, with only a few remaining spaces left open. Jin guessed a place like this would always be filled with lowlifes and thieves.

*Just like my wife.* He snorted in disgust.

Haun had sent a crewman to pay the docking fees for both

*Míng tian* and Prince Jarek's ship, *The Conqueror*. Jin stretched his arms over his head, as they waited for the man to return. He couldn't help the disdain he felt as he looked around. Normally, the sight would have held some fascination, but today he could only dredge up contempt.

"*Gē ge!*"

Jin turned at the familiar sound. It was his sister, Mei. Her stomach protruded drastically from her tiny frame, but she didn't move like a pregnant woman should. There was energy in her steps. Jin had known his sister was pregnant, but it didn't strike him just how far along she was until he saw her. He bit back a feeling of jealousy. Mei deserved her happiness and he would not begrudge her it.

Seeing her as she was now, Jin hardly recognized his sister. Her long hair was pulled back to fall in a long tail from the nape of her neck. She wore black, tight pants and a dark crimson shirt. Both hugged her like a second skin, proudly outlining her stomach. A gun belt slung low on her hips beneath her large belly, holding a phaser in the holster. The bottom of the holster strapped around her thigh. Jin knew her husband had given her the weapon. Jarek would give his life to protect Mei.

"*Mèimei!*" Haun yelled in answer, excited as he ran to greet their little sister. He lifted Mei up in a big hug, twirling her in a circle. Haun was ten years older than her, but the two had always been close. She used to follow him around, idolizing the very ground he walked on, and Haun in turn had treated Mei with a rare softness reserved for no one else.

As Haun let her go, Mei turned to where Jin stood, unmoving in his brooding state. He gave her a small smile, but it was all he could manage. Mei studied him, letting her soulful brown eyes run up and down over his haphazard attire and sunken face. Even pregnant she looked small and delicate. Mei had always been the tiniest of females, so slender and petite. She took a slow step forward, halting before taking another. Reaching for him, she wrapped her arms around his neck.

"Jin, Jin," she repeated his name over and over as if she could think of nothing else to say. "My poor Jin."

"How are you, Mei?" he asked, pulling her back so he could look at her face. There was a roundness to her features and she looked drained despite her energetic actions, but there was no hiding the fact that her eyes were happy. He was glad to see it. Jarek was indeed treating their sister well, just as he'd promised to do.

Mei laughed in distraction and glanced down to her stomach. "Fat and clumsy."

"Nonsense, *fea*." Jarek came up behind his wife, smiling. "You are beautiful."

"And you are delusional, *qin ài de*." Mei shook her head as she looked fondly at her husband.

Jarek dressed like a pirate. In fact, Mei had thought he was one when she'd first met him. Now they knew him for what he was, a prince doing his duty by his family by working as an ambassador in space. Mei was doing much of the same thing for them. They flew about the galaxies, learning of other cultures, making contacts and, most importantly, helping out when situations like this arrived. Jarek knew Torgan and the black market. He had contacts on the inside and could navigate the planet with ease. Here, none of them were princes. They were just men come to do shady business.

Jarek was a cat shifter from the planet of Qurilixen. He was broader than the Zhang brothers and very strong. According to Haun, the man was a good fighter, but his style utilized brute strength more than finesse. The man's long black hair was loose and he had it pulled away from his face to hang in braids at the temples. Black tattoos marked up one of his arms, the symmetrical pattern disappearing up his sleeve only to peek out of his collar by his neck. He was dressed in a loose white linen shirt, rolled at the sleeves, black pants and a gun belt. His calf boots were polished to a high gleam.

"Jin," Jarek acknowledged, smiling kindly before turning to Haun. "Haun. It's good to see you both again."

"We thank you for your assistance," Haun said. Jin was too busy brooding to do much beyond watching them talk.

"It's not necessary." Jarek slipped his hand around Mei. "You're family."

Haun nodded.

To Jin, Jarek said, "I've sent my men ahead to scout the area for a trap, just in case she knows we're here. Don't worry. We'll find her."

Jin nodded once. He opened his mouth to speak, but Jarek held up his hand.

"It's not necessary," Jarek said. "I'm only sorry we meet again under such circumstances."

* * * *

The city of Madaga was just as Jin imagined it would be having seen it from *Míng tian's* cockpit. It was a dusty spot, with adobe style businesses built of the brown-gray earth right next to larger complexes of metal and glass. The main trading compound where they were heading was inside one of the largest buildings.

Every disreputable low life creature imaginable came to Madaga--pirates, crooked businessmen, slave traders, bounty hunters, guns for hire--and they all centered in the main trading compound. The crowd was an unusual mix of humanoids and other alien creatures. Some looked like Líntiānese males with only minor differences--ripples of hard flesh across the brow, odd coloring, hairy bodies and long arms. One of the men had skin that reminded Jin of a reptile he had seen pulled out of the Satlyun River. The scaly flesh even glistened as if it were wet.

A giant of a man with crimson flesh and black eyes stood high above the crowd. Next to him there were two slight, pale creatures with what looked to be red-green eyes. The two pale men started pushing at each other and the big guy instantly pulled them apart by the backs of their necks. He held them away from each other, shaking them, even as they tried to kick at the other.

"Strange place, isn't it, *gē ge?*" Mei said to Haun, who was stopped from answering as two round blue creatures walked close by, staring at Mei's stomach. They made abrasive strange clicking noises as they spoke to each other.

"Don't worry, *fea,*" Jarek whispered to Mei. "They probably just think your belly's gorgeous, as do I."

Jin tried not to gag. There was nothing worse than hearing 'love talk' when one was depressed. He walked faster, trying to focus on the crowd. Large creatures that reminded Jin of insects buzzed overhead. They had two legs, six arms and a set of wings that could easily lift them over the crowd. Landing on the rafters high above, they pointed down into the complex. Jin looked away from them as he searched for Francesca, but he couldn't see her.

They passed near a round bar in the middle of the building, surrounded by tables. Several men were already drinking, maybe still going from the night before. Jin automatically veered off to order. He was starting to lose the numbing effect on his brain.

As Jin leaned up against the bar, he was surprised to see that Jarek had followed him. The man nodded once at the bartender, motioning him to leave them alone.

"I don't think you want to do that," Jarek said. "You might want your wits about you when you confront her."

Jin frowned. Who was this man to meddle in his ways?

"Besides, that one over there is foul enough to curl any stomach." Jarek nodded inconspicuously to a man who was so hairy he could barely make out his features. Small insects buzzed around his greasy head.

Jin laughed despite himself. "Is that what that smell was? For a second I thought I forgot to bathe."

Jarek chuckled before patting him on the shoulder. "I have four brothers, all of whom found love the very hard way. And your sister didn't exactly take it easy on me. I don't know what happened, but I know a broken heart when I see one. Nothing in life is what it seems and most sins can be forgiven. If your heart still wants her, then you must try and see past its pain."

Jin didn't move.

"It's not over until it's over."

"Mei sent you to talk to me, didn't she?" Jin asked.

Jarek grinned and nodded his head in agreement. "That she did."

"Thanks."

"Come on." Jarek lightly pushed him away from the bar. "Let's go track down this woman of yours. After you've dealt with her, if you still want a drink, I'll buy the rounds myself. We won't stop until they're pulling us off the floor of this place."

"I'll hold you to that." Jin allowed himself to be guided away from the bar. It helped knowing that he wasn't alone in the world. Besides, Jarek was right. He wanted his wits about him so he could best deal with Francesca.

"Sacred Cats!" Jarek laughed lightly. "I'll even buy you a Galaxy Playmate for the night if this doesn't work out, but only if you promise not to cause Mei any more worry in her condition. Oh, and you can't tell her."

Jin chuckled. His body wanted only Francesca and other

women paled in comparison to her, even now. However, if anyone could revive his lust, it would be a Galaxy Playmate. Part of him wanted to take one to bed just to spite his wife, but he knew he couldn't do it.

"Your sister is still giving me a hard time after all these months," Jarek said. "What is it about women? They can't just stay where they're told so you can protect them? They act like we're being tyrants when really we're only taking care of them."

"You tried to keep her on the ship, didn't you?" Jin smirked.

Jarek nodded. "Ah, you know your sister. She had to be involved. I tried locking her in our chambers, but she crawled through an air vent, stole my spare gun belt and ran out to find you guys before I could stop her."

"Mei always was one for adventure." Jin smiled as they approached his sister.

"What are you two talking about?" she asked, as if she hadn't sent Jarek to rescue Jin from himself.

"Your fondness for air vents," Jin answered.

Mei paled slightly before blushing. She slugged Jarek lightly on the arm. "What have you been telling him?"

Jarek tried to look innocent and failed. As the man swept his wife up into his arms, Jin had to look away. If anyone could give advice on how to make a happy marriage, it was Jarek. It didn't mean Jin wanted to see it though.

\* \* \* \*

Francesca took a deep breath. It hurt to move. She was pretty sure a rib had been broken in her last fray. If not broken, they were surely bruised. Her shoulder had been dislocated and she had been forced to pop it back into place herself by slamming it into a metal wall. The joint was still sore and it hurt to move it too much. Since she didn't have access to a medical booth or the space credits to pay for a doctor visit, she was obliged to suffer through the pain.

Damn Jin, the royal son of a Lophibian whore! The man had sent every bounty hunter in the known universe to bring her in. She wasn't safe anywhere. Already she'd been cornered five times since arriving on Torgan two weeks ago. It would have been more, but she stayed hidden most of the time in her firehole of a room.

Jin had her listed as a criminal wanted by an anonymous

royal family that was willing to pay handsomely for her safe return. She hadn't been wrong when she thought they might have her picture. They did and it was now posted on every Federation criminal poster she saw. Lucky for her, they didn't list her as a missing Princess, but simply as 'La Rosa, AKA The Rose'. If they had called her a princess, she would be caught and sold as a sex slave. Princesses had high value on the black markets. Many rich sleazebags would love to own one for their very own. And a princess with a wanted poster would be even more valuable because they could hold her crime over her head to prevent escape.

No, now she was just hunted for a preposterous reward-- fifty pounds of purple jade.

"Fuck-nut," she grumbled. It was clear they were trying to keep the Zhang Dynasty out of the spotlight, but someone would put the information together--purple jade, royal family. It could only be one of two empires on Líntiān.

Francesca knew she deserved to be hunted by the Zhangs. In fact, when the bounty hunters came, she didn't fight them off as she could have. Inevitably she got away, but not until after she let them get in a few good licks of a beating. Physical pain didn't cure the rotten ache she felt inside though.

Reaching behind her, she pushed at the wall. The old metal gave just enough so she could slip her hand inside. Grabbing the silk she found, she pulled it out. Wrapped inside the red robe she wore to her wedding was the Jade Phoenix. With one hand, she jerked the silk, causing the artifact to fall onto her lap so she could look at it.

Lightly, she ran her finger over the delicate bronze feathers, circling around the jewels inlaid into the metal. She had kept her promise to Chen Sun by taking the Jade Phoenix, but she had broken her own heart to do it. Now that she had the artifact, she couldn't sell it. If she did, the money would be enough to see a doctor and disappear forever. More and more that looked like her only option, but she couldn't bring herself to do it. Refusing to touch the stunning green stone on the bird's chest, she wrapped it back in the silk.

The room she'd procured for herself was as small as a prison hold and just as barren. Francesca didn't care. It was all part of her self-imposed punishment. Torgan wasn't exactly teeming with lodging for those who couldn't pay top dollar. There was no decontaminator, no food simulator and, by the look of the floor, a cleaning droid hadn't been in the place since it was built. Her neighbor had kept trying to watch her dress through a crack in the wall--that was until she'd stuffed part of her mattress into it and threatened to cut off the man's penis if he looked at her again.

A knock sounded on her door. Francesca didn't move. Her ribs hurt too badly.

"I'm looking for the one they call The Rose," a voice called. "She in there?"

"No," Francesca grumbled, her voice deep. She leaned over and worked the Jade Phoenix back into its hiding place. Pulling at the metal, she made sure it was bent back into place so no one would suspect the hiding place.

"Maybe you can tell me where to find her," the male voice persisted. "I need to speak with her."

"I don't know who you're talking about," Francesca answered, sitting back against the wall. So help him if this cretin made her get up off the floor! She grabbed her side, preparing to do just that if she had to. "Go away."

"I know you're in there, La Rosa," the man said. "I have a job that requires your delicate skills."

*A job?*

Francesca had to admit she was intrigued. She could use the space credits. Reluctant, and knowing it could be another bounty hunter trap, she asked, "What job?"

"Uh, well...." The man gave a short laugh. "I don't really want to talk about it here. Do you mind if I come in?"

Francesca frowned. This man was hardly behaving like a professional. If someone who knew what they were doing was coming to commission her, they wouldn't do it like this--not through a door. So who was he? Desperate man sent to desperate measures? Amateur bounty hunter? Someone very clever acting out of wits to throw her off guard?

Gritting her teeth, she pushed up from the floor. It took a moment of deep breathing, before she could lower her arm. Not bothering to fix her appearance, she hoped the disheveled state made her appear unattractive and surly.

She went to the door and pulled it open. The room was too cheap for even a hand scanner and the door swung in toward the room on hinges. A single man stood waiting for her on the other side. His hands twisted in front of him before he drew them to his sides, as if resolute to appear tough. He had short black hair, with glints of silver along his temples and looked too clean cut, as if he belonged at a doctor's convention more than a place like Torgan. That was except for his clothes. They were borderline working class--tight brown slacks, cream knitted shirt and short boots. Francesca took it all in, not drawing any conclusions until she heard what he had to say.

"Are you La Rosa?" he asked, swallowing nervously. "Are you The Rose?"

Francesca eyed him her mouth set grimly, and refused to answer.

"Mrs. Rosa... Ah... The Rose." The man held out his hand. She looked at it dispassionately and didn't take it. He cleared his throat and pulled back. "I'm--"

"Wasting my time," Francesca interrupted rudely. She couldn't help it. Her side really hurt and keeping a straight face was hard.

"I want to hire you," he said.

"Still wasting," she answered abruptly.

"Can I buy you a drink?" he offered.

A drink sounded really good to her, considering it would help dull the pain racking her body. She couldn't afford to buy herself one and decided to take the man up on his offer. If he was a bounty hunter, she might as well get something out of the deal before she let him beat on her. "Now you're speaking my language."

He stepped back so she could come out of the room.

"After you," she said. The man looked startled but stepped before her. Francesca kept at his back, letting him lead the way through the hall as she glanced around for trouble. The man looked at her several times, as if trying to make sure she was still following him. "How did you know what language I spoke?"

"Ah, the...." He faltered some but kept going. "There are posters with your information on them."

"You mean the wanted posters," she chuckled.

"Um, yes, yes, those."

"So, you think to turn me in for a reward?"

"Oh, no, no," he said, in what she imagined was his way of reassuring her. "I need to hire you ... for a friend."

"Your friend have a name?"

"Cap," the man answered.

"Never heard of him."

"He can pay."

"He'll have to. I'm not cheap." Francesca didn't say more as they neared the center of the compound. She should've known the man would have brought her into a crowd to discuss private business. It was so unprofessional of him. Perhaps he thought the crowd's presence would protect him if she decided he wasn't worth her time. Whatever his reason, it was too bad because it brought her out in the open.

Francesca moved through the crowd, doing her best to angle the man's body between those standing still and herself. She was glad she didn't wear her usual clothing. The loose shirt hid her womanly figure, even if the tighter pants did not. If someone recognized her here, she wouldn't have to worry about it until later. No one would chance snagging her in the middle of a crowd. To do so would draw notice to their cargo. No, they'd watch her, waiting in the shadows for their chance to strike.

The dark-haired man walked to the bar and Francesca found an empty table tucked into a private section--not that much of the bar area was private. Where she sat she could see the Federation posters flashing a round of wanted pictures. A few of the men she recognized. Some of them were even at the bar, watching the poster and cheering each time their face appeared. It was nothing new. Some men even placed bets on who had the highest payoff. Most of the men on the poster were people even the criminals wouldn't mess with. And then, she saw her face. Now why was it men wouldn't betray other men, but they had no problem turning on her?

*Fuck-nuts!*

The dark-haired man slid across the table from her, blocking her view of the posters. He set a tall drink in front of her and gave her a weak smile. Clearing his throat, he said, "To working together."

Francesca grabbed her drink and tried not to think about Jin or the lavish home she'd left behind. "I haven't agreed yet."

\* \* \* \*

Francesca groaned, moving to rub her head. The sound of metal on metal rang through her brain, causing a sharp pain to reverberate through her skull. Coughing, she tried to move, but her feet were stuck to the bed beneath her. She could barely reach her head as she tried to cover her eyes.

Francesca jolted to full awareness. What in the blazing star trails had happened? She pulled her arm again and again the sound of metal chains hitting steel jarred through her. How in the galaxies…?

Blinking rapidly, she looked at her wrist. It was shackled, as was her waist and her ankles. Whoever had her wasn't taking any chances that she would escape.

*I've been captured.*

Francesca's head throbbed, each pulse sending a new form of torment over her length. Her ribs ached horribly, but she could accomplish little to make them feel better. All she could do was take deep breaths and hope that time would stop her hurting. By the way the room jerked, she could guess she was on a ship. The metal room was small and lacked any lavish embellishments, but it was better than the dung hole she'd been sleeping in on Torgan. At least the bed she was strapped to was comfortable.

How long had she been out? What had happened? All she could remember was the dark-haired man smiling timidly at her as he handed her a drink, offering his nervous toast. Now her tongue was thick and a horrible aftertaste was in her mouth.

Drugged?

The thought angered her more than anything else. She was captured by some inept half-wit with some lame excuse about wanting to hire her?! Why in the known universes had she followed him from her room? Oh, she knew why. She had gotten greedy. She didn't want to sell the Jade Phoenix. Part of her thought if she kept the artifact Jin would come for her and another part of her felt closer to him when she held it. Now, she had no Jin and no Jade Phoenix. What she did have was a massive pain shooting over her body and the humiliation of being caught by some timid space cadet.

"Stupid, Francesca, really stupid," she berated herself. "You deserve whatever they decide to do to you."

## Chapter Eleven

Francesca opened her eyes only to be greeted by consuming darkness. She was still on the same bed with her body strapped down so she couldn't turn. The room lights were out and she didn't recall hearing anyone come in to check on her, though she imagined she was being monitored somehow. Earlier, she had passed out from pain while trying to escape her metal shackles and had no idea how much time had gone by since she was captured.

Francesca wondered if she could escape. She had no doubt she possessed the skills, but she no longer possessed the willpower. What did it matter?

Closing her eyes, she knew it wasn't important who had her now or what they did to her. In order to keep a promise to one love, she had betrayed another. She had fulfilled her vow to Sun. Vengeance was hers. How could Jin forgive that? Why would he want to? Whoever caught her had left behind the Jade Phoenix. Now it was up to fate to decide in whose hands the artifact fell.

*I have kept my vow, my master. I have taken the Jade Phoenix away from them. You are avenged. The Zhang Empire will fall.*

The words left her feeling bitter and cold. She never dreamt of the day when she could say vengeance was complete. What did one do after revenge? There were many tales of warriors, driven by revenge, but no one ever said what happened afterward. Maybe there was no afterward, no more of the story to tell. Maybe this was it. Her life ended in captivity, like a caged wild animal getting what she deserved.

*I have fulfilled my vow, Chen Sun. It is over.*

Even as she thought of her fate, knowing it for what it was--a bitter ending to a bitter life--she still wished it was Jin who had captured her first. She wanted his punishment. Her eyes closed, she willed her mind to slip back into her dreams. Jin was in her dreams, standing over her in anger. He hated her and still she would rather dream of him in anger than be in her reality without him.

* * * *

Jin looked around at Jarek's crew. They were a likeable lot of misfits. He had met them before when Mei had brought them home to meet their parents, but he didn't get to spend too much time with them before his sister had taken off. His gaze stopped on Evan without really seeing him.

Evan Cormier was a good man and highly intelligent. There was something about him that reminded Jin of Lian. Evan had gotten Francesca out of the room she was staying in and managed to drug her so she was captured without incident. It went smoother than Jin could have hoped for. No one was hurt and Evan made sure that no attention was drawn to either his wayward wife or the princes' crews. Jin rode back to Líntiān with Jarek as the Var prince transported Jin's cargo, the bound and chained Princess Francesca. They followed behind Huan. Some of his brother's crew didn't know why they were on Torgan and the Zhang family hoped to keep it that way. It wasn't widely known that Princess Francesca had run out on him.

As far as any outside the palace walls knew, Princess Francesca had been at his side since the wedding. Very few beyond the palace received transmissions from space and those who did most likely had never seen the princess. So, even on the very off chance that they were to see her Federation wanted notice, no connection would be made to 'La Rosa' and Princess Zhang Francesca.

*More lies.*

Though, he had to admit he was glad that his failure as a husband and a prince wasn't spread to the people. His humiliation was bad enough without the public opinion weighing down on him.

Jin shivered in disgust to remember where Francesca had been living. He offered her paradise and she chose the metal box with rusted walls.

*There is no love in that.*

The Jade Phoenix was on its way home, safely tucked away on Haun's ship. Its power had drawn them to it, hidden inside the wall of Francesca's dingy room on Torgan. It was all too easy. Really, they'd expected her to have sold it before they got to her.

"Mei's cooking," Viktor said, coming into the cockpit.

"She wanted me to tell you, Jarek."

Viktor and his brother Lucien were half human, half Dere. They had a milky white complexion that contrasted strangely with the red-brown and red-green of their eyes. Lucien was in charge of communications and Viktor was a mechanic.

"Thanks," Jarek grinned. Viktor disappeared the way he came.

"Mei cooks?" Jin asked. His sister never cooked. Sure, she knew how, they'd all had lessons, but...? Mei? A cook?

"It's her new hobby," Jarek said, giving a small grin. Jin had no desire to pry into the private joke between his sister and her husband. It would undoubtedly only lead to more insight into the couples unending love for each other.

"She's not bad," Rick, the pilot, admitted. He had a self-proclaimed affection for all women and an easy-going nature that went well with the mischievous glint that was constantly in his brown eyes. "And I'd never thought I'd say I liked having another woman on board since Captain Sam, but Mei's all right."

"Hm, thanks," Jarek drawled sarcastically.

Rick winked playfully. "No problem, Cap!"

"Sam?" Jin asked.

"She was Rick's captain before he signed on with me," Jarek answered. When Jin would ask more, he held up his hand. "It's a long story."

"Can I tell it?" Rick grinned.

"No," Jarek said, pointing at the controls. "You fly."

"Can't a guy have any fun around here?" Rick mumbled.

"You've had enough fun to last a lifetime," Jarek said. "Don't make me remind you what happened last time you had a little 'fun'."

"You got Mei out of the deal so what do you care?" Rick grumbled.

Jarek laughed softly to himself, smiling dreamily. "Yeah, I sure did."

"You know, you were a lot more fun when you were single," Rick said.

"And you were a lot more fun when you were kidnapped by drug dealers," Jarek teased back.

"But I wasn't here when I was...." Rick started.

"Exactly." Jarek slapped him on the shoulder and

motioned Jin to follow him out of the cockpit. "Let's leave him alone, Jin. Rick can't fly straight when he has an audience."

"Ha. Ha. Ha," Rick yelled as they left. The ship jerked hard to the right, crashing both Jin and Jarek into the wall.

"Rick!" Jarek warned amidst the pilot's hearty laughter.

"What? Wasn't me!" Rick yelled. "Honest! We hit a small black hole."

Jarek shook his head. "Sorry about him. I'd leave him somewhere but he only seems to find his way back."

Jin smiled. It was clear the two men were friends.

"So, I hate to press, but have you decided about our prisoner? I'd like to let one of the guys check her out. Evan said he detected something wrong with her when she answered the door."

Jin's gut tightened. "What kind of something wrong?"

"Nothing a medical booth can't cure, I'm sure. Evan wasn't sure what it was, but she might be hurt. And it wouldn't be a bad idea to make sure the drugs didn't have an adverse effect on her. They're perfectly safe and we've used them before, mainly on each other when we get bored in deep space. Oddly, Rick seems to get dosed the most. Once I found him naked and tied to the dining hall table."

Jin raised a brow.

"Don't worry, it's been replaced," Jarek laughed. "Anyway, it's always good to be extra cautious since we don't know exactly what type of humanoid line Francesca comes from."

"I don't think she knows," Jin admitted.

"I detect human in her," Jarek said, "if that helps."

"How?"

"Var senses," Jarek grinned. "I can sort of smell the difference. It's hard to explain. For my best guess, there is human in her and also something else. Maybe along the lines of Killian."

"Killian?"

"It's an almost extinct race mostly residing on Planet Bravon in the Solarus Quadrant.

"Isn't Bravon a myth? I didn't think anyone could survive in Solarus, something about too many suns." Jin frowned.

"No, I met a man from there once. He was a really gruff character. I guess he'd have to be since Bravon is the only inhabited planet in the quadrant. From what I understand, they have to stay under the surface and during the summer season temperatures can spike to nearly seven thousand degrees on the surface."

"Still sounds like a myth to me," Jin said.

"Well, possibly. I've never been there myself and frankly, I don't want to. The point is, when I walked by Francesca in the Torgan complex, I smelled the same thing in her that I did in that man. It's almost an ashy, smoky scent just beneath the surface. It was faint, but it was there. The Killians are said to be a strong race of people with superior strength and amazing learning capabilities and healing times. From what you and your brother have said about Francesca's fighting abilities and what Mei's told me of the Wushu Uprisings, it would make sense how one so young became so powerful and talented."

"I guess we'll never know for sure," Jin said. "She was an orphan."

"It doesn't matter. From what Mei says she's Líntiānese now." Jarek patted him on the shoulder, almost looking apologetic that he had brought the topic up. "Now that we're far from Torgan airspace, I'd say it's safe to untie her. There aren't many places she could go to that we can't find her."

Jin nodded.

"Mei even has all the ducts mapped out. Whenever she gets mad at me she escapes through the ceiling." Jarek pointed up to the grates above them. Jin shook his head. Trust Mei to do such a thing.

"My parents will be pleased to see Mei." Jin needed to change the subject. "Especially when she is so close to her time."

Jarek stopped and made a turn into the dining hall. "There's my sweet *fea*!"

"Ugh, I don't know how sweet I feel today. Your child keeps kicking me." She frowned, rubbing her belly for emphasis. "And Dev here is trying to get himself kicked off the ship by insisting I don't go up into the ducts anymore."

Jin looked to where his sister pointed. Dev was half Belvon, a demonic looking race with red skin. They weren't sure what the other half was. Aside from the intense coloring, he appeared humanoid, only larger. He was the ship's security force.

"Oh, Jin, have you met Dev?" Mei smiled at him, looking happy despite her grumping moments before. "Prince Zhang Jin, this is *Salebinaben Johobik en Dehauberkelsain en Thoraxian en Yyrtolzx Devekin.*" She motioned to Dev and then back to Jin. "Dev, this is my brother, Jin."

Jin nodded once. Dev did the same, even though they'd already met before Mei's introduction.

"You'd better watch yourself, Dev," Jarek said. "I think she's serious this time."

"And if I find her hurting herself or the baby, she'll seriously find herself tied to a chair," Dev threatened. Jin was surprised by the depth of the man's concern.

"Ugh, fine, no ducts until after the baby is born," Mei grumbled. "Now go away."

Dev grinned slightly and made a move to go, obviously proud to have won the battle of the wills with Mei.

"Hey, Dev, take Jin to find Lochlann. I think he's with Jackson in the commons playing cards." Jarek grabbed his wife from behind, kissing her cheek as she threw ingredients into a cooking pot. Vegetables sizzled sending their fragrant aroma over the room. "Jin here wanted to check in on Princess Francesca. Have Lochlann grab the handheld medical unit we found on Sintaz to examine her with."

Dev nodded in agreement. Jin followed the giant of a man in silence. He'd said no such thing about wanting to check in on Francesca, but he didn't need to. Obviously, his desire to be near her was apparent to everyone.

The commons area where Dev took him was equipped with a viewing screen, gaming tables, couches and chairs. The men clearly spent a lot of time there while in space. Jackson, a dark blond security officer who worked under Dev, played cards with Viktor.

"Ah-ha! Kiss my comet!" Viktor yelled, slamming down his hand of cards.

Jackson stared at it, grumbling as he tallied the scores on an electronic pad next to him.

"Lochlann," Dev said. "Jarek has requested that you get the handheld medical unit and go with Prince Jin to examine the princess."

Lochlann sat next to Evan, going over a star chart. Glancing at Jin, the man picked up the map and rolled it before handing it over to his friend. Evan took it, tucking the parchment under his arm. Dev turned, not waiting to see if Lochlann complied with the order and continued on down the hall alone.

"This way, prince," Lochlann said, as he passed through the commons door.

"Jin is fine," Jin answered. "Formality seems out of place here."

"You've got that right," Lochlann chuckled, relaxing some.

They walked in silence down the metal corridor. Lights shone in intermediate arches, rising overhead. Jin missed the palace gardens, the statues and beauty of his homeland. He was connected to it and found little to be enjoyed in what he'd seen in Torgan and on Jarek's ship. It wasn't so much that he thought his life was better, it was just better for him. He was tradition.

Jin needed to talk about something--anything to pass the time and keep his mind off Francesca. He'd yet to see her again, refusing to look at her as she was brought aboard *The Conqueror,* but he could feel her presence all around him. Maybe he was crazy, but he felt her, smelled her, even tasted her at times.

"Have you been with Jarek long?" he asked Lochlann.

"I was actually born on Qurilixen like Jarek was, but I'm of Draig decent, not Var."

"Draig?"

"I'm a dragon shifter, not cat. My kind lives on one half of the planet and Jarek's on the other."

"Ah, like the Song Empire and my family's," Jin acknowledged. "Are there any other powers on the planet?"

"No. Just us shifters. Believe me, that's enough. Most times the planet isn't big enough for both races."

"So you and Prince Jarek were childhood friends?" Jin studied the man closely. "That is how you came to be on this ship with him?"

"No, not quite. Our races were at war and have only recently declared peace. When I met Jarek, he was like I was--tired of the fighting and death. We grew up in war and had both seen friends die because of it. I can't remember the exact way it happened, but I guess we just hit it off. Perhaps it was that we both have the wanderlust in our hearts. One day we left for the high skies and we just kept going." Lochlann stopped and disappeared into a small room with a medical booth. Digging into a metal compartment, he pulled out a handheld unit. "Here we are. This should do the trick."

Jin frowned. "That's an ESC unit. Where did you get it? I was under the impression they didn't sell their supplies to outsiders."

"We, ah, found it on Sintaz awhile back." Lochlann laughed uncomfortably as he glanced down to where the handheld said, 'Exploratory Science Commission.'

"Sintaz? Isn't that a deserted ice planet? What were you doing there? From what I recall of intergalactic geography, only scientists land there for research purposes."

"Yeah, that's the one," Lochlann chuckled. "It's an ice block of a planet, all right. Colder than a corpse in the middle of winter."

"So what were you doing there?" he repeated.

"Um, well…. We were salvaging." Lochlann cleared his throat. "Oh, look, here we are. You want to go in first or shall I? I can give you a moment with your wife if you'd like."

Jin's hand shook as his thoughts were once again drawn to Francesca. Several months had passed and all he could think about was her. Now he had her and he was scared--scared that the feelings he tried to kill would rise up to strangle him, scared that he'd look into her lovely jade eyes and not be able to do what must be done.

A dull ache had settled in the back of his neck, radiating along his shoulders. His wavy reflection stared back at him from the metal door and he hesitated. Dark circles ringed his eyes, which were bloodshot from his excessive drinking. Though clean, his clothes were wrinkled and his disheveled hair was an overgrown version of his usual style. In all his life, he couldn't remember ever being so sloppily dressed and unpresentable.

He glanced at Lochlann. "You can go ahead."

Lochlann ran his hand over the door sensor, opening it. Compelled by an outside force, Jin couldn't help himself as he stepped inside the room before the man. Francesca was tied to the bed as he had requested her to be. She was too trained in the art of escape to risk leaving her unbound. A feeling of power washed over him as he saw her trapped. It would be easy to order Lochlann away. How he could make her suffer!

But he couldn't do it. His heart nearly stopped in his chest to look at her, only she wasn't like he remembered her. Her face was pale with shades of gray to her complexion. A bruise dotted under her right eye and her breathing was hard and raspy. Her lips, normally full and lush, were swelled beyond normal. Angry, he turned on Lochlann and hissed, "What did you guys do to her? I told your man Evan to be careful with her!"

"Nothing," Lochlann defended. "She was like that when Evan found her. We didn't touch her. I swear on my life, we didn't touch her. We did exactly what you asked. We drugged her and brought her onboard, no scene, no mess, and we tied her right where she is now to prevent her from escaping. From what Jarek told us of her skills, she's not one we'd mess with anyway. Besides, she's taken. Why would we try to impress a woman we can't have?"

Jin raised a brow at the last comment. He wanted to believe the man. Turning back to Francesca, he didn't say a word. Her closed eyes were darkened with black cosmetics, like when he'd first found her. The band stretched from temple to temple. She slept, though by the strained look about her features, it wasn't a peaceful slumber.

Neither one of them moved. Jin's hands trembled to touch her, but he held back, balling them into fists. Without looking at Lochlann, he ordered hoarsely, "Check her."

Lochlann moved past him into the room and began his scan. The laser went first over her face. "Minor facial damage," the man said as he worked. "We're showing an extremely sore shoulder, possibly an old dislocation and some swelling. Her chest is fine, lungs good... Oh, blessed stars. Ouch."

"What?"

"It looks like she's got a couple cracked ribs. They're fresh and haven't begun to heal yet. We should get her into a medical booth at once." Lochlann stood. "Holy Comet, this one is tough. Evan would've said something if he could tell she was injured. She must have blocked it from him."

"What are you saying?" Jin demanded.

"Evan can tell that sort of thing about people. He would've said she was in severe pain. The fact that he couldn't tell means she was hiding it well."

"I mean, she's been hurt? By what? Who?"

Lochlann frowned slightly, and said, "You'll have to ask her. I'd guess it's from a fight."

"With who?" Jin moved closer to her. His hands shook. Time had not cured him of his feelings, though it also didn't let him forget the hard lesson she had given him. He'd been willing to give her everything--his name, title, home, family.

Lochlann leaned over her and touched her side. Francesca mumbled and tossed in her sleep. "Oh, yeah, we got us a break here."

"What is she saying?" Jin couldn't move. He strained to hear her.

"She keeps saying something about the sun." Lochlann reached to feel her head. "Huh, she doesn't seem feverish. That mean anything to you? The sun?"

*Sun? Master Chen Sun.*

Jin took a deep breath and shook his head. He was a fool for not suspecting it earlier. Chen Sun meant more to her than just a master to a student. Even now she called for him.

"I'll get Dev. He can lift her into the medical booth." Lochlann left him alone with Francesca.

Jin stared at her. She mumbled again, but he couldn't make out the words. He didn't want to.

*I love you, Jin.*

She hadn't meant it. Jin didn't realize he'd clung to some small hope that she did love him, that she would have a good excuse for doing what she did, some noble reason. No. She did it for revenge. She did it for the man she truly loved. Chen Sun.

Francesca loved Chen Sun.

It made sense now, the way she refused to give up even when offered a glorious future as a princess. Few things could motivate a person to such an extent. Love and revenge. Francesca had both to drive her on.

Jin felt a little bit of himself die in that moment of clarity, as he stared at Francesca's face. The past became clear to him, as was his gift from the Jade Phoenix. He'd never cursed his blessing as he did in this moment. He should have known, but he hadn't wanted to see the truth for what it was. With that one word, the past broke free to be known.

*Sun.*

Jin understood now. He did not see the past like a play, but merely understood it for what it was. His family had hunted and killed the Wushu master, Chen Sun. Francesca loved him and she swore revenge. Taking the Jade Phoenix was the best revenge someone could take against them and tearing out his heart had just been a necessity to vengeance. He was a casualty to her personal war.

Blessed Ancestors! How could the spirits have done this to him? Why her? Why a woman who could never love him because her heart belonged elsewhere? They were fools, all of them! With their talk of curses and prophecies! He didn't break any curses and in the end the only damage done was to his own heart. Jin hung his head, not moving to wake her. There was nothing to say. He was defeated, not just defeat of the heart but of the soul. She'd won, totally and completely. He was a broken man without the will to fight her. How could he fight her? He understood her pain.

Francesca's heart was broken from her loss of Chen Sun. How could he fault her for fighting the pain he now carried within him? Francesca was lost to him, but it was worse than her death because he could see her and touch her, but he couldn't have her.

The marriage would stand. He didn't care about that. There would never be another for him. He would live out his days in solitude, away from Honorable City, away from every memory of her. And, perhaps, someday, he would finally be granted peace.

Lochlann came back into the room, Dev in tow. Lochlann freed her of her shackles. The giant red man kneeled by Francesca, gently scooping her up into his arms. Jin moved to leave, saying softly, "Please do what you can to fix her. I'm going to borrow a space pod and meet up with my brother. We'll send coordinates as to where to drop her off."

"But, you can't mean to...." Lochlann protested. Jin walked away and heard no more. It was over.

* * * *

Francesca gasped, coming instantly to full awareness. Blinking rapidly, she tried to move. A medical booth was closed around her body as she stood inside it and only her head stuck out the top. Her skin tingled as the machine worked, slowly repairing her injuries. Heat focused around her ribs and she knew the unit was in the middle of a repair cycle as it mended her bones.

The room was small, metal, like a ship's medical ward.

The medical booth's panel was pulled out from its side, but the screen was facing away from her and she couldn't see what part of the cycle it was on. Since she didn't know how long she'd been in it, she didn't know how much longer she had left. It could be minutes or hours.

Why were the men who kidnapped her fixing her? If she were injured, she'd be easier to control. She thought of the man who drugged her, ashamed that she was caught so easily. Maybe she'd wanted to get caught. Francesca did feel as if she wanted to be punished for her sins, for the life she'd led.

*It is done. You have your revenge.*

The words filtered through her head, but they brought little comfort. She didn't feel as victorious as she thought she would have. Instead, a hollow pit formed in her stomach. It was over. She now had nothing to live for.

*Jin.* His name washed over her, but it only made her feel worse. There was no way he'd take her back after what she'd done.

The unit beeped and the warmth around her ribs stopped. Francesca took a deep breath. It no longer hurt. She tried reaching along the edge to unlatch the unit, but couldn't find the groove to do so.

"Ah, you're up. Wonderful!"

Francesca jolted in surprise to see a milky white creature with brown-red eyes. She stared at him, trying to place where she'd seen him before. Then, a red giant of a man came to stand in the doorway behind him. The red guy she remembered. He'd been on Torgan with two pale creatures-- like the one who was now checking the medical booth's panel. Had they been spying on her?

"I'll tell the captain," the red man said.

"Thanks, Dev," the pale creature answered as he grabbed a chair from behind him and noisily pulled it in front of the control panel to the medical booth. He sat, all the time not taking his eyes off the screen.

Dev, the red beast, nodded at her in silent greeting and left.

"Who are you? Where am I?" she asked, still trying to find the groove to unlatch the unit's door. She grunted as she tried to bend her legs.

"Hey, easy there, Francesca. You were pretty badly beaten. We want to make sure you're healed before we get you out of that thing," he said. "This is about done on your ribs and then we'll do a complete scan of your organs to make sure they're all right. And to answer your questions, I'm Lucien and you're on *The Conqueror*."

"Which planet sent you for me?" she asked, rolling her head back. The unit beeped several times as Lucien set it up to do a complete health scan. She felt the tingling of the lasers starting at her toes only to slowly work its way up over her feet. Eventually, it would go over her entire length.

"What do you mean?" Lucien asked, studying her from his place on the chair. He leaned back, putting his hands behind his head as he kicked his legs out before him in easy repose.

"Just what I said. What planet are you working for? You're bounty hunters, right? Out to get a reward for capturing the elusive Rose? So which one is it? Ranoz? Quaser? Denat 7? Merca? Ticaron? Hungariz? The Zox Empire? Earth Moonbase Delta?"

"By the stars, you get around!" Lucien swore. "What are you wanted for on Ticaron?"

Francesca chuckled at the memory. "I stole a ring from Gretori Zothos on a dare. I can't remember what planet it was, but I did it on a dare one night when I was drunk. Turned out, he was really upset at its loss."

"I know of him," Lucien said.

Francesca lifted a brow. "That's who you're working for? He's still pissed about that damned ring? It was barely worth the time it took to sell."

"No, I've just heard of him. I don't think you have to worry about the Ticaron warrant anymore. I believe Gretori Zothos is dead."

"Pity. I guess I'll just have to work on keeping my numbers up," Francesca mused, just to give the impression of indifference. "So which is it then? Medical Mafia? ESC? HIA?"

"You're wanted by the Human Intelligence Agency? What did you do? Trade biological weapons?"

Instead of answering, she continued with her list, letting an almost bored quality enter her tone, "The Federation Military? The Medical Alliance for Planetary Health? Which, by the way, the MAPH is only a front for the Medical Mafia. If they got a hold of me, I doubt the legal end would be the ones to deal with me."

"Um, I'm getting the point, Francesca," Lucien said, chuckling.

"There's more," she offered.

"I'm sure there are," he agreed, reaching forward to touch the panel. The tingling over her ankle and shins intensified. "Small ankle sprain."

"Didn't feel it."

The intense feeling stopped and the machine moved up.

Lucien whistled lightly. "Looks like you tore the anterior crutiate ligament in your right knee at one time."

"Yeah, that and the cartilage tore in the other knee. I landed wrong jumping off a building. It hurt like a regil bite, but I don't feel it anymore."

"Well, why not let us fix them anyway?" he offered, smiling kindly. "You're already here and it's not like we have anywhere we need to be."

She shrugged. "Fine by me."

A man walked by the doorway. Lucien glanced up, "Oh, hey, Rick, meet Francesca."

Rick stopped and took a step back. Smiling, he winked and said, "What for? She's spoken for."

Francesca gave him a wry look, arching her brow. For bounty hunters they had a really easy way about them. In any other circumstance she would have liked them.

"Unless you're not happy, sweet cheeks." Rick grinned. "In that case, I'm Rick, pilot of this ship, one hell of a masculine specimen and great in bed."

"Go away now," Lucien ordered. "And never talk to the lady again."

"Hey, you stopped me." Rick winked at her and kept walking down the corridor.

"Uh, yeah, sorry about him. He's," Lucien shrugged, "an idiot."

The unit beeped again. Lucien frowned. Francesca studied him, slightly amused by his concerned look as he shook his head.

"What you find now?" she asked.

"You've broken all of your fingers at one time."

"All but the thumb," she corrected.

"Hmm." Lucien shook his head. "Try not to move them for a moment, the unit will reset the bones for you."

"Before you get all concerned, let me just help you out."

Francesca took a deep breath and looked at the metal grating along the ceiling. Seeing movement, she frowned. Someone was above them, watching. Absently, she listed, "Dislocated shoulder, split shoulder, multiple fractures, sprains, shin splints--those hurt like a *qingwa cào de liúmáng*. I had a broken wrist at one time and, *oh!* My neck is a little sore. I think I might have pulled a muscle."

Lucien let loose a soft sigh as he started keying in procedures into the machine. Francesca smiled slightly as the medical booth went to work. If anything, she was getting a lot of free medical stuff done. This was saving her a fortune--a fortune she wouldn't have bothered spending if it had been left up to her.

"You're going to be in here for awhile," Lucien said. "I have orders to check your blood work and do a full diagnostic."

"Tune me up like a spaceship, eh?" she laughed.

"Something like that."

Francesca kept her gaze above her. The person above them didn't move. She didn't let on that she saw, just stared blankly as she waited for the spy to act.

"So, you have many prisoners on board, or just me?"

"Uh, we only have one guest," he said diplomatically.

"Ah."

"So you speak Líntiānese very well," he said. Francesca quirked a brow and he repeated distractedly as he worked, "*Qingwa cào de liúmáng.*"

Had she said that? She frowned, realizing she had. The foreign words had just slipped out.

"Yeah, what of it?"

"Do you miss it? Líntiān?"

Francesca's stomach tightened. She had known that it was a distinct possibility that Jin had sent these men for her. He'd sent every other bounty hunter after her. She took a deep breath, suddenly frightened by the prospect of seeing him again.

Her voice hard, she answered, "No."

It was a lie, but he didn't need to know that.

"You do realize, others would pay much more for me," she said. "I don't know why you'd take me back to Líntiān."

"I hear it's a nice planet, a virtual paradise of the galaxies. Don't you want to go back?"

"The paradise part is embellished," she lied.

"I didn't think so when I was there," Lucien said, grinning.

Francesca laughed. The man was sneaky, she'd give him that.

"How much is he paying you?" she asked.

"How much is who paying us?" Lucien refused to meet her eyes.

"Prince Zhang Jin of the Muntong Empire. How much is he paying you to bring me back?"

"Nothing."

Nothing? Did that mean Jin didn't seek to get her back, but his family did? Francesca turned her eyes up. The person above her had moved, but now was still again. "Ah, his family wants me back. I see."

"I believe they do," Lucien agreed, nodding.

"Is there anyway to get you to change course? Any price?" she asked. "I don't wish to see Líntiān again. It's not really my taste of planets."

"I'm afraid not. We have our orders. It's straight to Líntiān." Lucien stood. "Try and relax as the unit works. I'm going to go get something from the food simulator. You want anything for when you're finished?"

"Phaser?" she asked, laughing lightly.

"Sorry, Francesca, that I can't do."

"Can't blame a girl for trying," she said as he left.

When she was alone, she kept her eyes above. "You know, if you want to learn something about me, just ask. Or at least learn how to sneak around better. Your lack of a creative hiding place is a little insulting."

It took a moment, but the person above her moved. Francesca watched as the grating was pulled up. A small, feminine hand poked out and soon a woman came after it. The lady grunted as she maneuvered her body through the small opening. Swiftly, she jumped out of the ceiling, landing behind the medical booth where Francesca couldn't see her.

"You are truly gifted, as they say," the woman said. Francesca shivered. The woman had a Líntiānese accent. "The Wushu master has trained you well."

"What do you want with me? Did the Zhang family send you to make sure I made it back to the hanging all right?" Her throat was tight and she didn't like the fact that she was trapped in the medical booth, unable to defend herself.

"Hanging?" the woman asked.

"Or whatever divine form of punishment they have planned," she said. "Hanging seems to be a galactic favorite, so I just went with that."

"Ah, so you believe you deserve to be punished." The woman stepped into view.

Francesca was surprised to see she was very pregnant. She glanced up. How did the woman move so fluidly if she was so far along with child?

"That speaks much of your guilt," the woman continued.

"I'm not denying what I've done," Francesca said. "Never really found the need to play innocent."

"I am curious. What crime do you think you are guilty of?" The woman looked her in the eye, searching and watchful.

"I stole the Jade Phoenix," Francesca said.

"A confession," the Líntiānese woman said, her tone strained. She was petite, her features almost fragile. Like her people, her skin was tan and smooth, though she seemed paler than other woman she'd seen on Jin's planet and she was dressed differently.

"Told you, I'm not big on playing innocent." Francesca winced, holding perfectly still as the machine went to work, healing old scar tissue on her wrist. The damage, while already healed, was extensive and painful to mend. "Besides, it's not really a secret. I took the Jade Phoenix."

The woman pressed her lips tightly together.

"I can't tell you where it is," Francesca continued, "if that's what you're planning on asking me about next. The truth is, at this point, I really don't know where it is. I'm sure I've been thoroughly checked when I was drugged so you know I no longer have the artifact. It's gone."

"Is this the only crime against my people that you wish to confess to?" she asked.

"What is all this to you?" Francesca asked. "What do you care if I hurt the royal family's pride?"

"It's very much to me," the woman answered. "I assure you."

"Fine, I'll confess. I'm pretty sure I broke a few traditions while I was there as well. But that really isn't my fault as you people seem to have a tradition for everything. I mean, really! You eat a certain way, walk a certain way, every little detail is done exactly the way it's been done since the dawn of human creation."

"You people?" the woman repeated, looking offended by the terminology.

"You bet your blessed space cakes, *'you people'*. Don't you dare look at me like I should take the words back. You're the ones who put yourselves so above other races. You hide out in a palace, stuck in your ways and traditions, you do everything so beautifully and right and perfect until a woman feels as if she doesn't deserve to be in your presence. You have a way for everything. What exactly should I have done? Stayed and felt inadequate for the rest of my life? Yeah, like I could really be some stupid princess married to the Faerian tale prince!"

Francesca was breathing hard by the time she stopped. Tears pooled in her eyes, threatening to spill over. She bit her lips together, surprised and ashamed that the words had come out.

"I have done all this?" the woman asked softly. Francesca didn't answer. It wasn't the type of question that required her to.

The machine beeped, finished with Francesca's wrist. It moved its attention to her shoulder. She stared at the woman, more frightened by what she'd admitted to than anything physical the woman could do to her.

The woman slowly walked to the panel. Francesca silently begged her to push a button that would kill her instantly so she no longer had to feel.

"You have had a hard life," the woman said, studying the screen. She ran her fingertip over the edge of the display, not pressing anything. "So many old wounds needing to be healed."

"Not so hard," Francesca lied, hoping to regain some of her dignity. "Just a few fights."

"You loved Master Chen Sun?" The woman's dark eyes met hers.

"Yes," Francesca answered. "I loved him."

The machine beeped as the woman pressed buttons, but the sound was so far away, so distant to Francesca's mind as she heard Chen Sun's voice in her head.

*If you have nothing to fear, you have nothing to lose.*

"And you believe the Zhang royal family had him killed?"

the woman's voice interrupted her thoughts.

"I know they did. I was there. I saw it."

"Very well." The woman nodded. "I will tell my brother of this."

"Your brother?" Francesca asked, stiffening.

"Jin," the woman answered.

"You are Princess Mei?" Francesca held her breath. This woman looked nothing like the royal family. Well, now that she knew the connection, she could see the resemblance in her features, but she was dressed so untraditionally and she was on a space ship with a crew full of men.

"Yes, my sister, I am Princess Mei. I am sorry you do not love my brother and I am saddened to know that the decisions of fate did not bless you as they have me. I love my husband and I wished for all of my siblings to find the same happiness as I have." Mei stepped closer and placed a hand on Francesca's cheek. A tear slipped from Francesca's eyes to hit the woman's hand. Softly, she asked, "*Zhe shi shen me?* What is this?" Mei wiped the tear with a gentle sweep of her finger. "So long ago and still you cry for Chen Sun."

Francesca didn't bother to speak, letting the woman assume what she wanted to.

"You rest. Soon we will be home." Mei nodded, pulling back. She walked toward the door.

"Your home, Princess Mei," Francesca said, trying to stiffen her resolve. "Not mine."

Mei glanced back from under her lashes. "You are a Zhang princess as well, my sister. And as a princess, you have a duty to your new empire. Like it or not, you are Princess Zhang Francesca. It was your own doing. Not even fate can change that fact."

"What do you know about fate?"

"Plenty," Mei assured her. "I'm happily married because of it."

Francesca snorted. "One couple."

"You need more?" Mei challenged. "Fine. All of my brothers by marriage have had fate intervene. King Kirill of the Var's wife was an HIA agent kidnapped by his father the day King Attor died. Then, Prince Quinn met his wife when she went to their planet to check it for bioweaponry. Pr--"

"This doesn't prove anything," Francesca interrupted.

"Prince Falke," Mei emphasized, continuing, "was kidnapped by Captain Samantha who used to captain most of this very crew before my husband took them on."

"He was kidnapped?" Francesca asked before she could stop herself.

"Yes, by a woman not much bigger than I am. And Falke is, well, have you seen Dev?" Mei waited as Francesca nodded. "Falke is as big as Dev. Imagine her surprise when she woke up the next morning with a naked guy like that chained in her room. She had darted him with a tranquilizer while he was in his shifted form and didn't know what she'd taken."

Francesca eyed the little Mei and tried to imagine her taking on Dev. It was hard to imagine the Zhang princess with Prince Jarek, especially if he was as big as she claimed Prince Falke to be. She looked at Mei's protruding stomach. A little thing like Princess Mei was going to give birth to that big of a man's child?

"Is Jarek…?" she began.

Mei followed her eyes down. "Oh, no. *Wode tian*! No. Jarek isn't as big as Dev. Though, he is plenty big, just not *that* big."

Francesca looked away.

"Then there is my husband's twin brother, Reid. He married a woman who stowed away on this ship." Mei laughed to herself. "I don't know why this popped in my head, but when Quinn was trying to woo his wife, he tried to do old Earth customs for her. He thought a little toy bear she called teddy was a real creature and he gave her this vicious looking stuffed creature for a present. The poor woman has to keep it in her living quarters."

"What does that have to do with fate?" Francesca asked.

"Nothing," Mei said, studying her. "You're not used to having normal conversations are you?"

Francesca didn't answer.

"Fine," Mei's expression faded into a stoic mask. "My point is that fate has a hand in everything. Otherwise, how could so many brothers from one palace find their perfect mates in such unusual ways?"

"Coincidence," Francesca offered, doing her best to act bored.

"You have had a hard life, haven't you?" Mei looked at her

in pity as she walked to the door. Shaking her head, she hummed softly and said, "So many old wounds needing to be healed."

## Chapter Twelve

*Imperial Palace of the Zhang Dynasty, Honorable City, Muntong Territory, Planet of Líntiān*

She was back.

Francesca stared at the gate leading into Honorable City. Its wide, gilded doors were stretched open, as if welcoming her into the palace fold once more. Torches were lit on either side, giving a soft orange glow to the pathways. Looking at Mei, she didn't feel so welcome. The woman hadn't talked to her too much since she'd been trapped in the medical booth, but her looks said what her voice did not. The princess was sad, disappointed, upset and she didn't hide it very well. It appeared to cause her husband great worry.

Francesca couldn't make her feet move, not because of the shackles chaining her ankles together, but because she knew Jin was inside the palace walls waiting for her. She didn't want to see him again. But, then again, if she saw how much he hated her then maybe it would kill some of her guilt.

Feeling a tug on her arm, she glanced up to Dev. The man's red skin glistened in the torchlight. It was late in the evening, but Mei had refused to bring her home in daylight. Apparently, Francesca's homecoming wouldn't be met with cheers of excitement from the Líntiānese people.

"You ever have to walk out in front of a firing squad, Dev?" Francesca asked her keeper. He didn't answer. "Ever feel like the entire palace was staring at you when you walked anywhere?"

"Look at me, my lady," he said. "Everywhere I go I get stared at."

"Ah, good point."

Dev pulled again, forcing her to move forward. "You must face your fears, my lady. The sooner faced, the sooner they will be behind you."

"You're a philosopher."

"*Hrumph.*"

Francesca had no choice but to hobble next to Dev into the

palace. Princess Mei and her husband led the procession, which consisted mainly of their crewmen. Evan, the man who'd drugged her, turned out to be quite intelligent. He walked next to Rick, Jackson, Lucien and Viktor. Since they were welcomed guests of the Zhang, no one stayed back with Jarek's ship. Lochlann on one side of Mei, as her husband was on the other. It was a protective gesture, most likely an automatic one since Mei would hardly be in danger in her own palace.

Francesca frowned as she stared at the tiny Mei. She was jealous of the woman. Mei had so many people who loved her and were ready to lay down their lives to protect her. Francesca had no one, not anymore. The only person who ever gave two space credits about her was Sun and he was dead.

*Jin,* her mind whispered. *Jin said he loved you.*

"Yeah, right," she grumbled under her breath. "He didn't even bother to come after me. Instead he sent his sister."

"My lady?" Dev asked.

"Oh, mind your own business," she growled at him. "I wasn't talking to you, beast man."

He answered her with a smile, the first genuine one she'd seen from him.

* * * *

She was back. Jin knew it even before Grandfather Manchu appeared to tell him the news. The spirit stood still before him, waiting for him to answer. The prince had no answer to give.

Jin took a deep breath, looking up at the giant statue depicting the ancient gods in tranquil poses. He'd made offerings since coming home with Haun, though he wasn't sure what he was praying for to happen. When he did wish for something, it was to kill the aching in his heart. His family tried to cheer him but he was inconsolable.

"Jin?" Manchu asked softly, his voice as weak as his transparent image.

"I heard you," Jin answered, his tone hoarse and low.

"Jin, I...." His grandfather drifted closer, reaching out his hand before letting it fall to his side. "*Duibuqi.*"

"I don't need your apologies, *lǎotou.*" Jin slowly stood, leaving his offering of a small vase on the ground. A single flame burned within the red center. "The worst is done. You got what you wanted. The Jade Phoenix is back. I am married and that is the only curse upon this household. Interfere in my life no more."

"But fate has brought her back to you. There is a chance--"

"What do you want from me?" Jin growled. "Haven't you done enough? I have done my duty and now I wish to be left in peace."

"Jin, I am still your ancestor. You will show me the proper respect--"

"*Zhùzuî*," Jin snapped, telling the old spirit to be quiet. He stormed out of the hall, leaving Manchu to stare after him.

"Well done," Zhang An said as he walked out of the Exalted Hall. Jin sighed heavily, trying to turn away from her as he walked in the opposite direction. It did no good, as the woman appeared before him on his new path, smiling.

"Don't you have a Sacred Chamber to protect? Or some ale to drink?" he grumbled, turning his back on her and walking the other way.

"*Xiâoxin*, Zhang Jin," she warned.

"Leave me be, old woman. I wish to see no more of the past coming to haunt me." He walked faster. An drifted by his side, completely unaffected by the rigorous pace he set.

"That may be, Jin, but you do not make the rules. The past is your gift--"

"My curse," he interrupted.

"And, being as it's your *gift*, you will know it and see it." An's smile widened.

"Do you have a point, or did the gods send you to plague me?" He stopped, staring her down.

"I speak of understanding your wife, the woman you willingly married."

Jin frowned. "Willingly? I was possessed by Manchu. Do not tell me it was willing!"

"Listen here, young one. Do not speak to me in such tones. I will whip you with the wind, if you dare so much again!" The wind stirred at An's threat, hitting him hard. "And do not claim you didn't marry the woman willingly. I offered you a way to end it. You could have tried her for her crimes, but you choose to save her. Now she is immune from our punishments because she took only what was rightfully hers as well as ours. I warned you of this, but you married her anyway. *You* made that decision, Zhang Jin. You."

"So I'm a fool," he cried. "Thank you for pointing that out. Is there a point to your ramblings or are you just enjoying my torment?"

"There would be a point if you would listen."

"I'm listening." He held his arms wide. Sarcastically, he urged, "Go on, wise one."

"Then stop talking," An ordered.

Jin opened his mouth and then snapped it shut, not saying another word.

"Good," she stated, her transparent form shaking slightly. The wind slowed to a gentle breeze. "Now, there is no changing the past, but there is a chance to redeem the future. Your bride is here. By learning her past, you can fix your futures."

"Great-grandmother, I already know. She was in love with Chen Sun. You all made the decision to kill him."

"Francesca told you she loved Sun? She said these words?"

"Yes. To Mei," Jin said. His sister had told him everything Francesca did on the ship. He even told him how she'd flirted with the pilot, Rick, though nothing came of the playful banter. Still, to think of it made him jealous. "So you see, the only hope the family has is that she'll choose to stay on Líntiān as a princess without causing us any more trouble. I have spoken to the emperor and he has agreed that a house shall be built for her in the countryside, in a place of her choosing. There she will be given servants and will be taken care of. She will want for nothing."

"What of you?"

"I will stay here at the palace. Or, if she prefers the life of the Muntong court, I will take the house in the country. It matters not to me where I spend my days." Jin sighed. The truth was, he would almost prefer the country, away from any reminder that he had a wife.

"And if she refuses to stay?" An asked.

"You know as well as I do she doesn't have a choice. At least not now. Perhaps in time she can leave."

"So you don't even plan to try? You are just going to roll over like a dog who takes his master's kicks?"

"What do you want me to do? She loves someone else." Jin closed his eyes as pain rolled over him. Did they not see? She loved someone else, someone whose death would always be linked to him and his family.

"The heart is not so small," An whispered, disappearing.

"But neither is it very forgiving," he answered, though no one was there to hear his reply. Knowing that he didn't have much of a choice, he steeled his nerves to go greet his wife. Mei and Jarek brought her back under the cloak of evening, but torchlight lit his way.

Jin didn't know what to think or believe anymore. Manipulation and lies were how they'd gotten into this situation in the first place. The altered scrolls, the Wushu Uprising, the past hidden from them all, these were all reasons why he was standing where he was now. He knew his ancestor meant well, but nothing good ever came of deceit. Jin was chosen out of all his brothers because he could see this. He was the past, understood it, and was burdened most by it.

Understanding didn't make it easier to bear. If anything, it made it harder. He couldn't hate Francesca for what she'd done because he believed he understood her reasons for doing it.

Folding his hands in front of him, he solemnly walked to the front entrance. His dark blue silk tunic shirt hung to his knees, blending into the darker night with the black silk of his pants. His ground shoes were quiet at he moved soundlessly over the pathway.

"Jin!" Mei rushed forward, wrapping her arms around him. She gave him a quick hug before pulling back. Jin touched her cheek and Mei grabbed his hand in hers, holding it there.

Jin glanced over his sister's shoulder. Francesca stood by Dev in a dark red gown that fell all the way to her feet. Her eyes met his and he couldn't breathe. She always had that effect on him. His heart beat slowed in his chest and for a long moment the dull sound was all he could hear, echoing in the caverns of his ears.

Francesca moved and the spell was broken. She lifted her wrists, gave him a wry smile and shook the shackles that bound her hands together. The chains clinked, sounding like tiny bells tinkling over the night.

Jin dropped Mei's hand, not saying a word to her. Slowly, he stepped forward to Francesca and said the only thing he could think of. "Welcome back."

"Thanks for inviting me," she answered coyly with no

trace of the sarcasm he knew the words to imply. A demure look crossed her lovely features and he read something deeper in the depths of her eyes, but she hid all emotion well behind her mask of indifference.

Jin glanced at Dev. The man nodded once and let her go. He moved to join his crewmen as Mei led her friends toward the guest house next to the royal chambers. Jin didn't move. His family had not come out to greet his wayward bride and he was left alone with her.

"How's the family?" she asked, making polite conversation.

"Better now, thank you." Jin motioned for her to follow. Her shackles clinked lightly as she walked beside him. "How was your vacation?"

"It was actually a little rough. People kept trying to beat me up and kidnap me. Funny, they seemed almost motivated to capture me." She looked at him from beneath her long lashes. "It was almost as if someone had paid them to come after me. I swear, I have never been so popular in my life."

"I guess you have one of those faces," he answered. The eerie politeness between them was making him sick, but what else could he do but play her game?

"Must have," she agreed. "I see your palace walls haven't crumbled and the Zhang Empire is still in power."

"Yes, though we did have a bit of a scare." Jin walked with her toward the bridge that arched above the Enchanted River. Stopping, he leaned against the rail looking down at the gently undulating waters.

"I won't tell you where it is." Francesca put her back to the rail and looked in the opposite direction. They didn't touch, but Jin could feel the heat of her body. He had missed holding her. Even now, he wanted to pull her close.

"I won't ask," he assured her, "for I already know where it is."

"You do?" Her round eyes studied him. "How?"

"We found it hidden in your room on Torgan."

"We?" She shook her head. "You mean your sister. You didn't come to get me yourself. You sent Mei."

Jin didn't answer. What did it matter?

"So what now? Prison? Death? Slavery?" She sighed, as if they discussed the weather. "What kind of torture do you have in store for me?"

"The worst kind, I assure you."

Francesca quirked a brow.

Jin turned to her, placing his hip on the stone rail. Crossing his arm over his chest, he said, "The most horrific punishment I can think of."

"Torture?"

"Marriage."

"Marriage," she repeated in disbelief, her cool expression disappearing into a look of surprise.

"To me," he said.

"Marriage to you?" Her stunned look was comical, only Jin wasn't laughing. She tried to chuckle, but the sound died halfway out of her mouth.

"Yes. Marriage to me." He'd missed looking into her jade eyes.

"Ugh, but...." She wrinkled her nose. "Why?"

"What punishment is worse than making you stay as a princess in the Empire you loathe so much? In an Empire you would see destroyed?" Jin reached for a strand of her hair, pulling it thoughtfully between his fingers. It curled around his thumb in a gentle caress. Looking up, he watched her expression to see how she would react to his closeness. He wasn't surprised when she gave nothing away.

"So am I to be shackled to your side? Do you really want to live like that? It seems more punishment for you than for me. How else will you assure that I stay put?" She watched his hand. The silky texture of her long hair was their first contact in months, but he felt as if every nerve in his finger jump to life, spreading his desire for her over his entire body. The mass between his thighs rose, hoping for a chance to relive the ecstasy only her arms could bring.

"I've thought of that," he admitted. "And I think I have a solution that doesn't involve chains."

"What's that?"

"Your word as a student of Wushu." Jin's hand trembled and he let her go. Shivering, he tried not to let his pain show. "Your word on Master Chen Sun's soul. Swear to him that you will stay here on Líntiān, as my wife. Swear that you will be dutiful and will honor your new family and I promise you that you will be given all the luxury of being a princess, and all of the freedom. You will be taken care of and, if you wish it, a house will be built for you in the country where you can live out your days in leisure and solitude. I won't force myself on you, Francesca, just so you know."

"That part was never a problem," she said, giving a small grin. Francesca looked over the small palace river. He heard the chains clinking, as if her hands shook too badly to keep them quiet. "You will take the word of a thief?"

"I will take the word of Master Chen Sun's lover." Jin took a deep breath. Pain racked his soul. Saying the words hurt much worse than he imagined they would as he practiced them in his head. It felt as if his heart and soul were being ripped out of his chest, leaving a hole where his happiness had once so briefly lived.

"You know," she said softly, gripping the stone rail so hard her fingers turned white.

"Yes. I know you loved him."

Francesca nodded in agreement. Her lips pressed tightly together and a tear slipped over her face. "Yes, I loved him."

The death of his soul was complete. Jin knew he'd never be whole again. Nothing mattered now. All was lost.

\* \* \* \*

Francesca took a deep breath. Seeing Jin again wasn't as she pictured it in her mind. She had tried to convince herself that she wouldn't care, that it wouldn't affect her, that all feeling she had was dead.

It wasn't. Her heart was very much alive and right now it ached. Hearing Chen Sun's name on his lips, hearing him speak of her love for the dead Wushu master only intensified her guilt. She had told Sun she loved him, had dedicated her life to avenging his death. Did she now betray him by feeling something for the heir of those who sentenced him to death?

Jin had no idea how right he was when he said marriage to him would be the ultimate punishment. Naturally, she would honor her word, especially if she swore on her dead lover. Only, the punishment was not how he envisioned it. It would be punishment because Jin would be hers, in all senses but the most important. Her connection to the past, her promise to Sun would keep her from being able demonstrate her love for Jin completely and that was if the Zhang prince would even allow her to show him. And after what she did in taking the Jade Phoenix, he would never truly love or trust her in return. She couldn't blame him. She didn't deserve his trust.

"Mei told you what I said?" Francesca asked, remembering her conversation with the woman. She'd regretted it every moment since.

"She did." Jin looked up at the moonless sky and breathed deeply. He looked so calm and collected. How could he be calm when she felt like she was dying on the inside? "She said you spoke of your love for him and that you believed my family had him killed."

"They did. I saw everything."

*If you have nothing to fear, you have nothing to lose.*

Sun's words repeated themselves in her head. As she looked at Jin, she felt as if she'd already lost so much. Maybe she never really had any of it to begin with. Maybe love wasn't meant for her.

"I had already suspected as much. Tell me, how is it you were there and yet you live? If it is as you say, then the Zhang guards would not have let one with your skills live."

Francesca took a deep breath, not wanting to remember. She closed her eyes and the past came rushing in around her.

*We are all motivated by our desires. There are all types of seductions. The seduction of the flesh is the most obvious. The rogue seducing the untried virgin even more so. But there is also the seduction of an object worth having. The seduction of greed, lust, hate. What seduces you, sweet Francesca? What is it you desire most?*

It was the last lesson he'd taught her. His words had been rushed, as if he tried to communicate everything in the brief second he had to speak.

*Those are the questions you must ask yourself at every turn. To know yourself is to know truth. The beginning and the end of all things is inside you. Tonight, something ends so that another may start and someday you will finish it. You must promise me not to let all I've taught you die. You must promise me that you will destroy the ways of those who come to destroy me. Our ways must live. The actions of a few should not kill the ways of many.*

*How?* She had asked him.

*The Jade Phoenix. Go after the Jade Phoenix. Its power will lead you down the right path.*

Sun had pulled away from her then. She wanted to follow, but couldn't. He'd tied her up while she slept. The man had known death was coming for him and he didn't try and run.

For days he'd been plagued by visions of what was to come. He had refused to tell her anything. After his death, she knew he had seen his own end. He'd spoken of ending and beginning. That night his life ended and her life of vengeance began. She'd promised him she would never forget what he taught her. He asked her to take the Jade Phoenix, to destroy the ways of those who came for him. That was what she'd tried to do. Had she failed? Or did her actions somehow fulfill what Sun had told her to do.

*To know yourself is to know truth. The beginning and the end of all things is inside you.*

Francesca frowned. Blessed Stars! Why did he have to speak in his accursed riddles?! Why couldn't his message have been clear? A list of things that must be done?

*One, take Jade Phoenix. Two, sell Jade Phoenix. Three, let the Zhang Dynasty fall.*

No, instead she got, *Go after the Jade Phoenix. Its power will lead you down the right path.*

Not for the first time, she wished Sun was in front of her so she could shake him. What *exactly* did that mean? All she could do was translate it the best she knew how, and that was what she thought she'd done. She'd taken the artifact off the planet. What happened now that they had it back? Was this the path she was to take? To stay here as a princess? In ten years was the opportunity to end it all going to cross her path? How long did she wait? What did she do in the meantime?

"Francesca?" Jin prompted when she didn't speak.

*To know yourself is to know truth. The beginning and the end of all things is inside you.*

Maybe that meant she was to go with her feelings for Jin. The urge to stay was perhaps Sun's way of telling her to stay. Is that what he meant? Before coming to the planet, she had contemplated his words endlessly until she'd thought she understood. But now she was realizing they were not so simple. Jin's eyes beckoned her to speak. Without conviction as to her true path, she answered him.

"I was tied and bound. Sun told them I was his sex slave and they fought for a long time. Finally, after they killed him, they let me go. At the time, I knew very little Lintiänese so I can't tell you what they said to each other. Only later did I upload the language files, but by then the words had faded completely." Francesca's voice was dead. She remembered the night well. They'd just made love, so sweet and tender. Sun had been her first. How young she'd been, so grateful to him, and how wise he had seemed to her.

"Do you remember anything about the guards at all?" His tone was soft, inviting her to share.

Francesca took a deep breath and then another. She hoped she was doing the right thing. "No. But I remember Sun. There was always a sadness to his eyes, as he looked out over the stars. He longed for his home, a home he'd been exiled from."

"He told you he was exiled?"

"How would you phrase it? Your guards chased him out of the lands, killed all his friends, his family, his children. His soul was broken when he found me."

"Do not blame me for the deeds of my ancestors. That was long ago, years before I was born and Chen Sun was older than I am now. Do you even know how old he was? For I am only now beginning to understand how the outside world views age. Others do not live so long as we do."

"Yes, I'm sorry. You're right. I shouldn't have said you. I meant the guards of your ancestors attacked the Wushu village."

"And those ancestors are dead. My grandfather was in rule when the order was given and he was influenced by the will of his parents. I never would have ordered the annihilation of the Wushu followers."

Francesca laughed softly. "Don't call Sun an old man. He looked forty to me."

"We Líntiānese do age well," Jin agreed, giving her a ghost of a smile. "So that night you vowed to take the Jade Phoenix? To destroy us?"

"Yes. Sun used to talk about its power and how it fed the Zhang Empire."

"Then there it is. The whole affair laid out before us." Jin sighed. "At last, the truth."

"Yes. There it is."

"Thank you for telling me the truth, Francesca. I know now all that has happened between us could not be helped. Things have occurred as they were meant to. I know you don't want to be here, but I urge you to take my offer. Give me your word you will stay here, on my planet, as my wife and that you will not try to destroy us again. In return, I promise you I will let you live in peace. We will not have to see each other except when it is necessary. For all that has happened, it is not so bad a punishment, is it?"

There was no way for him to know how bad a punishment it was. Jin said nothing of love, so neither did she. Perhaps they were beyond that now. How could there be love and trust after all they had done to each other? She stole. He sent bounty hunters after her. Francesca was well aware that it was mostly her fault. In knowing this, she understood that she didn't deserve to ask his forgiveness. And that was if he'd ever loved her at all. It was possible he'd just been using the words to manipulate her, as she had manipulated him on their wedding night. When she told him she loved him, the words might have been true, but she said them for the wrong reason.

"You have my word, Jin. I will stay on this planet as your princess." The words were cold, as cold as she felt on the inside.

"Thank you."

She nodded once.

"Ah," Jin reached into his tunic and pulled out a small metal key. "Here, let me see your hands."

Francesca held out her hands and he freed her from the shackles, letting them drop to the bridge. Taking her wrists in his warm palms, he rubbed her sore flesh. Her skin tingled where he touched her. The desire she'd been trying to keep at bay as they spoke washed over her in a sudden undeniable wave. His fingers became caressing as his movements turned from administering to stroking.

"My ankles," she whispered, shivering at his nearness. She was afraid to say too much, as if doing so would break the magical spell weaving between them. Over two months had been too long a time to be without his touch. Sex had never been a problem between them, in fact it seemed to be the only thing they could get right.

Jin let go of her hands and kneeled before her. Francesca looked around. They were all alone. She couldn't even detect any guards. Swallowing, she looked at the orange torchlight glowing on Jin's dark hair. She loved to watch the way he moved. He was a man of dignity and grace. The traits were bred into him and yet warred with other emotions in him as well. When she looked at him, she saw shades of a man wanting to get out, a man trapped behind decorum and trained to the point that honor was all he knew. There was nothing wrong with honor, but it saddened her to see a man so controlled by it. Honor and duty made him marry her and that said enough. She had no doubt that if he didn't have to, he never would have taken her as a bride.

"I'm sorry you married me, Jin," she whispered. If he heard her he never showed it and she couldn't bring herself to say the words aloud again. *But I'm not sorry I married you. I tried to be, but I can't.*

Jin lifted the hem of her gown and reached for her foot. His hands wrapped around her ankle as he worked to free her. The shackles clanked on the ground. Jin stayed where he was, rubbing her ankles as he had her hands. When she didn't protest, he grew bolder, running his fingers higher along her calf. He touched the back of her knee and she gasped in pleasure at the intimate contact.

Francesca's head fell back on her shoulders. Her heart pounded in excitement and just a trace of fear. Jin always had this effect on her. Their troubles faded until all she could feel were the primitive urges of her body radiating from between her thighs. It was easy to embrace the physical pleasure when everything else between them brought such heartache and pain. She willed him to reach higher beneath her gown. Her hips wiggled slightly and he looked up. His gaze bored forward, piercing her to her soul, beckoning her not to stop him. She looked into his eyes and a silent understanding passed between them.

Anticipation made her giddy. Her breathing deepened. He grew bolder, running his hands up and down both of her legs. Francesca braced her hand on the railing, leaning her butt against the hard stone for support.

The cool night air caressed her thighs as he lifted her gown higher. She wore no undergarments beneath the thick silk and his harsh breathing sounded over them as he reached her naked hips. Digging his fingers into her flesh he pressed his face close to her stomach. The shackles clanked as he pushed them out of his way with his knee. Her body ached and she longed to feel his delicious mouth on her sex, pleasuring her.

*I've missed you. I've missed this.*

Jin rubbed his cheek along her thigh, massaging her with the silk. Slowly the material rode further up and his face met her inner thigh. His lips brushed her naked skin, as he kissed a hot, wet trail along the delicate flesh.

His teeth nipped her. Jolts of pleasure shot along her nerves until every inch of her burned with desire. Her nipples ached for attention, but her legs were too weak for her to let go of the rail. Jin bit her again, soothing the ache with his tongue. The tip swirled a haphazard pattern to the crease where her leg met her hip. With each brush of his lips, the more aroused she became until she was sure her thighs would explode from the pressure. Groaning, he centered himself over her. His hot mouth intimately captured her as his tongue parted her moist folds. The sound of his voice vibrated his pleasure over her. He kissed her gently, focusing his attentions on the hard bud he found waiting for him.

Francesca moaned softly, rocking into him. The stars surrounded her, blurring her vision as her eyesight dimmed to everything around her. Jin's mouth sucked greedily at her taste and the sound of his private kiss only aroused her more. His fingers dug into her hips, hard and grasping. His tongue went deep, riding up into her body.

Without thought, she rode his tongue. Teeth grazed her clit and she cried out softy. "Ah, yes. Yes."

Francesca came, shivering hard as she jerked against his mouth. When he pulled back, her thighs were sticky from their passion.

Jin stood. His mouth captured hers and the sweet taste of his kiss was on her lips. The pleasure of her climax still warmed her blood, running like a euphoric drug throughout her senses. Weakly, she wrapped her arms about his neck, unable to control the need for more.

Francesca smelled only him, the natural scent of his body. Pulling him roughly into her kiss, she warred with him for control of the passionate embrace. She thrust her tongue into his mouth. Each time she was with him more of her mind slipped into the mindless fog. She felt safe in his arms and couldn't force her mind to listen for danger beyond them. With Jin, she felt no danger from the outside world. Nothing out there could hurt her as much as the man in her arms.

Jin pressed his tight erection against her stomach. She remembered all too well the feel of him inside her, the way he could move his hips in a perfect rhythm. The Líntiānese palace disappeared until there was nothing else--only Jin and what he was doing to her.

Suddenly, he pulled back, his erection still pressed tightly against her. He was breathing as hard as she was and his look held desperation and pleading. His dark eyes reflected the torchlight in their depths, so real that it looked like flames actually wrapped around his pupils for a brief moment.

Francesca moaned, grabbing his face and forcing him back to her lips. She kissed him deeply until she had conquered every last inch of his mouth.

Aggressively, he pressed her tight against the rail as she reached between them to pull up his silk tunic. She succeeded and the length of his chiseled body fitted to hers, firm and unyielding, until every flex of his strong hips seemed to grind his erection into her softer stomach. Parting her thighs to let him rock more intimately against her, she wished his pants would just melt away.

He ground his arousal along her, stimulating her sensitive bud through his clothing. She moaned into his mouth, lightheaded from his deep kiss and unwilling to break it to get air. Frantically, she pushed at his waist to untie his waistband. He broke the kiss, gasping for breath as she caught hold on his naked shaft.

A growl sounded it the back of his throat. He ripped her gown open, revealing a breast as his palm cupped her, squeezing the mound as he pinched her nipple hard. Jin was tense, rigid to the point of demanding. He looked dominant, virile, strong, and so very beautiful outlined in orange torchlight. It wasn't just his tight, muscled body either. It was in the way he held himself, the gracefully superior way he moved against her.

Francesca stroked him as she parted her thighs. He grabbed her hips. Lifting her up, he angled his body to hers. It didn't matter that they still wore clothing. The need to feel him was too strong. She clutched at him, pulling him closer.

Jin guided himself into her willing body, pushing hard as he filled her completely. Her body hung precariously over the rail, but she wasn't scared. Jin held her hips tight, keeping her from falling. Wildly, he pumped into her, hitting hard against her core as he buried his face against her naked chest. His hot mouth brushed along her exposed nipple and he sucked it hard between his teeth.

There was so much heat and friction that she couldn't help but moan his name over and over, urging him to take her harder and faster. He did, moving with swift speed in and out, in and out. She arched her back, taking all he had to give.

"*Bâobèi,*" he groaned against her breast. "*Nî hâo mêi.*"

She smiled at the compliment as he told her how beautiful she was. Francesca wanted to be beautiful--for him.

Pleasure exploded throughout her body and she was unable to scream even as her mouth fell open. Jin only thrust harder, forcing her to ride out her climax. He pumped into her trembling depths, his movements becoming jerky as he neared his own release.

Suddenly, he stopped. His hips jerked one last time as he came inside her. Francesca closed her eyes. For a long moment they didn't move, their bodies pressed tightly together. Her body soared to know that he could still be with her like this, that he didn't hate her too much to have sex with her. It might not be love, but it was something and she clung to what they had with both hands and refused to let go.

Jin pulled away. The cool air caressed her skin as her silk gown fell around her legs. After he righted his clothing, Jin held his arm to the side, silently motioning to the end of the bridge, urging her down the path with him. The shackles stayed on the bridge as he walked with her in silence. Francesca didn't want there to be words between them. Not now. What could they really say to each other?

Going into the royal chambers, Jin opened the door to his room before stepping aside to let her go in first. He didn't protest as she went to his bed to lie down. Exhaustion overtook her and she didn't want to think. Jin crawled in beside her, not touching her as they both fell asleep.

## Chapter Thirteen

When Francesca opened her eyes, Jin was resting on his side, studying her intently. He wore a dark green bathing robe with black dragons on it. It was belted along the front. He smelled fresh and exotic, like he'd already been in the decontaminator and his skin glistened as if he'd rubbed herbal oil on it. Her first sleepy instinct was to smile, but his words stopped her.

"You said last night that Chen Sun found you. Where did he find you?"

Pushing up from the bed, she held her disheveled gown to her chest and slowly stood. One of her shoes had been kicked off in the night and the other was still on her foot. Kicking, she flung the remaining shoe off and walked toward the decontaminator. It was the only place she could think of to hide her face from him without running out the door. "Can't we leave the past be? Do you really wish to discuss this more?"

"I am your husband. I think I have a right to know these things," he said.

Francesca lifted a brow as if to say 'Oh, really?' and slid the door to the decontaminator room closed. When she was out of sight, her expression fell and she held completely still. She took a deep breath, doing her best to keep her breathing calm so he couldn't hear its staggering pattern.

"Would you tell me as your friend then?" he called from the other side. "If not as your husband?"

She rolled her eyes, not really mocking him but more herself. "Are we friends?"

"I think it might make for an easier time together, don't you? Unless you prefer to fight me all the time."

Francesca slipped out of her gown. His voice was muffled by the door, but she could understand him fine.

"He bought me at an auction," she answered as she stepped into the unit. A tear slipped over her cheek and the decontaminator's lasers automatically targeted it, drying the moisture instantly.

There was a long pause. "So you really were his s-se...."

"Sex slave?" she offered. Another tear fell and that one was cleaned up just as fast as the first.

"You were?"

"No."

"Then, why did he purchase you?"

Francesca shook her head. Lasers scanned over her body, their green light tickling as it ran over her form. She lifted her hair, making sure it was thoroughly cleaned. "To save me. I was an orphan raised by a religious sect. The monastery was raided ... *blessed comet*, it must have been fifteen, sixteen, maybe even up to eighteen years ago now. Honestly, I can't really tell you, I lost track of time there for awhile and the monastery wasn't big on personal information like ages and birthdays, let alone things like keeping track of the years. Truth be told, I didn't even know how to tell time until I met Chen Sun. As for my age, we guessed at it one night and I've kept track by that ever since."

"So you do not know what your parents are?"

"No one ever told me if they knew. I assume humanoid." She took a deep breath, not saying more.

"Go on. What happened after the raid?"

"I was brought to the Torgan slave auctions. I had a knack for escape and got away. From there I lived in the Torgan ductwork for a time before they flushed the pipes and out came me in the dirty flushwater supply. The men who found me didn't know what to make of me so they decided to earn some extra space credit. I was put on the auction block and that's when Chen Sun found me. He said I had spirit."

"What made him think that?" Jin's voice was closer. Francesca jumped and looked at the door. She could see it easily from her place in the decontaminator unit. She had no idea why she felt so shy this morning, when that had never been a quality she possessed before. She saw Jin's shadow through the white of the thin door. His hand was lifted against the frame, but he didn't make a move to enter.

"I bit the ear off of one of the auctioneers."

Jin laughed. "Now that does not surprise me."

Francesca kept an eye on his image. The shadow of his finger traced absently along the door.

"And he taught you Wushu?" Jin asked.

"Yes." For a moment, her eyes clouded as she remembered. "He started my training. He said I had a natural aptitude for it. I've always had stamina and healed fast and am a quick study."

"And who finished your training?"

"I did." Francesca couldn't stop herself from answering. Jin asked, and she answered. She wanted him to know about her, wanted to tell him, wanted him to understand so maybe someday he'd forgive what she had done, even if he couldn't forget.

"How was that?"

"The night the Imperial guards kill ... *came*, I found some old manuscripts with translations written in so that I could understand them. Sun had left them where he'd known I would look. I devoted every moment to study and I even picked fights for practice. As my talent grew, I became bolder, stealing small and then bigger. I am hardly a master, but my talent increases. Perhaps someday I will have perfected the art."

"What if I asked you not to practice it? To let the art form die?"

"I wouldn't agree. I can't Jin. I promised Sun on his dying day to continue the way of Wushu."

"What if I asked you to teach me?" His voice had softened. "Would you now consider me worthy of learning?

Francesca took a deep breath. Teach Jin Wushu? Stepping from the decontaminator she made her way to the door. Her hand shaking, she pushed it open. His eyes met hers. He was serious.

"I thought your people didn't approve of Wushu." She watched him closely as he answered.

"Maybe they were wrong." His expression didn't falter.

"Why do you wish to learn?"

"Because the ways of the past should not die." His lids fell over her gaze, shading his features from her. She loved the look of his face, the shape of his eyes, the darkness of their depths. "Because I believe it is not the art that caused the problems of the past, but a man. Master Ming Bo started the Wushu Uprisings. He and his followers. The tradition is not to blame, but those who misused it."

Francesca swallowed. Was this what Sun had sent her to do? To give Wushu back to his people? Did he know that the Jade Phoenix would be recovered? Did he see this in his dreams?

*The Jade Phoenix,* Sun had said to her. *Go after the Jade Phoenix. Its power will lead you down the right path.*

Was teaching Wushu her path? All this time she thought she was supposed to bring down his killers. Was instead her goal to reform them?

Very carefully, she whispered, "Before Chen Sun died, he said to me, 'You must promise me not to let all I've taught you die. Our ways must live.'"

"Does that mean you will teach me?" Jin cupped her cheek, pulling her gaze back up to his.

Francesca nodded. When Sun had spoken the words, this might not have been what he had in mind, but in a way it did fulfill his wishes. The truth was, she no longer knew what he had in mind. All she could do was do her best to honor him and that's what she'd done. Teaching a Zhang prince would ensure the legacy of the Wushu lived on.

Jin lowered himself to his knees and bowed his head before her. "Then I become your willing student, Master Francesca."

Francesca shivered. "I'm not a Master."

Jin's eyes met hers. "You are the only one we have. Do you accept me?"

Francesca reached out, placing her hand on Jin's head as he bowed once more. Standing naked before him, she stated, "I become your willing Master, Pupil Zhang Jin."

Jin surged to his feet, a grin on his face as he lifted her around the waist. Carrying her naked body to the bed he flung her down and crawled on top of her.

"This wasn't the lesson I had in mind, Pupil Jin," she laughed as Jin stopped to kiss each breast. His sudden burst of energy surprised and excited her. Her heart beat hard against her chest.

"Ah, well, perhaps I should take you on as my pupil." He pulled the belt free and parted the front of his dragon robe, revealing that he was completely naked beneath.

"You think to be a master in the bedroom?" she asked, grinning. Never had she felt so giddy. With Sun, there had always been an overwhelming sadness between them. There was love, but it wasn't carefree or without its wounds. Scars from the past had affected them both. With Jin, there was something else. She refused to say deeper because that didn't seem fair, but it was what it was and it definitely was different.

"I have ways I have yet to show to you, my princess." Jin traced his finger from her neck to her navel.

Francesca shivered, running her hands into his hair. She couldn't help thinking yet again that they might fail when it came to emotions, but this part they were pretty good at. "Well, if you put it that way, I become your most willing pupil, Master Jin."

"Mm," he chuckled against the valley of her breasts, nestling his face between the two globes. "I like you calling me Master."

"Aren't you forgetting something?" Francesca looked down, seeing his dark hair against her skin. Running her fingers into the soft locks, she toyed with the ends.

"Oh, yeah." He ran his hand down her stomach and cupped her sex with his palm.

"No," she laughed. "Do you accept me as a pupil?"

"Mm," he nestled between her breasts before lifting up to look at her. "Yes, I become you most willing Master, *bâobèi*. Now turn on your stomach so I can explore my pupil."

\* \* \* \*

Francesca looked around the table as she played with the two ivory eating sticks. She'd almost forgotten the horror of her first taste of Líntiānese dining culture, but now it came back to her full force. The table was larger than before with two floor cushion seats added to accommodate Jarek and Mei.

Like the first time, the plates were handcrafted pottery, but instead were painted with gold stripes on red. As Jarek and Mei told stories from their time together in space and discussed Mei's upcoming labor, Francesca skated the sticks over the table. At least this time they weren't sitting in silence staring at her, and the hall wasn't crowded with nobles as it had been before.

Jin caught her eyes, as he was silently watching her in the seat beside her. He gave her a small smile. There was an easiness between them that hadn't existed before. She was scared of saying too much about it for fear she'd ruin it.

"What are these things called?" she asked softly, holding

up the sticks to Jin.

*"Kuay tzu,"* he said, cupping the small bowl and taking a drink. "Chopsticks."

The soft sounds of the family's conversation were punctuated by the more robust sounds coming from Jarek's crew who were seated a few feet away at their own table. There were no guests in the large hall, just the two tables. Francesca noticed that everything was still precise with decorum, but the family seemed more relaxed. Rick smiled at her and winked. Francesca had begun a friendship with the playful man while on the ship and knew he was offering to help make her husband jealous. The last thing she needed was trouble. She shook her head slightly and he laughed before looking away. Jin caught the gesture and turned around to study the other table. When he again looked at her, he'd quirked a brow. Francesca shrugged nonchalantly and quickly pretended like she was interested in what Mei and Fen were discussing about baby names.

"What do you think of Shaming?" Fen asked. The woman smiled at her. They hadn't spoken since Francesca's return, but the princess didn't seem to be holding a grudge. Francesca had worried about that since Fen had been so nice to her the first time she was there.

"For a boy or girl?" Jarek asked, confused.

"Boy, of course," Fen said. "And for a girl, Rong or Da-Xia."

"Huan Yue," Haun offered.

"Or Shu Fang?" the empress added.

"I was thinking Sying," Mei said. To her husband, she offered, "It means star."

"I like Star." Jarek nodded thoughtfully.

"No, Sying," Mei corrected.

Jarek frowned. "But my people will understand Star."

"Don't your brothers, the other *ten nai* princes, have children?" Fen questioned Jarek.

*"Ten nai?"* Francesca quietly asked Jin.

"Tiger men," he answered just as softly.

"Ah." Francesca nodded in understanding. Jarek's brothers were shifters as well.

"What are their names?" Shen asked.

"Korbin, Roderic, Payton, Aliya and Emma," Jarek answered with obvious pride.

The Zhang family made faces of uncertainty.

"A-li-ya?" Fen repeated, looking at Lian for confirmation.

"This will be a royal child," the emperor said delicately to Mei, as if it needed explaining. "He must have a name he can be proud of."

Francesca watched Jarek to see if he was insulted. He shared a look with his wife, but didn't seem upset. He winked at her and they both took a drink of the sweet liquor.

Servants brought the food, placing it on the table. Red dishes with gold stripes matched the dinnerware. The empress served the meal, giving Francesca an extra helping of the steamed red flowers from the nearby farmlands.

"Francesca favors the *hong jio ju*?" Mei asked.

"She is a *sù shí zhe*," Lian said.

Mei laughed, shaking her head. "No. She ate meat on the ship every day. In fact, she hardly ate anything else."

The royal family turned to look at Francesca, who in turn looked helplessly at Jin. Her husband smiled, but didn't offer any help.

"Uh, the religious observance is over," she answered faintly.

The emperor and empress nodded, satisfied with the answer. Mei quirked a brow, nudging Jarek in the ribs with her elbow when he started to chuckle. They'd gotten into a religious conversation on the ship and both knew she was lying. Jin hurriedly changed the subject.

"I like Park," Jin said, "for a boy or girl."

"Huh," Jarek said thoughtfully, turning to Mei. "Parker."

"Park," Mei repeated. "I like it."

"Parker," Jarek said under his breath.

"We'll discuss it later," Mei answered just as softly.

The emperor stood raising his bowl. The hall instantly quieted. "Finally, names are chosen. Park and Park!"

The hall cheered. Mei and Jarek exchanged looks. In unison they said, "Park it is."

The emperor sat and it was one of the rare times Francesca had ever seen the stoic man smile.

"And when might we expect a child from you?" the empress asked, looking directly at Francesca and Jin. "Now that you are home, I expect Jin has explained our expectation to you."

Jin made a weak noise and Francesca could feel the blood

draining from her face.

"Hmm, I see," the emperor said.

Francesca busied herself eating the silky flower petals as the next course was served. Thankfully, she wasn't considered the guest of honor and was saved from having to eat something with eyeballs still intact.

After dinner, Lian suggested the family retire to the Imperial Gardens for afternoon games. The emperor stood, reaching for his wife to help her up, prompting the others to follow behind them. Jarek's crew was invited to play and they eagerly accepted, but insisted that they first must leave an offering of liquor for Zhang An's spirit. From what Francesca could gather the woman had made a prediction for them about their lives being affected by the five Líntiānese elements and it was driving them crazy because they couldn't figure it out.

"Come with me," Jin said softly as they left the dining hall, grabbing Francesca by the hand. He pulled her behind him, as he walked away from the others toward the front of Honorable City.

"What? Why?"

He stopped. "Do you really wish to stay here playing games and answering uncomfortable questions about babies, which by the way is all my mother's doing. Or would you rather get out of here?"

Francesca glanced behind them at the others before turning back to him. "What did you have in mind?"

"Come on. Follow me." Stopping at the front gate, Jin pushed at a stone. It slid to the side and he spoke, "Transportation for two."

Francesca stared at the stone in awe. "You do have the palace on computer, don't you?"

Is that how they caught her the first two times? Had she set off some kind of special alarm? And why didn't it go off the third time?

"Some of it," he answered. "I would've shown you if you'd have stuck around long enough to learn anything about my home."

"Oh, trust me. I learned plenty about your home when I was here last time. It's all any of you could talk about. I felt as if every conversation was a lesson in Líntiānese culture." Francesca cleared her throat and affected a Líntiānese accent. "You see, Francesca, the silk worm came from Earth and eats mulberries. That is how we get clothing. And this button is called a frog. See that carving on the door? Those are gods, made to protect those who enter into the Exalted Hall. And jade, oh, jade is so precious to us. Jade is like our virtues. It represents wholesomeness, intellect, righteousness, music, art, sculpture, honesty, earth and the heavens, truth, justice. All the things you are not."

"I never said that," Jin denied, appearing appalled. "Not once did I mention silk worms."

"Ah!" she hit him in the arm.

He laughed, before catching himself. Clearing his throat, he affected a serious air. "I never said you weren't virtuous."

"You never said I was."

"You...." he hesitated. "What do you want me to say, Francesca? You are a thief. You stole from my family. I gave you trust and you stole from me."

How could she deny it? Francesca knew better than to even try. Luckily, she was saved from answering as a large craft pulled up in front of them. From what she could see, no one drove the vehicle. The dark brown wood was accented with gold and red. An eye was painted on one side next to the Líntiānese character for the Zhang family name and a large metal hook hung from the front.

"Is that a...." Francesca frowned, looking up at the giant sails. "A boat? Who is driving it?"

"It is called a *tu di hang*. It means land boat or land craft and it is programmed to pull up to the front of the palace. It has self-navigation, but the outer core is designed after," Jin paused. "Never mind. *Duìbùqî.* I know you do not wish to hear about our culture."

Francesca looked at the land craft and decided that maybe her first step would be to learn all she could about her new homeland. Jin was proud of what he was and she needed to respect that. If she showed an interest, maybe she could prove that she was willing to try.

*Small steps, Francesca. Do not rush anything. You want this friendship to work.*

"Actually, go ahead and tell me," she said.

Jin looked at her surprised. She made a face at him and he cleared his throat.

"All right," Jin said, looking back at the vehicle. "The

design is based off of the ancient Junk ships from Earth, before they knew of space and other planets."

Francesca laughed. "Can you imagine? Thinking that you're the only beings of people out there? How archaic. Humans actually thought they were the only species in all these star systems."

Jin chuckled. "I've heard that long before that they believed their Earth was flat and if they got into their boats, they could sail right off the side of the planet."

Francesca couldn't contain herself. "Okay, now you are making that up! No one would believe that, not even a primitive culture."

"Possibly. An ancestor told me the story when I was a child."

"Ancestor? Do you mean like your grandparents? Are they still alive? Have I seen them at the palace and just didn't realize it?"

Jin looked down at his hands and made a weak sound. "Ah, no, not alive, but you did meet my grandfather, Manchu, in a way."

Francesca's brow rose. "You're going to have to explain that one as well."

"The day we met at the *Qi-zi* ceremony," Jin began.

"*Qi-zi*? As in wife?" she asked, arching a brow as she looked at him in disbelief. "That was a wife ceremony?"

"Yes. Women come in hopes that a match will be made with a prince." Jin grinned. It was the charmingly arrogant smile of a man who knew his marital worth.

"Is that why you asked for me? You had to pick someone and I was better than anything else you'd seen?"

"No, that wasn't it."

"Okay. So you hoped that your family would forbid the marriage and you wouldn't have to marry anyone at all? You picked me to make them mad."

"No." Jin moved toward the land craft and ran his hand over the protruding, decorative eye. It lit up and scanned his palm. The red light blinked twice before the side opened and a wooden stairway came out from the side. It lowered to the ground for them to walk on.

Jin held his hand out hovering along her lower back and guided Francesca to the stairs, without touching her. She grabbed the rail, holding her silk gown to the side as she stepped up the steep incline to the oval deck. Wooden walls wrapped all the way around the sides. Three stiff canvas sails were unfurled overhead. Their large span cast shadows over the deck. Toward the back a small row of steps led up to a small platform that overlooked the distance.

"The sails can capture the wind, but they are not necessary to make the land craft move. We've combined the ancient designs and modern technology. The ship hovers over the land and…. Do you see that?" He pointed at the hook. "It is an anchor for weighing down the ship as it stops and there," he pointed toward the back, leaning over the side, "is the back rudder for controlling the movements so that we may drive manually if we have to. However, the virtual controls make for a much smoother ride."

Francesca stood beside him, leaning over the rail. Their arms brushed and she turned to look up at him, not seeing the rudder. Jin stepped back, coughing as he moved away.

"Were you rebelling against tradition?" she asked, not letting him off the hook too easily.

"Ah, no."

"Fine, don't tell me why." She openly frowned at him. "I believe you were saying something about the *Qi-zi* ceremony?"

"You want to know why I picked you." Jin refused to meet her gaze.

"Isn't that what I've been trying to get out of you since you did it?"

Jin glanced up, looking apologetic. "The truth is I didn't pick you."

Francesca froze. "What? No. I heard you. I was there. You pointed at me and said that you chose me to be your bride. The whole hall heard you. You did pick me, Jin."

"I didn't pick you, *bâobèi*. I never would have picked you." Jin gave her an almost repentant smile as he looked at her.

"Don't call me *bâobèi*. You can't say something like that and then call me *bâobèi*." Francesca scowled at him. The breeze stirred around her, flapping the sails. "You said you were compelled."

"Yes, compelled by my ancestors. One ancestor in particular." Jin glanced around, looking up at the sails. "My grandfather."

"He convinced you," she asked, confused.

"He possessed me. I had no choice." Jin took a deep breath. "His spirit entered me and made me act."

"Your dead ancestor possessed you," she repeated in disbelief. Well, that was a new form of rejection if she'd ever heard one. He didn't want to pick her, he was forced by dead people to do so. Throwing her hands to the side, she mumbled, "Wonderful."

"Does this really bother you?"

"No," Francesca lied. He searched her face for a moment and then, as if he believed her, nodded. Looking around, she said, "So, you going to teach me to drive this thing or what?"

## Chapter Fourteen

Jin pressed the accelerator on the computer console, making the *tu di hang* go faster. The lush Líntiānese countryside flew by in a blur. The red of the giant *hong jio ju* flowers blended against the blades of the yellow-blue grasses. In the background, a forest blocked out the horizon. They were far from the palace, having driven over the land at high speeds.

Every once in a while they'd see a few farmhouses that were clustered close together to form a village, standing out against the pale blue of the cloudless sky. Líntiān truly was as close to paradise as any planet in the known galaxies. Jin was happy to be home. Space was not for him. This was where he belonged--on Líntiān.

He wondered if Francesca could ever feel the same. She didn't smile as she looked over the land. The wind whipped her hair, trailing it behind her head in long, dark trails. In the blue silk gown, she looked like she belonged. That was until he saw her face. Her features weren't those of a Líntiānese woman. Jin didn't care, and barely noticed the fact anymore. She was beautiful, more beautiful than any other woman he'd ever laid eyes on. He wanted to tell her, but couldn't make the words come out. There was an uneasy truce between them and he didn't wish to break it.

"There!" Francesca yelled, pointing in the distance to a hill that overlooked the valley they traveled in. Near it was the forest. As he turned the craft, the trees slowly came more into view, their spiny leaves pointing upward toward the sun. The leaves traveled with the sun, pointing always in its direction. At night, they would fall down, only to rise again on the other side as the sun came with the dawn.

"That is the *Hsi Yang* Forest," Jin said. "It is short for *Guoh Yuan Hsi Yang*, which means 'orchard of the setting sun'."

"That is where I want my house," Francesca said. Jin didn't meet her eyes, but could feel them on him. "You said I could live outside the palace in the countryside. I want a house right there. A small one--"

"You are a princess," Jin interrupted. "Nothing is small. There are guards and security. A wall will have to be built around the--"

"No, no walls," she said. "I want to see the landscape."

"But--"

"I can take care of myself, Jin. I'll bend on a few guards, but I don't want big walls blocking everything out. I want to see the countryside. If you put walls around me, I'll feel caged. I'll go mad like that."

"I will speak to my father on it," he conceded.

"Talk all you want. You build them, I'll have them torn down." Francesca smiled. "Yes, this is the place. No one owns the land do they? They won't be upset with me for living there?"

"It will be an honor for them." Jin slowed the land craft and the wind died suddenly as they drifted at an easier pace.

"Who owns it? Let's go make sure. I won't be a bother to anyone and I won't take anyone's land from them. I'd have the people's permission first." She gave him a stern look.

"Now? You wish to inquire about it now?

"Why not? We're already out here."

"But, there are no…." Jin looked behind them. They were all alone.

"What? You need a procession and horns announcing your presence to go anywhere? Come on. They are people. We are people. We'll sit down and ask, like people." Francesca elbowed him to the side to take the electronic helm. "So, which way?"

Jin pointed toward the hill. "Just a ways past the other side."

"At least you know who owns it," she said. "That's a start, Jin."

"What do you mean to imply?" He wasn't sure if he should be insulted by her words or not.

"I mean that these are your people and you and your family shut yourselves off from them like they carry the blue plague. Aren't you even curious what goes on outside the palace walls?"

"We are told what happens beyond the palace walls."

"I'm not talking about some general's report. I'm talking about seeing for yourself. Do they have festivals? How do they celebrate? Who makes the best food in the land?"

"The palace chefs," Jin said with certainty.

"How do you know? Have you tasted everyone's cooking?"

"Why would I want to impose upon them?"

"You could look at it that way, or you could think of returning the favor and inviting your host to the palace. And I mean invite, not decree."

"You suddenly have very definite ideas of how things are done here," he said.

Francesca bit her lip and reached into her gown. Pulling out a folded scroll, she handed it to him. "I was going to give it back. Last night, after you fell asleep, I snuck into the library and did some reading up on what it is I've agreed to be. I wanted to know what I'd gotten myself into."

Jin looked at the scroll. The once rolled parchment was folded from where she'd carried it. The keeper of the library would be annoyed by that fact as it was an old document. The writings were about decorum and what was expected of the royal children. It was meant to be a learning tool for the very young, but since Francesca was new to her title, he supposed it was a good place for her to start. He just wished he knew she was reading it beforehand. It would have been nice to have been prepared for her sudden attacks on the way they did things.

"This is just a guideline," he said. "We use it to train royal children in the very basic ways. Not everything is set in stone."

"Oh, so you do leave the palace?" Her wide eyes stared at him, prying away at pieces of his soul.

"No. Not really."

"Then, you invite peasants to the palace to dine?" she asked.

"Um, no. We don't really do that either. Nobles come."

"Ah, so what part of this scroll is just a guideline?" Her smile was mischievous, daring him to argue with her.

"The home you are looking for is over there." He ignored her baiting and pointed to a small cluster of farms. He steered the land craft in the direction of the village. A wooden sign with three Líntiānese characters flapped in the wind before the main road leading in front of the first houses.

"What does that say?" Francesca asked, pointing at it.

"*Tan jau dern.* Searchlight. This village is the first called when someone or something is lost in the *Hsi Yang* Forest. It was established as an outpost to the palace and eventually turned into a farmstead as men brought their families to live with them here."

"I'll give you points for knowing that much," she said, winking.

"Thank you," he answered wryly.

Villagers came out to greet them, surprised looks on their faces, as the *tu di hang* came to a stop. Francesca smiled at them, but they weren't comforted by the look. They whispered to themselves, gesturing frantically at the royal land craft.

"By the way," Francesca said as Jin lowered the stairs to the ground. "Any chance you have some uploads at the palace?"

"What kind?"

"Your language files for one. The one I used was incomplete."

"I think you're doing all right," he offered.

"Thanks, but I'd like one anyway. And also reading and writing."

"You know, it was said that the Wushu learned calligraphy the old way, through years of daily practice."

"Well, being as I am technically the only Wushu master left, there really isn't anyone around to teach it to me, is there?"

"I'll see what I can find."

"Thank you." Francesca's smile grew as she stepped down the stairs. Jin knew it was possible the villagers didn't recognize her as they had yet to lead the procession through the villages to introduce the newest princess. Actually, it was possible some of them didn't recognize him, but for the royal dragon print on his long tunic.

"*Ni hao,*" Francesca said to everyone. "Hello."

"*Ni hao,*" the villagers answered timidly, one right after another. They looked more at Jin than at her. As Jin stepped down, they bowed low to the ground. Francesca arched a brow.

"You are not going to change millenniums of tradition in one day," he whispered to her in the star language she was comfortable in, so the people couldn't understand if they heard him. "Get used to the bowing."

"Oh, the bowing I don't mind," she said, grinning. "Who doesn't like to have people worshiping at their feet?"

Was she teasing him?

"Stand, please," Jin said in their native tongue so they could understand him.

"Prince Jin, you honor us." One of the older men stepped forward. Jin could tell by his clothing that he was a man of power within the village. Like the other farmers, his clothes were earth-toned in color and simple in design. The browns and dark reds matched the colors of the planet because they were crafted from natural fibers. On their heads, they wore saucer-shaped hats woven from the bark of the spiny trees found in the *Hsi Yang* Forest. They offered protection from the sun when out in the fields all day tending the *hong jio ju* crop.

"I have come to present my wife, Princess Zhang Francesca, to the village," Jin announced. The people instantly turned to her bowing low as they'd done to him.

"Please, stand," Francesca said, stepping forward. Jin made a move to stop her, but he was too late. She'd already reached one of the women and was holding out her hand. The woman looked at it and stepped back. The woman's wrinkled hands were soiled from the fields and she wouldn't dare touch the princess. "It's all right."

The woman looked at the others and slowly held out her hand, not touching. She kept her dirty palm up so the princess could see it. Francesca took the hand and clasped it without hesitation. "Hello, I'm Francesca." The woman drew her hand back as the princess let go, glancing at it in surprise. "And you are?"

"Ye Xiu," the woman said softly.

"Very nice to meet you Xiu." Francesca moved to the next person and held out her hand. "*Ni hao.*"

Jin watched, amazed as she took the time to introduce herself and greet every person in the village, even the children. The villagers appeared confused by the interaction, especially the village elders, but they weren't rude as the princess paid her respects.

After Francesca had finished, she turned to Master Pan the head elder. "If you are not too busy, I would love a tour of your village."

Master Pan's chest lifted slightly as he nodded once. Jin shot his wife a rueful smile and fell into step next to her. In her language, he said, "You are determined to stir the pot, aren't you?"

"I have no idea what that means," she answered in kind, "but yes. Yes, I am. If these people are to be my neighbors, it will be better if they like me. Besides, I don't cook and someone is going to have to either show me or feed me. In my experiences, working folk tend to be the best at both things."

"Ah, so that is why you wished to know who the best cook in Muntong was." Jin laughed. Master Pan stopped and the prince motioned him to continue walking. He fell quiet as the elder gave a tour of the small village. There wasn't much to see, but Francesca politely inquired about everything, occasionally requesting that Jin translate some sign for her or elaborate when she didn't understand what Master Pan said.

The village of Searchlight was like many others in the empire. The homes were clustered close together, each with their own private family garden. They were modest dwellings, but pride had been taken in their construction. Aside from the homes, the village shared barns and meeting houses. Only a dozen families lived in this particular village, making for a very tightly woven community.

After the tour of the outside, Master Pan invited them to join him for tea in his home. Jin followed Francesca's lead, enjoying the way she interacted with the commoners. He had to admit, he was a little out of his depth, as his family had never before talked with their subjects on such a familiar level. Seeing children staring at him from behind a barn, he stopped and bowed, palm to fist, to them. They scurried away in a fit of excitement.

Master Pan's home was as modest as the rest of the town, but it was clean and had lovely decorations upon the wall. An old scroll listing his family's many great deeds was in the center. Stained wooden planks made up the floors and walls. From the front room, there was a view of the courtyard garden. Artistic pots held plants along stone walkway and dried herbs decorated the arches leading outside. Latticework screens, hand-painted with delicate trees and forest scenery, were placed along the wall, ready for use should they need to block off a portion of the room.

"This is lovely," Francesca exclaimed, running her finger along the edge of the screen.

"Thank you," Master Pan said, smiling at his wife as she shuffled in to place a tray on the table. She placed the earthenware cups on the table and began to pour the tea. "My wife painted them."

Francesca's grin widened. "Mistress Pan, you must let me commission you to paint screens for the home I plan to build for myself. Naturally, only if you have the time and do not mind. I will pay you for your time, of course."

The woman stopped mid-pour and looked at her husband.

"Your highness is not going to live at the palace?" Master Pan asked meekly.

"Actually, I wished to discuss building a home on the big hill that overlooks the valley and the forest. Do you know the one I speak of? It has an outcropping of rocks on it shaped in an arc." Francesca drew her fingers mimic the rock formation.

"Yes, your highness, I do." Master Pan didn't move. Jin almost felt sorry for the man. When Francesca put her mind to something, she wouldn't be easily swayed. It was apparent the elder didn't know what to make of the new princess. Jin himself didn't know what to make of his wife.

Jin took Francesca by the elbow and led her to sit. She did and Master Pan joined them at the table. Mistress Pan handed the princess the first teacup. Francesca took a sip. "Mistress Pan, you must permit me to impose upon you more. I simply must learn how to make this."

Jin looked at Francesca in surprise. Who was this woman? She was hardly the Wushu thief come to plague him, the one he thought he knew how to predict.

"Y-yes," the woman stuttered, nodding. "Thank you, princess. It is an old recipe my mother taught me when I was a young girl."

Master Pan looked sternly at his wife and she snapped her mouth shut. The woman filled four more cups and set them on the table, one before each of them and an extra on the end where no one sat.

"When I build my house you must come and visit me. I wish to hear all about it." Francesca took another sip. "Now, Master Pan, as I was saying about the hill. My husband tells me you are the man who I need to speak with. I would like permission to build a home on it."

"The princess seeks permission?" Master Pan looked at Jin in surprise. "From me?"

Jin sipped his tea and motioned absently back to Francesca. "My wife desires permission, as not to insult the people who have made their homes in the area."

It was a long moment before the elder spoke. "I do not see why it would be a problem, princess."

"Wonderful!" Francesca clapped her hands. Jin was sure he'd never seen her so excited. He set his cup down and studied her. She reached forward and lightly touched Master Pan's hand. "Thank you."

He nodded, but didn't answer. Jin knew the situation to be highly unusual for them and it would take them awhile to warm up to his wife.

"Mistress Pan, I will be in touch with you about the screens and the tea." Francesca stood and bowed slightly. "Thank you for your hospitality, but I'm afraid we must be getting back."

The couple bowed in return and Jin led his wife from their home so they could take their leave of the village. When they were back on the land craft, speeding away from Searchlight, he said, "This pleases you?"

"Very much so," she answered.

"I have to know, are you up to something? The way you were acting in there, it was," Jin paused, "unlike you."

"There are many things you don't know about me, Jin," she said quietly. "Not everything I do is an act. Some things are sincere."

"Are you implying you act when you are at the palace?" he questioned in surprise.

"Some." She nodded. "You all stare at me in the palace, expecting me to do something wrong. I don't blame you, but it does put a lot of pressure on a person to behave a certain way. I like the idea of being out here. If I must stay on the planet, I would be in an area where I'm not constantly watched and judged."

"We have reason to watch," he reminded her.

"I know and I can't change that. I had reason to do what I did." She lightly touched his arm. "Here I have a chance to be more that just the woman who tried to destroy an empire. I have a chance to live in peace."

"I didn't realize you were so unhappy at the palace." His stomach tightened. This was a side to his wife he would never have suspected. There was an honesty to her, as if in this moment there were no games, no scheming or lies.

"You never asked." Francesca moved to the side of the land craft as they neared her hill. Jin set the coordinates and slowed the vehicle before going to join her side. It was a beautiful location. Lifting her hand, she said, "This is how I used to picture how I'd want my home when I was in the monastery. It wasn't here, but it was like this--a hill, trees, a small creek and a family. Naturally, the house looked different than the homes here, but the concept is the same. This is what I want, Jin. I want to live here. You said I could."

Jin nodded. The view soured as he looked at her dream, for it would keep her away from him. The reality of how their married life would be struck him in that moment. She would be here, he would be at the palace, and rarely would they meet.

"It will be yours," he said quietly. "However you wish."

"No walls?"

"No. No walls."

"And will you help me find the people I need to design it and build it?"

"Yes. It will be taken care of." The words tore at him, but what else could he say?

"And I can hire local craftsman to decorate it?"

"Yes."

"And can I have a scroll to put in the front room like Master Pan had? I couldn't read it, but I would like something to hang on the wall. And I'd like one more thing as well."

"What's that?"

*Anything, Francesca.*

"I want to start a school to teach Wushu to children. The art should be shared, not hidden. I'll follow whatever guidelines I must and adhere to whatever precautions your family deems necessary, but I want to teach what I know." She pointed to the hill. "And this will be the perfect place to do it."

Jin took a deep breath. Would his family agree to such terms? Would the nobles? The ancestors? Looking at her face, he suddenly didn't care. If she wanted it, he would find a way to give it to her. "Yes, Francesca. You can have it any way you wish."

She smiled, a genuine smile. It was an expression he'd never seen in her and his heart stopped to witness it now. He took a step back. How he wished he was the one to put that look on her face! But instead, it was a dream of something else. Jealousy burned. He wished he could be her dream, a life with him, a world with him, a house with him in it. But it wasn't.

He'd bared his soul to her once and she'd left him. Jin would not do so again. He swallowed down his pain and went back to the controls. The land craft sped at his command and he drove them back toward the palace. Francesca stayed at the rail, silent as she looked over the countryside. He imagined she planned her life and it was a life that didn't include him in it.

\* \* \* \*

"When we were at Searchlight, why did Mistress Pan put a full cup of tea at the end of the table where no one sat? Did she think someone else was coming to visit?" Francesca looked up at Jin, eyeing him from across the many scrolls she'd taken from the walls. He seemed exasperated by the fact she demanded they get started on the plans to build her new home right away, but she couldn't help it. A fire burned inside of her and she was excited to see a school built honoring Chen Sun and what he'd taught her. Now, more than ever before, she believed this to be her path. This is what Sun had wanted her to do.

"She left it as offering to the ancestors," Jin answered, glancing up from the rolling parchment he studied quietly. They were in the library. Rolled scrolls lined the walls in giant columns. Symbols were carved along the shelves, tiny words keeping the texts organized.

"Oh," Francesca turned back to the architectural drawings, not seeing them. "But, she doesn't really believe that the ancestor will come and drink it, does she?"

"The ancestor might," Jin answered.

"But, ghosts are not real."

He looked up and sighed, setting the parchment down. "How do you know?"

"Well...." She glanced around them.

"There are ancestors around us even now," Jin said.

"Jin, I know what you're saying, that the dead never leave us. They are always in our hearts, and so forth, but I mean she doesn't literally believe that, does she?"

Jin turned to the side and looked at an empty table next to them. "Pardon me, would you mind showing yourself to her?"

Francesca laughed. "Stop teasing me!"

"Uh-hem" Jin pointed at the table.

Francesca glanced over and gasped. Startled, she stood too quickly and knocked over her chair. A transparent figure of a young man sat staring at her, wiggling his fingers. He was dressed as she'd seen Jin, but the cut of his clothing was slightly different. Opening her mouth, she tried to speak, but words failed her.

*Ghost.*

*Spirit.*

"Princess Francesca," the spirit said in acknowledgement, bowing his head. His voice whispered, sounding as transparent and airy as he was.

"Ah," she squeaked. "Dead."

"Yes," the spirit answered with a smirk. "Dead."

"This is Zhang Ho," Jin introduced. "He was killed in battle long ago. He's my great-great-great-great-uncle."

"Five greats," Ho corrected.

"Ah, my apologies," Jin said.

The spirit nodded in acceptance and turned to look at the empty table.

"What's he doing?" Francesca whispered, still awestruck.

Ho glanced back up and reached to the table. As soon as he touched it, a transparent scroll appeared. "I'm helping you find a way to have your Wushu school."

"Oh," Francesca said, her mouth working before she managed, "Thank you."

Ho again turned his attention away and slowly dissipated into thin air.

"Is he still there?" Francesca asked. Jin nodded. She looked around the library. "Are there more?"

"A few," he said.

Francesca glanced around, stunned to see images of the dead appear to her. Their bodies shimmered from nothingness and they looked at her, some smiling, some not.

She backed up toward the door. Jin stood, following her as she rushed outside.

Francesca turned in a circle. "Are they everywhere?"

"They can be," Jin said.

"And...." She took a deep breath.

"They mean you no harm," he said. "Most of the time they ignore us and we them."

"Your grandfather really did possess you to claim me, didn't he?" She bit her lip, trying not to cry. Jin nodded. "You really didn't want to marry me, did you? And that's how you knew I was breaking into the Sacred Chamber. One of them told you, didn't they?"

Jin nodded. "Yes. My great-grandmother Zhang An. She watched the Sacred Chamber. On our wedding night, she was celebrating with the others. That is how you slipped past that night undetected."

"So it had nothing to do with skill?" Oddly, the thought didn't relieve her as much as it should. Her heart was too heavy with the knowledge that Jin would never have married her if the spirits didn't make him do it.

"No, not really. In fact, many of them are frightened and impressed by your skills." He didn't move and his face was horribly blank. "You only see them if they wish for you to. Or, in my case, I always see them. It started soon after I met you. An said it is because the Jade Phoenix blessed me with knowledge of the past. It's how I figured out what happened to Chen Sun. It's why I was chosen to marry you."

Francesca tried to keep a straight face, but couldn't. She opened her mouth, but couldn't go on. Spinning on her heels, she tried to get away from him. Instinct took over and she began to run, hard as her feet hit against the sidewalk. Her eyes scanned for spirits, but she couldn't see anymore of them.

"Francesca!"

She heard Jin running behind her and it only made her go faster. Suddenly, an image of a transparent hand whipped by her face, carrying the breeze with it. She jolted, tripping on her long gown. By the time she righted herself, Jin was by her side.

"Fran--"

She didn't let him say the word. Punching at him, she hit his jaw. Jin blinked in surprise. The rage felt too good and she didn't give him time to question her as she swung for him again. Jin blocked her blow. She hit at him again, this time adding a kick to the combination. The silk of her gown fluttered as she moved. Jin took up her challenge, fighting back. They sparred over the pathways, kicking and punching, sweeping and blocking.

Francesca let loose all of herself on him, her full skill empowered by her broken heart. She kicked his ribs and he returned by knocking her in the chest. Flying back, she landed on her feet, skidding to a stop. Instantly, she ran forward, jumping in the air to meet him above the ground. Their bodies tangled and they fell hard.

Her eyes met his and the sounds of their grunts echoed over Honorable City. Guards came from their hiding places to watch. Neither of them cared as they continued on.

"Is this what you want?" he demanded, striking her face with his arm. "You wish to fight me?"

"Yes," she growled, grabbing his hand and flipping him over her shoulder. He landed on his back only to kick his feet into the air and land on the ground. She nodded. "You are more skilled than I thought."

"That's because you never give me a chance to prove myself worthy of you." Jin twisted out of her way as she charged him. "You always hold part of yourself back."

They exchanged punches. Blood trickled over her mouth. She loved the familiar salty taste. It was comforting, familiar. A matching wound dripped from his mouth and a bruise shadowed his jaw.

"It is I who am not worthy of you, Zhang Jin. You said it yourself. You were compelled by your dead grandfather to marry me." Suddenly he stopped and dropped his guard. It was too late for her to stop her motion as she jumped into the air and slammed her foot into his chest. The wind wheezed out of his lungs and he stumbled, landing on the ground.

Instantly she felt horrible. Rushing to him, she leaned over him. "Jin?"

"Is that what this is about? You're mad at me because I told you the truth?"

Francesca was breathing hard. She fell to her knees and buried her face in her hands. "Yes."

"Do you wish me to lie?" His words were stunted and he hadn't moved. She peeked at him, seeing that he gripped his chest.

"I wish you to love me," she whispered. "I wish for you to forgive me."

"I cannot compete with the memory of a dead man, Francesca. Why would you have me love you when you cannot love me?"

"Who asked you to compete?"

"You did. You admit you loved him, Francesca. You came here and stole for him. Everything you have done since I've met you has been because of him!" Jin rolled onto his side and pushed up from the ground. It was slow going but he finally made it to his feet. He stared down at her. "Nothing you do has been for me."

"You're right," she said. "I promised Sun I would come here and I have kept my word. He saved me from myself, Jin. He saved me and I owed him. But...."

"But, what?" Jin yelled, his features animated with frustration. "What?"

"I fought so hard to do what I promised because...." She took a deep breath. "Because I never loved him the way I love you." Francesca got to her feet. "Because I felt like I betrayed him by loving you. He saved me. I was grateful and looked up to him. He was the only family I had. But he longed for his dead wife and compared to that memory, I was nothing. I tried to be, but I see now why I could never have been Chen Sun's dead wife. I know why I could never have had her spot in his heart. Yes, I loved him, but...."

Jin didn't move, as he stood clutching his stomach. She wanted him desperately to say something.

"But not as I love you. His memory does not hold power over me. Not anymore because I love you, Jin." Francesca bowed her head, feeling as if the breeze would knock her over. She swayed on her feet, the fight all gone from her. Jin had the power to crush her and she waited for him to do so. Weakly, she repeated, "I love you."

Still he didn't answer.

"I understand." She nodded. "I am not worthy, I know that. I lied and stole and have done things you can never forgive. But, you did love me once, didn't you? On our wedding night, you looked at me and you did love me then, didn't you?"

"Yes, I loved you then," he whispered.

Francesca started to cry. "I ruined it, didn't I? I do not ask for you to forgive me, for I did what I had to. I only wish that fate had brought us together under different circumstance."

"And I wouldn't change a thing," he said.

Francesca blinked, chocking on a sob as she moved to cover her face. Tears soaked into her sleeve. Jin came forward and touched her arm. "Do you lie to me now, *bâobèi?*"

"Chen Sun told me that we are all motivated by our desires and that there are all types of seductions. If you know what you desire, then you know the truth within yourself. Then he asked me what it is I desire most. I couldn't answer at the time, but I know now. You. I desire a life with you the most. It is you who has seduced my every breath, taken hold of my very soul from that first moment. I desire you, Jin. I love you and it is a life with you that I want more than anything. If you can find it in yourself to love me again, I promise that your happiness, our life together will be what motivates me because it is what I desire more than anything in the galaxies."

Francesca took a deep breath, not sure whether to allow herself to hope at his silence. Slowly, a smile spread over his face.

"That is my desire as well." Jin touched her face. "I never stopped loving you. The moment you left is the moment my soul died and it only now is reborn with your words."

Francesca yelled in relief, throwing her arms around him. Jin groaned at her affectionate attack and she instantly backed off. He grabbed his ribs and gave a sheepish laugh. "Do you think next time you can tell me what's on your mind without breaking my ribs?"

Francesca laughed, slipping an arm under his to support him as he began to walk. "I'll do my best, *ài rén*, but I can't promise anything."

The End

Don't miss out on collecting these other exciting
Harmony™ titles for your collection:

Clone Wars: Armageddon by Kaitlyn O'Connor (Futuristic
Romance) Trade Paper 1-58608-775-4
*Living in a world devastated by one disaster after another,
it's natural for people to look for a target to blame for their
woes, and Lena thinks little of it when new rumors begin to
circulate about a government conspiracy. She soon
discovers, though, that the government may or may not be
conspiring against its citizens, but someone certainly is.
Morris, her adoptive father, isn't Morris anymore, and the
mirror image of herself that comes to kill her most definitely
isn't a long lost identical twin.*

The Devil's Concubine by Jaide Fox (Fantasy Romance)
Trade Paper 1-58608-776-2
*A great contest was announced to decide who would win the
hand of Princess Aliya, accounted the most fair young
maiden in the land. The ruler of every kingdom was invited--
every kingdom that is save those of the unnaturals. When
King Talin, ruler of the tribe of Golden Falcons learned of
the slight, he was enraged. He had no desire to take a mere
man child as his bride, but he would allow the insult to go
unchallenged.*

Warriors of the Darkness by Mandy M. Roth (Paranormal
Romance) Trade Paper 1-58608-778-9
*In place where time and space have no boundaries, ancient
enemies would like nothing more than to eradicate them
both, just when they've found each other.*